HEXES AND HOLIDAYS

BLOOD AND Bells

HEXES AND HOLIDAYS

BLOOD AND Bells

CJ HOLMES
MICHAEL ASHWOOD

CITY OWL
PRESS

This book is a work of fiction. Names, characters, places, and incidents either are products of the author's imagination or are used fictitiously. Any resemblance to actual events or locales or persons, living or dead, is entirely coincidental and not intended by the author.

BLOOD AND BELLS
Hexes and Holidays, Book 1

CITY OWL PRESS
www.cityowlpress.com

Cover Design by MiblArt. All stock photos licensed appropriately. Characer Art by Pixel Art Studio.

Edited by Tee Tate.

For information on subsidiary rights, please contact the publisher at info@cityowlpress.com.

Print Edition ISBN: 978-1-64898-603-1

Digital Edition ISBN: 978-1-64898-604-8

CITY OWL PRESS
Escape Your World ♦ Get Lost in Ours

Also by C J Holmes & Michael Ashwood

CJ HOLMES

Labyrinthine

Thrones of the Forsaken, Book 2 (coming soon)

MICHAEL ASHWOOD

A Song for Lost Things

For anyone who's ever tried to hold Christmas together with lists, string, and spite—and found something wonderful in the chaos.

Chapter One

HOLLY

The first thing I notice when I step into the town square is the absence of the tree.

Not just any tree—*the* tree. The one that's taller than every building in Willow Creek, so brightly lit that the town had to file for separate permits from NASA. It's the crown jewel of our Winter Wonderland Gala, the literal centerpiece of the town's festivities and the sap-filled, beating heart of our community.

And it's gone.

In its place is an empty patch of churned-up snow surrounded by a few crushed ornaments, and what looks suspiciously like elf-sized footprints leading away from the crime scene.

Elf footprints are on-brand for the Christmas vibe that Willow Creek has going on, but these are completely wrong. They're sharp little dents that clash with the sugar-cookie rooftops and underscore the absence of lights and other decorations that adorned the square only a few hours ago.

The town is supposed to be a winter wonderland, a place where Hallmark movies are made. Usually, the square is a picture-perfect postcard with fresh snow, twinkling lights, and enough hot cocoa flooding the air to warrant an FBI investigation. Now it looks like Christmas sneezed glitter and then went for a lie-down.

I clutch my clipboard to my chest like it's a certified flotation device, breathing in the square's usual cinnamon-cocoa aura and getting...nothing. Just cold.

This can't be happening.

Not now.

Not one week before the gala.

The logical part of my brain tries to reassure me. Maybe the tree was moved for maintenance? A quick redecoration? Maybe someone has sent it for a quick spruce up. I wish that unintentional pun brought me joy, but I'm almost positive it's a pine tree. Deep down, I know the truth. Someone, or something, has stolen it.

I've barely slept all week. The Gala was my chance to prove to myself and everyone else that I'm capable of putting on a Christmas that would dazzle. A Christmas that means something. That matters. Not just another small-town festival. Willow Creek's Winter Wonderland was my one shot.

My mom built her reputation on events people talk about for years.

This was supposed to be the start of my career.

And now, it could be over before it even started.

I crouch to pick up a shattered ornament—a tiny red bauble split right down the middle. The sight of it is oddly personal, like Christmas itself has taken a direct hit.

I scan the area, hoping to see something positive, but the whole place is in disarray. Strings of lights droop pathetically from the lampposts, and half the candy cane decorations have toppled over. The giant inflatable snowman, our second-most beloved decoration, lies half-deflated and face-down in the snow like he's missed his cue and is taking it very personally. With one resounding wheeze, it seems to resign itself to its fate, collapsing even further and declaring it's had enough of this world. I'll be tempted to join him if this farce continues.

"No, no, no," I mutter, shaking my head.

My fingers turn ice cold, despite my gloves. There's no time to panic. I just need to find a solution. A replacement tree. Extra decorations. Maybe a miracle or two. Move Christmas? Is that an option? Maybe I could hammer together a bunch of coat stands and paint them green, and—

"It's gone, isn't it?"

The voice that interrupts my backup planning is smooth, deep, and laced with just the right amount of smugness to set my teeth on edge. I don't need to look to know who it is, but I do anyway. Sure enough, there's Niklaus Draven, leaning casually against a lamppost like he doesn't have a care in the world.

Nick, as I begrudgingly call him, is one of the town's resident vampires. And not just any vampire—the *annoyingly perfect* kind. He's tall, dark, and infuriatingly handsome, and he knows it. He's dressed in a black coat so tailored it could probably double as body armor, and his jet-black hair is slicked back, except for one rebellious strand that curls over his forehead, giving him the air of a rom-com villain who moonlights as a cover model.

Those freakishly silver eyes that dazzle like moonlight gleam in the streetlamps, giving him that unholy vampire glow that somehow manages to be both creepy and frustratingly handsome. They're like polished mirrors, equal parts unnerving and unfairly attractive.

"Not now, Nick," I snap, turning away and brushing snow off my coat. "I have enough problems without adding a sarcastic vampire to the list of things I have to worry about."

"Oh, come on, Holly," he says, his tone dripping with amusement. "I was passing through and noticed something seemed...off. Missing, perhaps?"

"Spotted the absence of the giant, seventy-foot spruce tree, did you? Incredible sleuthing. You must be a whiz at finding Waldo."

"I think it's a pine?"

I count backwards from ten, giving up at eight.

He steps closer, scattering snow as he moves. "Touchy, aren't we? I assume the missing tree isn't intentional?"

I whirl on him, brandishing my clipboard like it doubles as a stake. "Why would I intentionally remove my own centerpiece?"

"I don't know. I'm not an event planner. Does it add a touch of drama?"

"Do you have *any* idea how much work goes into this gala? The tree is the centerpiece, Nick. The centerpiece! Without it, the whole event is ruined."

He raises an eyebrow, clearly enjoying my meltdown. "I had no idea Christmas trees were this vital to your well-being. Do you want to hear my theory about how it came to disappear?"

"Is it anything like your theory on how vampires and garlic came to be associated due to an over-seasoned *spaghetti aglio e olio?* Pass. I don't need conjecture," I say, resisting another jab with my clipboard. "I need solutions. Unless you know where I can find a replacement tree the size of a small skyscraper on thirty seconds' notice, go bother someone else."

Nick doesn't budge. If anything, his smirk widens, revealing the slightest hint of fangs. "Oh, but I *do* know something you don't."

I fold my arms, glaring up at him. "If it's anything except the tree's exact location, I don't care." I use my very best hardened stare to convey my irritation to him.

He leans closer, and I catch a faint whiff of something dark and spicy, like cinnamon mixed with danger. "Your little tree problem isn't an accident."

"I didn't think the tree magically uprooted itself and went for a stroll down Main Street."

"Let's just say there are some less-than-festive forces at work in Willow Creek this year."

Before I can tell him exactly where he can shove his cryptic nonsense, a loud crash echoes through the square.

As I whip around, a string of Christmas lights skids across the snow, and a group of small, pointy-eared figures darts after them.

They're giggling like maniacs, their tiny boots kicking up snow as they dart between the lampposts in a blur of red and green.

"Are those..." I crane my neck. "Elves?"

"Yes. Rogue elves," Nick says, stepping up beside me. "Nasty little creatures. They're like feral cats with opposable thumbs and better teamwork. They smell worse though."

"Why? Why are there elves?"

"Well, when an elf—"

"Stop."

The tallest elf, standing at an astronomical two feet tall, stops long enough to kick over a candy cane decoration, cackling like it's the funniest thing in the world. His companions cheer him on before scampering off into the shadows, their mischievous faces and pointy ears blending into the darkness.

I press my hands to my temples, willing myself to stay calm. "You have *got* to be kidding me."

"Looks like someone's been naughty this year," Nick quips, far too cheerful for my liking.

"Don't make this worse."

"Oh, I'm not. I'm simply observing." His silver eyes practically twinkle. "Fact is, you've got a supernatural problem, Frost. Lucky for you, I'm an expert in dealing with these kinds of things."

A small, disbelieving noise escapes me. "You're an expert at being a pain in my planning spreadsheets."

Another crash sounds, this one louder than the last. The elves have tipped over one of the nearby market stalls, sending a cascade of gingerbread cookies into the snow. My heart sinks further as the cookies are crushed into the snow, and I scream at this fresh disaster. The elves giggle again, the sound high-pitched and eerie. Like tiny little gremlins, they scurry off, delighted with the shiny lights they've stolen.

Nick tilts his head, watching me with what might almost pass for sympathy. Almost. "Holly, be honest. Do you really think you can handle this on your own?"

"I've handled parties going wrong before."

"This is a bit more specialized than what you're used to dealing with," he says, gesturing to the chaos. "Rogue elves are tricky. You'll need someone who knows how to handle them."

"And you think that someone is you?"

He grins, his fangs catching the light. "I'm a vampire, Holly. Chaos is my specialty."

I blink at him, then laugh. It's not a happy, amused sound. It's the kind of laugh you let out when someone tells you something so ridiculous your brain briefly short-circuits.

"Nick, the last time you got involved in town business, the entire Harvest Festival had to be moved because you turned the corn maze into a bat habitat."

"I added ambiance," he says smoothly. "I can't help it if mortals lack an appreciation for theatrics."

"Theatrics? You had cotton candy bats dive-bombing children."

"They were harmless. Besides, the children seemed to enjoy the thrill. Bam. Bat in the mouth. They loved it. Their parents simply overreacted."

This is exactly why I don't want his help. He collects chaos like other people collect snow globes, and I'm fairly sure the label on the bottom says "For Niklaus Draven's amusement only." Willow Creek doesn't need his drama. I definitely don't need his scheming and backstabbing. What I need are solutions, and I'm coming up short.

He steps closer, invading my personal space with his aggravating calm and cologne. Infuriatingly, he smells like cinnamon and night air. My treacherous lungs inhale again before my brain can file a complaint. God, the vampire is attractive and he knows it, weaponizing it against every girl who comes his way. I refuse to let myself become another entry in his mental guest list of admirers.

"Frost, I'm aware my methods and your methods tend to meet somewhere around mutual disapproval. But the town tree is gone, your Winter Wonderland is teetering on the edge of becoming a festive disaster, and—" he gestures lightly to the chaos "—this is precisely the sort of thing that spirals."

There's less performance in him now. More memory, perhaps.

"I've seen what happens when it does. One mishap becomes two, becomes panic, and then something people remember for all the wrong reasons." He glances back at me. "My coven and I like it here, Holly. We were rather hoping to stay. Possibly even attempt this 'community spirit' I keep hearing about."

"You? Community spirit?"

"Try not to faint. I'd never hear the end of it."

"Let me fix this for you, Holly. Rogue elves are nothing to scoff at and you need someone who understands their nature. Their quirks. Their weaknesses and how to exploit them."

"Let me guess," I say dryly. "You're an expert on rogue elves, too?"

"I've encountered them before."

"When? At some secret vampire-elf mixer I didn't hear about?"

"Vampires and elves don't mix," he says with a smirk. "Too many territorial disputes. But I've dealt with rogue creatures enough to know how to track them, and how to stop them before they cause more damage."

Before I can argue further, there's another crash, followed by a shrill laugh that makes my skin crawl. One of the elves has climbed onto the inflatable snowman and is using a broken candy cane to puncture it. Repeatedly. It wheezes again, deflating in slow, agonizing defeat.

"Fine! You want to help? Be my guest. But if you so much as *think* about turning this into one of your dramatic stunts—"

Nick holds up a hand, mock solemn. "Scout's honor."

"You were never a Scout."

"True. But I am an excellent vampire."

With a wholly unnecessary flourish of his long coat, he walks toward the elves like he's auditioning for a gothic superhero role. Walking isn't even the right word. He's strutting. I follow reluctantly, muttering under my breath about terrible decisions and the inevitability of this blowing up in my face. But I do need those elves to leave, and if I'm honest, they creep me out.

As we approach the center of the square, an elf notices us. Its tiny, pointy face scrunches up in a snarl, and it hisses like the aforementioned feral cat.

Nick stops, tilting his head like he's studying a particularly interesting bug. "You see that, Frost? Classic rogue elf behavior. Aggression, lack of self-control, and an unhealthy attachment to destruction."

"Aggression, lack of control, and destruction," I deadpan. "Should I get you a mirror? Are we going to do something about it, or are you here to give a TED Talk on elf psychology?"

Ignoring me, Nick scoops up a handful of snow. He packs it into a tight ball, his movements deliberate and precise. He presses his feet into the snow, almost as if he's taking up a position, and then he waits, watching the rogue elves as they cause more havoc on Willow Creek. They haven't come for us yet, seemingly quite happy to destroy whatever decorations remain in the town's square.

Against my better judgment, I scoop my own handful of snow. It's cold, obvious, and exactly the kind of plan you make when your Plan A was "giant municipal tree."

"What are you doing?"

"Engaging," he says simply, then hurls the snowball with unerring accuracy.

It smacks a rogue elf square in the face. The elf lets out an indignant screech, stumbling backward and landing on its tiny butt. For a moment, the other elves freeze, their beady little eyes darting between Nick and their fallen comrade.

Their lips curl back and the glee in their faces disappears, replaced with a look of sheer violence and unadulterated anger. They've morphed from impish creatures into true terrors, but Nick simply bends down, picks up another handful of snow, and forms it into a densely packed ball.

He throws, scoring a direct hit. Another rogue elf flies backward and lands in a snow drift, leaving only its curled, red shoes and bright green tights visible. It shrieks as its legs start to kick, and I laugh, unable to contain myself.

The elves glance at each other, their expressions shifting to something akin to uncertainty. One lets out a low, guttural hiss, its head swiveling toward the others as if waiting for a signal. Another elf, its crooked hat askew, growls in response but takes a hesitant step back. Nick holds up another snowball and waggles it at them. Slowly, their aggression begins to waver, their confidence faltering like a deflating balloon. As though reaching some unspoken consensus, they spin on their tiny heels and bolt, their retreat a flurry of jingling bells and mismatched shoes skidding on the icy ground.

They scatter into the snow-laden streets, their bright green and red forms growing smaller and smaller until they vanish entirely into the swirling flakes. One elf pauses briefly at the edge of the square, shooting a final, venomous glare over its shoulder before disappearing into the shadows.

For a long moment, the square is still, the eerie calm almost as unsettling as the chaos that came before it. The faint jingle of a half-smashed ornament rolls across the cobblestones, its sound muffled by the snow. A crooked candy cane dangles precariously from a toppled wreath stand, leaving its red stripes smeared as though the fight had bruised even the decorations.

Wreckage litters the square—the deflated snowman, shattered ornaments, the trail of glittery destruction leading off into the distance like festive breadcrumbs left by tiny vandals. Somewhere in the rubble, a strand of Christmas lights flickers weakly, its cheerful glow now a pitiful reminder of what this square used to be.

A single bulb blinks in the wreckage—brave, if not especially helpful.

"Well," Nick says with a dry chuckle, "that was fun."

"Fun?" He gets a look. It does absolutely nothing. "The square is trashed, the tree is still missing, and I have maybe a week to fix this. All you did was whip a few snowballs."

Nick shrugs. "Details. The important thing is, we know who took your tree, and we can follow their trail before it gets snowed over."

"Oh, good. That's reassuring."

"Even better, I'm going to help you fix this."

"You are?"

He holds his hands out as if framing a picture. "Think of it. Frost and Draven. Christmas partners."

I groan, burying my face in my hands. "This is a nightmare."

"Don't worry, Frost," Nick says, his tone uncharacteristically gentle. "We'll get your tree back. After all, Christmas is about miracles, isn't it?"

"You're enjoying this, aren't you?"

He smirks, his silver eyes gleaming. "Immensely."

Of course he is.

Chapter Two

NICK

Holly didn't technically agree to team up, but she didn't actually refuse either. So when she announced she was going home to "shotgun melted chocolate," I told her I'd be in touch.

My house is nestled among the rolling hills that make up the northern border of Willow Creek. I refuse to call it a castle—too on the nose—or a manse, which sounds like something a dentist names his cottage. So a house it is, and a house it shall stay, until something grander comes along. A 'mere' three-wing affair on forty acres of prime real estate, complete with an underground mausoleum and, charmingly, a built-in movie theater that seats forty. Last night we watched *The Lost Boys.*

I'm thinking of nonsense to stop myself from thinking about Holly. Grinning like a teenage nitwit who scrawls bad poetry. About her eyes. It's undignified for a mysterious Lord of the Dark. I've lived for eight centuries. Dined with Eleanor of Aquitaine. Destroyed entire covens because they remarked poorly on my scarf.

I will not grin over a woman.

Still.

Holly Frost.

A vexing problem. One I'm strangely eager to solve.

Her chestnut hair never quite behaves, catching the light in warm, unruly strands. And those green eyes of hers are startling bright, like freshly cut leaves, always a step ahead, as if she's already decided how the conversation ends and is waiting for the rest of us to catch up. She's been a riddle since we both arrived in Willow Creek, almost at the same time.

We disagreed immediately. We've been consistent about that.

I make a small, disgusted sound. Holly Frost is the definition of adorable, and I need to get my head straight. If any other vampire hears me talking like this about a human, I'll have to end them out of sheer embarrassment.

It's nearing dark as I make my way through the ornate, cast-iron gates that surround the grounds. Beyond them, the house rears up in true gothic silhouette—steep gables, brooding stone, ivy that refuses to mind its manners, and gargoyles who judge on principle.

The humans of Willow Creek have, thankfully, learned that most of what Hollywood says about us is nonsense. We don't explode in daylight. That would be wildly impractical. Six months in, and they've mostly stopped waiting for us to combust.

Crinkshaw, my body man, waits by the front door. I found him in a British graveyard sometime in the early sixteenth century, and, against all reason, kept him. He's a grim, emaciated ghoul—gray skin stretched too tight, bones making unwelcome appearances, and he provides the general impression of something that ought to remain politely buried.

He's also remarkably gifted at saying the wrong thing at precisely the wrong time.

A ghoul entirely without humor.

"You were right, Crinkshaw." I throw my jacket at him, and dust poofs from his shoulders as he catches it. "Rogue elves. As you predicted."

"Marvelous, Sire," he says in his grave-scraping voice. "Glad that they weren't those bothersome, haughty, highborn elves. Their height alone is a burden, and their moral superiority is enough to make the strongest choke. Were you able to fend them off?"

"With ease. Lucky that you sensed them coming. It's a rather neat trick of yours, and I'll have you teach me some day. But here's something you couldn't have predicted. They stole the giant Christmas tree."

Crinkshaw hangs my jacket, and we make our way through the cavernous lobby that keeps the drama outside. Inside, it's all beeswax polish, lamplight, and heat from overworked fireplaces—past the Monet I acquired from the man himself and the rocking chair I've never liked. Both wear tinsel and garland with disreputable cheer. Someone's draped tartan throws over the leather settees and strung warm fairy lights along the picture rails, as if daring the gloom to take a night off. My coven has been hard at work ensuring virtually every square inch of available space is covered with Christmas decorations.

Strictly speaking, vampires are forbidden from participating in Christmas. Oh, not the trappings of it. We can decorate and exchange gifts and the like, but the magic—the feeling of warmth and fellowship and seasonal joy—that is beyond our reach. There's a tale behind that and one I don't care to dwell on, but this season is always bittersweet. None of this, however, stops the coven from decorating as immortals are strangely festive. We've learned that life never stops. If we don't stop to appreciate the moments of joy when they appear, they often stop coming altogether.

"The Christmas tree?" Crinkshaw says, as we make our way to the kitchen. "Sire gives me too much credit, including the assumption that I know, or care about, a giant Christmas tree."

"It's the centerpiece of their winter festival. The Willow Creek Winter Wonderland. And, before you ask, Holly Frost was there too."

Crinkshaw's sunken eyes adopt an agonizingly slow crawl of surprise, like a glacier reconsidering its route. "I don't believe I would have ever asked about Holly Frost."

"Now you don't have to. She was there."

"Stupendous, Sire. And the elves?"

"I can't say with certainty if they would have asked about Holly. It never really came up."

Crinkshaw inhales deeply, despite not needing to breathe. "I meant that I would enjoy hearing about how you drove off the rogue elves."

"I threw some snowballs at them," I shrug. "I put a small drop of my power in each one, just enough to give them a scare."

We reach one of the many kitchens in my home, and like everything, it's impressive. It's also indecently cozy: copper pans glow, cloves and orange peel scent the air, and a mismatched congress of oversized mugs waits by a humming kettle like loyal footmen. Walnut worktops sit on top of bespoke cabinets, and even though we don't technically need to eat, the stove is large enough to serve a restaurant. Crinkshaw enjoys baking, and it's a curious habit of his I've never understood, although I've enjoyed its benefits. It's a little larger than the coven needed, but I wanted to be sure that we had enough space for several wine fridges, and the kitchen fitters were insistent that this was the only way to fit them in.

I sit at the oversized kitchen island, watching Crinkshaw as he limps around it. My thoughts sprint.

"We have a bigger problem to deal with, Crinkshaw, and I fear that we must solve it. Why did they steal Holly's Christmas tree?"

"Sire seems...notably preoccupied with Holly Frost."

"Don't be ridiculous, man. I'm simply concerned about the tree and the saving of Christmas. The Willow Creek Winter Wonderland is the most important festival for this town, and vampires always get the blame anytime something supernatural goes wrong. This hardly feels like the moment to let everything collapse. And I don't care for the insinuations buried in your dusty tone."

"I have but the one voice, Sire. Would you care for dinner?"

"Get on with it, then. And call for Ronan. I'd appreciate his advice."

Crinkshaw limps to the blood fridge to prepare me a fresh bag. I narrow my eyes, making sure he selects a good one. Vintage varies, and standards must be maintained.

The arrangement is simple: we don't hunt, and in return, we don't cause problems.

It's worked well enough.

It would work significantly better if Holly Frost would stop intruding on my thoughts.

Twenty-three other vampires make their home here. Most have been with me for centuries, although I'm reasonably relaxed about their comings and goings. They often disappear for decades at a time as vampires tend to be somewhat transitory. Some were wary of my idea to move, but life had become stale in Canada, and most were looking for something different. Willow Creek represented an exciting, new challenge, and the bar we opened is keeping some of my more restless brethren occupied.

I'd assured the mayor that we'd be the kind of vampires that didn't cause trouble. That meant no feeding off people without consent, no public spectacles of fangs and violence, no exploding into clouds of bats, or anything that might scare people. Just quiet, neighborly coexistence. I swore up and down, left and right, and in every way possible that we were civilized and had given up such unbecoming tendencies centuries ago. It wasn't a particularly burdensome promise, given the fact that we aren't savages, and the residents of Willow Creek have been mostly receptive to our presence. It perhaps doesn't hurt that vampires tend to be jaw-droppingly attractive.

"I have heard tales of battle!"

A roar from the entrance of the kitchen pulls my attention. Ronan bursts through the archway, filling the space with his enormous presence. A Celtic warrior turned vampire, he's never quite let go of the old ways. He retreats to a wood cabin he built on the grounds whenever modern life becomes too offensive, which is often. I convinced him to stop carrying an axe at all times sometime around nineteen-twenty, though I'd wager he still has at least ten knives hidden on him.

Today, he's in a leather jacket, jeans, and heavy boots, looking less like a relic of the past and more like he's about to start a bar fight. The V-neck tee is too casual for my taste. His fire-red hair falls around his face, and even I need to tilt my head to meet his gaze.

At least he's moved on from tartan.

Crinkshaw hands him one of the several glasses of blood he's already prepared, and Ronan guzzles it in a single swallow. He slams the ornate glass onto the marble counter hard enough to shatter it.

"There was a battle," he continues, "and yet, where was Ronan? Brave Ronan? Was he in the midst of combat, guarding the back of his leader? Or was he instead tucked in the library, a quiet shadow of the warrior he used to be, toothlessly reduced to eating soup and watching reruns of *Mad About You?*"

"I thought you adored that show?"

"Helen Hunt is a treasure." He nods. "My point stands."

"You don't have to worry, Ronan. The battle was a non-event. Over before it started. Crinkshaw, here, was right when he read the signs. Rogue elves have descended on Willow Creek."

"Rogue elves? Pah. Disgusting creatures. Barely worth the time it takes to fight them. Not nearly as elegant as their full-grown cousins, who stand a proper eight feet and make for worthy adversaries. They're a challenge worthy of the mighty Ronan. Still, I suppose their diminutive cousins are a passing diversion. They are well and truly bested?"

"Obviously." I sip at my glass. Bitter, with a hint of sweetness. Lovely. For a being that only exists on necromantic flesh, Crinkshaw has a surprisingly subtle palate. "Well, at least temporarily. You'll be delighted to hear that the game is only just starting. We have another nasty problem to contend with."

"Finally." Ronan slams his giant, meaty fist on the table. His blue eyes glimmer at the promise of battle and brawling, and his reddish hair falls over his face as if it's seizing the opportunity to attack. He leans forward, flexing his muscles, and I have to admit that they are impressive. "This place has made me weak. A new enemy is what we need. Tell me what horror descends that we might face it, as brothers."

I lean forward to deliver my news. "The giant Christmas tree is missing."

Ronan frowns and stares at me for several uncomfortable seconds. I wonder if he misheard my quite exciting announcement. I'm about to repeat myself when he finally speaks.

"Apologies, Nick. My hearing has likely atrophied along with my battle prowess," he says. "I think I heard you say a Christmas tree is missing."

"Correct."

"Mm-hm. How is this incredibly mundane event exciting?"

"Holly Frost is involved."

"The event planner? The one who nearly set the town on fire last year?"

"That's her. And she's single, in case you were wondering."

"No one is wondering, Sire," Crinkshaw interjects.

Ronan shakes his head, and his hair mounts a small rebellion. "I came for battle, and you talk to me of spruce?"

"They're historically pine," Crinkshaw adds, ignoring the arching of my eyebrow.

"Quiet, ghoul." Ronan points at me. "You cannot be serious, Nick. I came here ready for violence, not festive forestry. Does the tree at least contain multitudes of demons? Tell me what you've drawn us into now."

In brief, I tell him of the missing tree, the snowball fight with the rogue elves, and how cute Holly's nose looked when she was agitated. It crinkled like a curious fox sniffing out trouble, equal parts endearing and mischievous. It was impossible not to smile when she got that look, even in the midst of chaos.

Ronan glances at Crinkshaw. "Has he been like this all night?"

"Utterly disastrous and besotted? Yes."

"You're both missing the point," I say. "Holly Frost has a problem, and by helping her, we can help ourselves. This is the biggest event of the year. The most important of the seemingly infinite festivals Willow Creek holds. If we fix it, we stop being tolerated by the town and start being useful. Acceptance is far more valuable than polite nods."

I straighten slightly.

"Although," I add, "if acceptance happens to increase patronage at the bar, I won't object."

Ronan rubs his nose. "Rogue elves though? It's like fighting children. Nasty, stupid, sharp-toothed children. They smell."

"Worst case scenario, you get to punch an elf as hard as you can." I clap him on the shoulder. "I'll tell you what, we'll make a sport of it. We can have a competition to see which one of us can punch an elf further?"

Ronan's eyes light up at the promise of elf-punching, and Crinkshaw shuffles toward the door. The ghastly creature makes a noise that, coming from anyone else, would be a note of dissent, but from the desiccated ghoul who haunts my house, it could simply be his bones creaking.

"I'll have you beat by two meters, or not at all." Ronan cracks his knuckles. "Alright, then. It stands. Preferable to reruns of *Desperately Seeking Susan*."

"Brooke Shields is a treasure," Crinkshaw deadpans.

"Perfect." I drum my fingertips together, a visual calibrated to radiate the leadership qualities I'm well known for. Ronan looks impressed, and *I'm* impressed with myself for having convinced him that I'm still exceptionally awesome after all these centuries.

"We'll start our investigation tomorrow," I decide, taking a large mouthful of the drink Crinkshaw poured me and letting its taste tickle my taste buds.

I'll get to see Holly again.

Not that I care.

Chapter Three

HOLLY

The Knit and Kettle coffee shop fogs its own windows like it's proud of being warm. Carols crackle from a retro radio, and the café smells like honey, espresso, and the snug comfort of freshly baked things. A fire nestles in the recessed hearth; along the mantel, knit stockings and twinkle lights do their level best to out-cheer winter. Every table has a poinsettia and a tiny tealight. I slump into a corner chair and try very hard not to be charmed.

My Christmas sweater has acquired permanent glitter thanks to yesterday's chaos, and my mittens steam on the radiator like exhausted hedgehogs. The barista slides two chunky mugs across to us—peppermint mocha for Marcy, gingerbread latte for me—both crowned with whipped cream and a dusting of nutmeg.

My best friend sips her drink, her gaze heavy with barely concealed amusement. Her long, dark curls behave like they've signed a contract with a shampoo company. Mine attempt 'curl' and achieve 'festive static'—as if I lost a fight with a helium balloon.

"Soooo," she says, drawing the word out like she's savoring it. "How's the Christmas festival prep going?"

The glacial stare I send Marcy is cooler than the icicles hanging from the frozen gutters outside. "Fantastic. Nothing says festive spirit like rogue elves destroying half the town square and stealing the centerpiece of your event."

"Rogue elves?" she snorts, nearly choking. She dabs at her mouth with a red-and-white striped napkin that bears an uncanny resemblance to elf hosiery—and to the stockings that flashed across my vision as they made off with the Christmas lights. "You're kidding."

"Do I look like I'm kidding?" I ask, gesturing at my frazzled hair and the faint glitter embedded in my Fair Isle knit. Even my beloved clipboard slumps in defeat beside the sugar caddy. "They wrecked the entire square. The tree is gone. And to top it off, Nick *bloody* Draven decided to show up and..." I wave my hands vaguely, searching for the right words. "...do his whole brooding, smug vampire thing."

I stir my latte with a gingerbread man until his head falls off. Accidental. Mostly.

"As in *the* Nick Draven? Mr. Tall, Dark, and Infuriating?" Marcy slurps her peppermint mocha and leans in closer, eager to hear the gossip.

I groan, letting my head fall to the table with a dull thud. "Yes, *that* Nick. He's impossible, Marcy. He showed up in the middle of everything, all silver eyes and fangy smiles, like he owns the place. And then he had the audacity to act like he was helping."

Marcy snickers, and I want to throttle her. She moved to Willow Creek after a spectacularly bad breakup and we quickly became good friends. She hasn't quite let go of the fallout, which means everyone else's love life is now apparently community entertainment.

"Well, at least he isn't Josh," she says.

"Low bar," I mutter.

"Did he help?"

"No," I snap, lifting my head only to be faced with Marcy's knowing look and deep brown eyes that refuse to let me get out of this. "Alright, technically, he helped, inasmuch as he chased the elves off. But he was insufferable about it and, apparently, he wants to help me track the tree down."

She grins. Widely. "Sounds nice of him."

The barista sets down a plate with two cranberry-orange scones and a ramekin of clotted cream because the Knit and Kettle understands emotional triage.

I scoff and chug back my gingerbread latte, slamming the festive cup down on the table in protest.

"He'll want something in return. He always does."

Marcy rests her chin on her hand. "Sounds like your mind is already made up about him. What did he do to earn you eternal wrath?"

The fire crackles in the background, and for a moment, I watch the flames as they twist and leap. I wish I had that kind of energy, that ability to keep burning, no matter what's thrown my way. Right now, all I feel is the creeping dread of what else could go wrong, especially now that Marcy's got me talking about Nick Draven.

"He just... turns up," I say, dragging my gaze back to Marcy. "Exactly where I don't want him. Offering opinions. Judging everything. It's like I can't do anything without him appearing out of nowhere to comment on it."

Marcy's smile widens.

"I swear he's doing it on purpose. Like I've personally offended him by existing," I add. "He waltzes into town and thinks he can do whatever he wants because he's—what's the phrase he used? 'Older than Christmas.'" I roll my eyes. "And don't even get me started on that ridiculous blood bar of his."

Marcy snorts again. "You mean *Hemoglow*?"

"Yes, *Hemoglow,*" I say, mimicking air quotes. "Who names a bar that? It sounds like a vampire nightclub designed by a marketing committee and a fog machine. He turned a perfectly nice, old tavern into some vampire haven where people actually volunteer to let him and his friends drink their blood. And somehow, I'm the one who gets side-eyes in this town for saying I don't think it's right."

"The place is popular," Marcy says in a tone that suggests she's about to say something scandalous. "You've seen the line outside on

Friday nights. Honestly, if Nick wanted to have a nibble, I'd probably roll up my sleeve and ask if he wanted it shaken or stirred."

She giggles and rolls her eyes suggestively, and then her hair decides to join in, adding more insult to injury. Marcy isn't remotely interested in Nick, or anyone else for that matter, but she likes a good flirt from time to time. She also enjoys winding me up, and that, apparently, isn't a challenge when it comes to a certain vampire.

My fingers pull at the sleeve of my Christmas sweater, adjusting it unnecessarily as I scoff. "Do you know how ridiculous you sound?"

Marcy laughs, leaning back in her chair with a smug little smirk. "I'm just saying, if Nick Draven asked me to volunteer, I'd consider it. Those cheekbones? That jawline? He could ask me to alphabetize his blood fridge and I'd probably swoon."

"You're gross," I say, shaking my head. "Also, never say 'blood fridge' in a café where pastries are trying their best."

She shrugs. "Fine, but you're deflecting. What's the *real* issue with him? You've had it in for him since the day he arrived, and while I get it —vampires, blood bars, smugness—this feels more personal than that."

The conversation's sudden change of direction catches me off guard. My gaze flickers back to the fire, the flames licking at the logs with lazy persistence.

"It's not personal," I lie, and even my latte foam judges me.

"It's *totally* personal," Marcy counters, her grin widening. "Spill."

I press my lips together, reluctant to dive into the mess that is my history with Nick. But Marcy's enthusiasm is unrelenting, and I know she won't let it go.

"Fine," I say with a sigh. "The first time we met, he told me humans were 'predictably small-minded.'"

"That feels like he was joking. You're really that bothered by something he said that long ago?"

"Okay. Two things." I sip my coffee, thinking about what I'm about to say and how childish it sounds. "When I told him I was the event planner for the Christmas Gala, he laughed at me. He actually laughed. Like I'd said I was hosting a gala for squirrels."

Marcy winces. "Oof."

"Yeah, *oof*," I echo bitterly. "He's been condescending since day one. I know Willow Creek has other events. You handle Valentine's. Amy does Easter. But Christmas is mine, and it's important to me. My mom pulled strings to get me this job. If I can just make it work, really work, it's the kind of thing people notice. If I pull this off, I stop being 'her daughter' and start being me."

I huff out a breath.

"And now, I'm supposed to believe he's suddenly interested in helping? I don't buy it. He probably thinks it'll be entertaining to watch me fail."

"You're not going to fail," Marcy says, suddenly all steel wrapped in a cable-knit.

I let out a humorless laugh. "You're confident."

"That's because I know you," she says simply. "You care too much to let this year's gala flop. Besides, it's not just about the tree or the decorations. You've been working on this for months. The whole town can see how much effort you've put into it."

I toy with corrugated sleeves. Warmth leaks into my fingers. It's ridiculous how much I need that. I've been under more pressure than I want to admit, and although it's been difficult, I know that the town is counting on me. I've got to deliver the Willow Creek Winter Wonderland and make the gala the best we've ever had—for the town, as well as for myself.

"It's more than that," I admit softly. "More than the gala. It's about proving that I'm not...a complete disaster."

Marcy frowns. "Who said you're a disaster?"

"No one," I say quickly. Too quickly. "Not outright, anyway. It's just... the expectations are always there. My mom built her career on events people still talked about years later, and I'm the one who set a town wreath on fire during last year's Christmas festival." I bury my head in my hands. "There's a video. It has views. More views than this town has people."

Marcy snickers, failing to hide her amusement.

"To be fair, the wreath *was* impressive," Marcy says. "It's more that wrapping it in enough fairy lights to illuminate an oil tanker with only one extension cord has consequences."

She gets a look. It joins the pile of looks she's ignored before.

"Exactly my point. People remember the disasters. And this gala is my chance to prove I have what it takes. That I can do this. That I can do something that matters."

"I don't think anyone expected you to proactively plan for a tree kidnapping by stray elves."

"This is Willow Creek. Normal around here is what other people call a government inquiry."

"This is just a small blip."

It's more than a blip to me.

It feels like everything.

Every late night spent poring over plans, using every ounce of energy to make this event perfect, it all feels like it's teetering on the edge of collapse. And the worst part? If it does fall apart, I don't know if I'll be able to convince myself to try again. The gala was supposed to be my moment, my chance to show the town—and my mom—that I'm more than a backup plan. But all I've managed to do is make a mess of everything. And now a literal vampire wants to help, which is either fate being kind or fate being bored.

Marcy leans forward, her expression earnest now. "Holly, you've got nothing to prove. Anyone who knows you can see how much heart you put into everything you do. You're not your mom, and you don't have to be. You're *you.* And honestly? That's more than enough."

I blink, her words catching me off guard. "That's disgustingly sweet, Marcy. Are you feeling okay?"

She laughs, tossing her napkin at me. "Don't ruin the moment, Frost. I'm trying to be a good friend here."

I smile despite myself, the tight knot in my chest loosening a little. Maybe she's right. Maybe I'm putting too much pressure on myself. But then the memory of the destroyed square and the missing tree flashes in my mind, and my shoulders sag again. This gala is supposed to make everyone feel like Christmas is magical, even after the awful year that Willow Creek's had, and I can't help but think I've let everyone down. Again.

Marcy reaches across the table, giving my hand a reassuring squeeze. "You'll figure it out. You always do. And if Nick Draven wants to help, let him. Even smug vampires have their uses."

"Like driving me up the wall?" I mutter.

"Or driving you against a wall?" she adds, because friendship is suffering.

"Marcy!" I swat at her, and heat rushes into my face.

"Seriously, Holly," she laughs. "Don't let him distract you. You've got a town rooting for you, even if they don't always say it. And if anyone can pull off a miracle, it's you."

I manage a weak smile, Marcy's confidence in me a balm I didn't know I needed. Her words sink in as I stare down at the remnants of my gingerbread latte, and it's not like I haven't heard similar encouragement before—my mom always tells me I have potential, that I'm capable. But potential is a nice word for not quite there yet. And that's the weight I've been carrying for as long as I can remember: the need to prove I'm more than the quirky girl who makes mistakes. More than the daughter of the Hollywood event planner. More than the girl who thought she could make a flaming wreath work.

The bell above the café door jingles, and a gust of icy wind sweeps in, carrying with it the scent of snow and pine. I glance up and freeze as a familiar figure steps inside.

Nick Draven.

Of course.

What's a peaceful morning without a dash of smug vampire to spice things up?

Snowflakes dust his dark hair and coat, the sharp lines of his face somehow making the cozy café feel like the wrong backdrop for him. His silver eyes scan the room briefly before landing on me, and a slow, infuriatingly confident smirk spreads across his lips. Even in the soft light, he has that prowly elegance—like a wolf who learned table manners and now critiques cutlery. And naturally, because the universe hates me, he looks completely unfazed by the cold, the chaos, or life in general.

"Speak of the devil," Marcy murmurs as he saunters toward the counter. "The staggeringly, stunningly gorgeous devil."

The snowflakes surrender on Nick's shoulders, and he dusts them off with theatrical care, the way some men check a watch they don't actually need.

"Don't you dare say a word," I hiss, already regretting every life choice that's led to this moment.

But Marcy just sips her mocha, her eyes gleaming with mischief. "Who, me? I wouldn't dream of it."

Chapter Four

NICK

Holly is easy to spot when I walk into the Knit and Kettle. I invariably notice everything because I'm a vampire. For instance, there are six customers in the café, four women, two men. Behind the counter, two teenage girls. Wool coats steam by the radiator; mittens drape like sleepy animals. A retro radio crackles with carols, and someone's scarf smells of pine.

Mr. Patel, the town's salt truck driver, sits by himself, doing a crossword puzzle and blowing on a hot mug of tea through his four remaining teeth. He took over this winter and drives the gritter like it's a sacred duty.

At the table over is Meribel, a reserved and elegant siren who runs the vinyl shop. She came to Willow Creek a few years ago, and there's a rumor that she's lost her voice over some mishap with an enchanted microphone. That doesn't stop her from trying to teach everyone else about the magic of harmony.

Most folks in Willow Creek are like that. Charming, eccentric, and a little out of place, until they end up here.

I notice that Holly has a slight sag under her eyes today. Not enough sleep after her Christmas tree was stolen. Her hair has more than its usual slight fray at the edges. One of her fingernails is ragged.

She's exhausted—poor thing—and the Fair Isle sweater looks like it lost a minor skirmish with static.

She'd be devastating in strong colors. Navy. Claret. Even plum. Today's pale green tries its best. She's still—infuriatingly—radiant. I wonder what magic she uses.

Holly Frost doesn't act like other humans.

Most are...intrigued by me. Curious. Sensibly impressed and occasionally wary.

She isn't.

Since that first meeting, she's barely tolerated me. I've offered advice. Assistance. Insight. Dashingly charming jokes. All of it, apparently, unwelcome.

Vexing.

And now she sits there, biting her fingernail, while her friend looks at me exactly as mortals should. Marcy understands the situation perfectly. Holly does not.

Not that I care.

This is about securing our place here before anyone has the bright idea to reconsider it.

Marcy waves at me, and I give her my three-out-of-ten smile. I've developed a scale, one I really should have patented. A one or two handles most humans. I save anything higher for when I want something.

Four would be enough to make every woman pay attention, and anything higher requires a fainting couch and smelling salts. A ten would knock the socks, and every other item of clothing, off whoever I aimed it at. I've rarely had cause to use it.

My heightened senses do a second sweep of the room, catching every detail: the hum of the espresso machine clashes with the gentle scrape of a spoon against porcelain, the faint tang of cloves mingling with the scent of old wood and spilled cream. A headless gingerbread man floats in Holly's latte, which feels pointed.

These small things used to bore me. Lately, they've become oddly comforting. Perhaps immortality makes a hobby of the mundane.

Holly sips her coffee and checks her phone, pointedly ignoring me. I swallow a fresh wave of irritation, and I wonder what that's all about.

"May I?" I ask, gliding towards the empty seat.

"Please," Marcy gushes.

Holly grunts at me.

It's typical. It's impolite at the very least. And despite this behavior that borders on rudeness, I will remain a gentleman. Polite charm costs nothing, so I turn my attention to Holly's friend. I dip my head, take her hand, and bow over her knuckles—old-world manners, not a bite.

"I don't believe we've seen each other in a while."

Holly's friend turns bright red and stammers out, "I've been doing chocolates. Making chocolates. For my store. The chocolate store. It's the one with the chocolate."

I murmur encouragingly at her, quite pleased by how flustered she is, and turn up my smile by one notch. Marcy blushes with enough intensity that it's possible her heart might explode. This is an appropriate response. It's how any normal human being should respond to a vampire as old and important as me.

Holly continues to pointedly ignore me. I cough at her. It gets her attention, and she raises her head.

Finally.

"Yes?"

"How are you, Holly?"

"Peachy," she says, though she obviously isn't. "Where are we on the elf problem?"

I clear my throat and adjust the napkin over my lap while gesturing at the teen behind the counter. I catch the barista's eye and mime a cup. She nods—table service appears to be a seasonal miracle—and I turn back to Holly. While the stimulant effects of caffeine do nothing for me since I turned, I still rather enjoy the taste. Technically, the Knit and Kettle doesn't do table service, but I am a vampire, and so the girl will inevitably do as I ask.

"You seem particularly intense this morning."

"I suppose for an immortal, human trivialities like days and weeks are barely worth noticing," she snaps. "But to us, they matter. The festival is in a week. We have no tree. You said you'd help. So fine. Help."

It's impossible to miss how the light filtering through the frosted window plays on Holly's face, and I once again note that the weariness she carries seems heavier than usual, as if it's woven into the loose threads of her sweater or the way her hair rebelliously frizzes at the ends.

I've seen humans unravel before, but with Holly, it stirs something unfamiliar—a tug, faint and persistent.

Marcy's eyes widen at Holly's demeanor, and I struggle to keep the smile glued to my face. Thankfully, the server comes over with my coffee and places it in front of me. I thank her, and she scurries off, and I pick up the steaming hot coffee and take a sip.

"Ah," Marcy exclaims. "Careful, you'll burn your mouth."

"I can't be hurt. At least not by coffee." I set my drink down and raise an eyebrow at her. "And you'd be surprised how much heat I can withstand."

Marcy melts under my attention and innuendo, which is as it should be. Another useful reminder that Holly's continuous wall of disdain is the anomaly, rather than the rule.

Of course it is. I'm delightful.

This is a Frost problem, not a reflection of me in the slightest.

Holly punctures that thought with a cough.

"That is the worst line I've ever heard in my life, and a man once asked me if I was a fruit because I look like a *fineapple*," she says.

"To business, then," I say. "It's not quite that simple. Rogue elves are a tricky business. Anyone can chase one or two off, but making them stay gone—that's the trick."

"How long will it take? I can't have them flitting around while I figure out what to do about the tree."

"Ah." I raise a finger. "Which brings us to an important distinction. What's the priority: getting rid of the elves, or getting the tree back? We likely can't do both at once."

Her brow wrinkles quite wonderfully as she considers the question, and it becomes obvious how much this matters to her. I can't recall the last time I cared about something enough to worry over it. How interesting. Perhaps I've spent too much time buried in paperwork. Mortals and their dilemmas are far more entertaining.

"Tree first," she finally says. "I can't risk its absence. The whole festival is anchored around it. It would look stupid when the dancers I've hired to perform 'Dance around the Christmas Tree' don't have an actual Christmas Tree."

"Smart choice. And finding it will likely solve the other problem. The elves appearing at the time that the tree disappeared is hardly a coincidence. I suspect they have it. We can do both."

"So why," she says through gritted teeth, "did you ask me to pick one or the other?"

"Oh," I say, waving a hand. "It sounded more dramatic."

"I knew it!" She bangs the table, earning a frown from the married couple at the table by the window. "You're not serious about this at all. This is a diversion for you. Something to occupy your time."

Holly's voice is blade-sharp and cutting. Her words are not particularly scathing—I've heard worse over the centuries—but they carry a heat, a spark of passion that my kind rarely gets to experience.

I shouldn't want to stoke that fire.

And yet, I do.

I find myself wanting its heat, drawn to it as if I were a moth. Perhaps this is part of what I find so thoroughly confusing about Holly Frost. She's like oil to my water, the heat of summer when all I want is winter's cool, and I cannot stay away from her.

"That's all life is," I say, wondering if philosophical musings might impress her. "Doing things to occupy your time. Opening a bar. Sitting here having a coffee. Would you prefer it if I helped by making more time appear or something? How would that even work? I'm not a wood sprite."

"Wood sprites can make time appear?" Marcy asks. "Since when?"

"They're distantly related to genies. They're a bit like a cross between a stopwatch and a photocopier. Terrible at parties, by the way."

"You're going to need to circle back on all of that."

Humans know so little of the supernatural world. It's complicated, and the lineages and classes of creatures can be difficult to understand and recall, even for someone as old as me. The problem of human lore and their silly books and movies has only made this worse, and I hope I won't have to explain all of it.

There are better things to do.

Like figure out why Holly is so cross with me, when all I've done is try to help.

Before I can explain further, Holly interrupts. "This is a waste of time. You were never going to be serious about this."

She rummages through her purse, muttering under her breath at me, until she emerges with a crumpled bill, which she throws on the table. As she stands up to leave, I grab her wrist. Her frustration radiates off her in waves, palpable even to the humans around us.

I rise and step into her path, close enough to catch the faintest trace of her scent—citrusy, warm, alive. It shouldn't affect me the way it does. Nothing about her should. And yet, here I am, grasping at any excuse to keep her from walking out of the Knit and Kettle and out of my life.

"Holly. Please. I want to help. I'm sorry I tried to be funny."

She snatches her hand away and puts a wool beanie on her head, preparing to exit.

"I have to go. I have things to do. Including finding a new tree and cleaning up the town. Then I see if Amazon has any elf repellent. You never know. They have Nicholas Cage pillowcases."

There's something about that last bit that causes her voice to break, and I feel a stab of sympathy. When was the last time I felt anything even close to that for a human? Several centuries, at least.

"Stop." I edge a little nearer to her. She is really very close to me, and her scent deepens. Oranges. Blood oranges too. Lovely. "Holly, let me help. I can help you get your tree back. Let's at least try that first before you resort to panic buying merchandise."

"You still haven't told me any ideas you have to help." She looks up at me, and I find the smallest glimmer of hope in her eyes. I very much want to turn that glimmer into something bigger.

"I don't know where the elves have taken your tree." She scoffs and forces me to pivot to stop her from walking out the door. I try again. "Wait. I said I don't know where the elves took it, but I know someone who does."

"Who?"

"Mímir."

"What?" She stomps her foot in frustration. "That's your answer? That's your great vampire solution? An ancient, severed head?"

"I wouldn't go near that thing, Holly," Marcy says.

"Well, duh, Marce," Holly replies. "There's no chance that thing's coming near me."

Holly perfects the art of unimpressed, and I have to confess that I'm unsurprised. Mímir has a reputation, and it isn't good. He's not nearly as bad as everyone thinks he is, but he likes people to believe that he's unpleasant because it keeps them from bothering him. I can understand and empathize with that, especially when most humans are utterly infuriating. Admittedly, he's got a bit of a temper, and he doesn't have an exactly cheery disposition, but I don't imagine many would when they've spent an eternity living the way he has.

"He's fine," I say, smoothly, using every ounce of my vampire charm. "I've known him for ages. He knows...well, everything. He knows literally everything. We'll ask him who took the tree."

"I don't feel like losing parts of my memories, thanks," Holly says.

"Oh, that." She's referring to the price Mímir demands for his information, and she seems rather hung up on it. "We'll work something out."

I flash her a two-point-five grin.

Nothing.

"I said no theatrics." Her voice is low and threatening. "And the first thing you suggest is a desiccated old head who spits out riddles in exchange for memories. This is your idea of a sane, sensible approach to the elf problem?"

"Holly," I keep my voice gentle. "Your town is seemingly plagued by mythical creatures from the beyond. Its inhabitants are invariably supernatural or connected to them in some way. Given the context, this is a remarkably measured approach."

"He's got a point," Marcy says. I give her a four-point-five smile, and she gasps a little, gripping her cup as if it's the only thing tethering her to reality.

"Whose side are you on?" Holly asks.

"His. *Oh my god.* His."

Holly makes a sound that suggests deep regret before turning her attention back to me. Her gaze is steady, but there's a flicker of something in her eyes—hesitation, maybe, or the barest trace of trust she doesn't want to admit. Holly has a way of looking at me like she's sizing up an enemy on the battlefield, one eyebrow quirking slightly as though she's daring me to prove her wrong. It's as frustrating as it is fascinating.

And I have to admit, I like it.

"Fine." The word comes out attached to a frustrated breath. "We'll try it your way. We'll visit Mímir, but if this doesn't work, I'm trying something else. But no more theatrics and weird, supernatural mumbo jumbo."

"Scout's honor." I quip, happy to return to the running joke again.

Holly doesn't look reassured.

"Let's get going."

Chapter Five

HOLLY

I've made some questionable decisions in my life, but this one is in the top five for all-time worst, and it's climbing the ranks at record speed. I've never really wanted to meet Willow Creek's relic that time forgot.

Everyone knows the story. Mímir was once human. A keeper of infinite knowledge, consulted by gods and mortals alike. Then someone decided to sever his head, likely over a disagreement about his prices. Rather than dying like a sensible person, Mímir persisted. Now his disembodied head sits on a frosted stump in the middle of a forest, trading riddles for memories, each one adding to the patchwork of experience stitched into his consciousness.

It's eerily silent as Nick and I make our way deeper into the woods. Each step we take sinks into the snow; the sound louder than it should be. My scarf keeps puffing steam into the collar of my coat, and a pocket hand warmer clicks softly against a thermos of cocoa I absolutely didn't bring for Nick. Above us, bare branches lace the sky. When the wind stirs them, they whisper like paper lanterns. It's the kind of place you'd expect to find a body in a murder mystery—or maybe something worse.

Our trip to Mímir is taking longer than I expected, and I'm not dressed for this kind of excursion. The conditions aren't helping, and this isn't the festive trip through a snow-covered winter wonderland that Nick promised me. I knew this was going to be worse than he made it out to be, and my gut is screaming that this is only the beginning.

"This feels…ominous," I mutter, my voice barely above a whisper.

Nick, of course, looks entirely at ease. His perfectly cut coat billows slightly as he strides ahead, his hands stuffed casually into his pockets. He doesn't even bother to glance back at me when he speaks.

"The forest won't bite." He pauses, throwing a smirk over his shoulder. "Those rogue elves might if they ambush us. They could descend on us from trees like drop bears."

"Not funny," I snap, tightening my scarf against the chill. "What's a drop bear?"

"Well, they're Australian, if I recall right. A distant cousin of the koala. They lurk in trees, waiting for unsuspecting maidens to pass underneath them before they fall from their branches and knock them unconscious. They don't enjoy wintry weather."

He's teasing, and I refuse to give him the pleasure of getting a rise out of me. I ignore him and continue to plow through the snow.

The faint sound of jingling bells grows louder as Nick and I trudge deeper into the depths of pine trees. It is not the cheerful jingle from carols. It's slow and weighty, as if sleigh bells forgot their song.

"I feel like I'm walking into a horror movie," I mutter, my boots crunching on the frozen ground. "What is that?"

"Festive ambiance." Nick shrugs. He is so disarmingly calm that the forest practically blushes and cues gentle snowfall. "You don't need to worry, Holly. Mímir doesn't bite. He doesn't have the teeth for it. Literally. They got pulled out years ago after they started showing signs of decay."

"An immortal, all-knowing severed head that lives in a forest has a dentist? How does flossing even work?"

"He's got a phone."

That raises about forty new questions, and I briefly consult with my clipboard on where 'learning about the telephony habits of a decapitated life coach' should be listed.

"Forget I asked."

The forest clears, and we step into a small, circular glade. It's quiet, but it's the silence of absence, not the silence of peace, and I shiver. The sun shining through the small opening bounces off a carpet of perfect, untouched snow. In the center is an ancient oak stump, gnarled and covered in frost. Atop it sits what can only be described as one of the single most bizarre sights I never imagined I'd ever witness.

It's a nightmare dressed in holiday cheer; the sight of it turns my blood cold.

"Is it wearing a Santa hat?"

Nick chuckles, brushing snow off the stump like he's welcoming an old friend. He brushes his hands together and steps back, delighted with his efforts.

"Festive ambiance."

Mímir regards us from his frost-silvered stump. His features look carved from old stone, the kind that remembers stories, and his sunken eye sockets glow red. A knitted Santa hat perches at a hopeful angle. Someone has looped soft tinsel around the stump and a single strand of multicolored Christmas lights winks with patient persistence.

I blink, certain I've lost my mind. "This cannot be..."

"Mímir." Nick bows. "I see you're in a festive mood."

The head's mouth opens with a dry click, a sound like wind through a keyhole. It groans, and every single hair on the back of my neck stands on end. Even the trees around us whisper in fright as the head wakes up, as if we're all waiting nervously to find out what kind of mood he's in.

"Niklaus Draven," he rasps, his voice like gravel scraping across metal. "And with him, Holly Frost."

I take an instinctive step back. "Why does he know my name?"

Nick chuckles, completely unfazed. "He knows everything. It's his defining trait. Holly, meet Mímir. Mímir, meet Holly Frost."

Mímir hums, the sound unsettling and calm at once. "Frost. Apt. The air about her is oranges and worry."

I glare at Nick and adjust my hat, hoping that its acute angle conveys how thoroughly unsettled I am.

"I don't like this."

Nick only shrugs. "It's fine."

I don't know why I expected anything from the vampire in the way of support. He stands beside the stump, completely at ease, as if the pair of them are about to start a carol concert. It's as though chatting with a severed, glowing, tinsel-covered head is the most natural, normal thing in the world, and Nick doesn't flinch or falter under Mímir's scrutiny, his calm so absolute it borders on arrogance.

Watching him, I can't help but wonder if this vampire is immune to fear or if he simply doesn't care enough to feel it.

"We seek your counsel, Mims. We need your wisdom."

The head gurgles, and I look forward to a few months of nightmares from this experience.

"You're aware of the arrangement," he intones. "Thus our pact is spoken; thus our bargain stands. Time is a fleeting arrow, memory's tethered strands. What was sought is granted; the cost lay in our hands."

"Not happening. I'm out. So long, Draven. Enjoy your tete-a-tete with Severed Seagal over here. I'm not giving it one of my memories. I still have a recurring nightmare about third year when I called my professor 'mom,' and even that one's staying."

The air grows heavier, as though the forest itself is holding its breath. The faint jingling of the lights around Mímir's neck is almost mocking, a grotesque parody of holiday cheer. Even the snow beneath my feet seems unnaturally still, muffling the sound of my shifting boots. The chill is more supernatural than seasonal.

Nick holds up a hand, silencing me with a frustratingly calm look. "Relax. I told you. I'll pay."

"Generous," Mímir says, his tone dripping with mockery. "What knowledge do you seek, bloodsucker?"

Nick ignores the jab. "A Christmas tree. Stolen from Willow Creek by rogue elves. Where is it?"

Mímir's gums mash together as he chuckles, an unsettling rattle that seems to reverberate through the frozen forest, making the trees groan in response.

"Ah, the tree of light," he rasps, the words oozing from his tongue like old honey. "It stands where glitter gathers, snow flurries, and mischief keeps watch. Seek the unlit star and the path will show itself."

His eyes glow brighter, their red almost hungry, as if he relishes the confusion that haunts the air between us.

I throw up my hands. "Great. Cryptic riddles. So helpful."

Nick smiles. "It's part of the fun."

"You have incredibly bizarre ideas of what constitutes fun."

Mímir's glowing eyes hold steady, unblinking. "Mind the Hollow of Mischief. The elves guard it closely, even though their hearts are twisted by betrayal and their minds consumed with chaos. Outwit their leader, the one with the crooked crown, fur-lined and heavy with red."

The clearing darkens at his words, the once-cheerful flicker of his lights now a sinister pulse, and it feels more like a forgotten ornament lurking in the attic. The snow beneath me shifts as it stirs in response to the riddle, and the wind howls across me, bringing anything but seasonal cheer.

Perhaps Christmas has decided to hold its breath.

"The Hollow of Mischief?" I ask. "That sounds completely safe and not at all horrifying."

"It's only a name," Nick says, gently, as if that helps.

"Mm-hmm. And 'crooked crown'?"

"A metaphor," Nick says, clearly guessing.

"Minds consumed by chaos?"

"A tautology."

"Do you even know what that word means?"

"Something to do with tacos?"

This is definitely not the experience I expected. So much for assuming a treaty with an immortal head would be straightforward. Nothing about this is reassuring. Nick isn't taking this seriously. That much is obvious now. His involvement is only making things worse. More complicated. More ridiculous. Harder to control.

A mistake.

Mímir's jaw creaks open one last time. "Beware, mortals. One wrong step, and you may lose more than just your way. Mind the bells that do not ring and the red that walks in winter." His red-rimmed eyes zero in on Nick. "Now, as to payment."

"Right." Nick places his palm to Mímir's brow where faint runes glimmer.

The air shivers the way heat does over a road, and a thin silver thread lifts from Nick's temple and settles into the stone. He inhales, eyes closed, then releases the breath and lowers his hand.

"All done," he says. "Thanks, Mims."

"That's it? You lost a memory?"

Nick nods. "I've been alive a long time. Got a lot stored up there. For a vampire, this is more like housecleaning. I don't even remember the memory he took."

"Now, that's a tautology."

"We'll get dinner later." He knocks on top of Mímir's head. "Mims, what did you take?"

"Your quarrel with Shakespeare about the names of Romeo and Juliet. He wanted to call them Cecil and Mildred."

"Brilliant pen, questionable naming instincts," Nick says, amused. "'Mildred, Mildred, wherefore art thou, Mildred?' It never quite sang."

Nick laughs at his own joke as these two quasi-immortal beings casually discuss things that happened five hundred years ago, and my brain quietly gives up. This is insane.

The glow in Mímir's eye sockets dims, the red hue fading until it's little more than a faint ember. The eerie light flickers like a malfunctioning Christmas light left out in the cold too long. It stutters once, twice, before sputtering out completely, leaving only the soft, cold glare of sunlight to cast long shadows over the clearing. The strand of lights along the stump returns to a steady twinkle, like a nightlight someone refuses to unplug in December.

Nick claps his hands together, looking entirely too pleased with himself. "See? That wasn't so bad. It was helpful."

I stare at him, incredulous. "You call that helpful?"

"Extremely."

I mutter under my breath as we leave the glade. The forest seems darker now, the trees pressing in closer, their branches casting long, spindly shadows over the snow.

Nick is completely unfazed, even though we've just been given a warning from an ancient, severed head about rogue elves, a cursed tree, and an ominous place called the Hollow of Mischief. Not exactly the kind of thing you brush off lightly if you're mortal. It's annoying, the way he saunters through life jingling like pocket sleigh bells, while I try not to hyperventilate into a gift bag. He moves like someone who's made his peace with long years. I have not, and I'm in a hurry, and Nick Draven hasn't been human in a very long time.

The silence in the forest grows heavier as we continue our trek back to town. The chill sinks right down to my bones and refuses to let go. A shiver runs through me, and I try to ignore the sense of being watched, as if something in the trees is waiting for us to make the wrong move. The wind stirs, carrying the faintest scent of pine and something metallic. Somewhere far off, a bell rings in town, thin and bright. I picture windows steaming in one of the beignet bakeries and a row of sweaters drying by the radiator.

"So, the Hollow of Mischief," I say, breaking the silence. "Do you know where that is?"

Nick glances over his shoulder, his silver eyes glinting even brighter now. "I've been in several." He grins at his terrible joke, and my cheeks turn scarlet. "But this one could be a bit trickier to make our way into."

The urge to strangle him rises, and it's briefly satisfying to consider—until I remember it wouldn't end him or put me out of my misery.

"You don't know where it is, do you?"

"Not exactly," he says simply. "But we'll find it."

I give him a long look. "And you're sure about that?"

"Of course," he says as though it's the most obvious thing in the world. "It's Christmas. Everything's a little more magical this time of year, right? We just have to follow the signs."

"Right," I mutter under my breath, reassured about nothing. "I suppose we'll be following a star and hoping it leads us to a baby and a manger next."

It's hard to tell whether my frustration comes from his carefree attitude or the unsettling feeling gnawing at me as the wind picks up, howling through the trees like some kind of warning. The snow is falling heavier now, and the path ahead looks just as creepy as when we started, the forest pressing around us like it's trying to keep us here. I glance toward the distant lights of Willow Creek, a small beacon of normalcy, and a sinking feeling settles in my stomach.

"We're not getting anywhere like this," I say, my voice tense. "We've got to head back into town. If we're going to get that tree and stop whatever this is, we need a plan. And we're not going to find it out here, in the middle of nowhere."

Nick falters slightly, his gaze flicking toward the darkened woods behind us. He nods, as if weighing the idea. For a moment, one glorious moment, he looks like he's actually thinking about things properly, like he's finally taking something seriously.

"You're right. We'll regroup. Over eggnog. Perhaps a mince pie might help?"

Maybe not.

"An eggnog?" I repeat, incredulous. "After what we just heard, your solution is a Christmas treat?"

Nick shrugs. "What's the point of fighting the supernatural if you can't enjoy the finer things in life? Eggnog is holiday spirit in a cup. It's a survival tool at this time of year." He stops and gives me a look I can't quite figure out. "Just because serious things are happening doesn't mean we have to be serious about them. Life is supposed to be fun."

"Oh? That's your ancient wisdom, Saint Nick of the Undying? Life is supposed to be fun, is that all?"

He stops so fast I slam into his back. He turns, suddenly serious.

"The best purpose I've found in life is to savor it. Like warm cocoa with the people you love. If you find better, send me a postcard."

With that, he spins and starts walking back, hands tucked in his pockets, clearly enjoying the absurdity of it all. Watching him for a second, confusion and frustration tangle together—a vampire telling me to lighten up feels like a failure so astounding that it doesn't have a name yet.

But part of me knows he might not be wrong. Maybe all of this would be easier to deal with if I just went with it.

With a sigh, I follow him.

"If we're getting eggnog, mine's getting an extra shot," I say. "And I call dibs on the biggest mince pie."

Chapter Six

NICK

We make our way back to town, not quite arm in arm, but closer than before. Holly's been quiet, but at least she hasn't complained about the cold or the fact that all we got from Mímir was a cryptic riddle. Given her usual fire, her silence seems like progress.

She's discouraged. It shows in the way her shoulders hunch and the drag of her steps. We made real progress today, but she doesn't see it. Now doesn't seem like the time to say I told you so.

Eggnog will help.

Telling her about the Hollow of Mischief can wait.

With luck, things will feel more settled by then. There's something about Holly Frost that gets under my skin in a way that unsettles me deeply. Not bad, exactly. Not as such. Just confusing. Strangely warm. The heaviness in her steps and the way she grumbles about the cold are increasingly difficult to ignore.

More concerning is the fact that I bent the truth about the Hollow of Mischief. Its nature is perfectly clear. I know exactly how to get there, but the walk back didn't seem like the right time to gloat. Not when her nose was all crinkled up like discarded wrapping paper. Describing it as anything other than a pocket dimension surrounded by evil, buried beneath a mountain of misery wouldn't have been comforting, and anything more accurate requires an advanced degree in Eldritch Geography with a minor in Quantum Physics.

The truth is, it's difficult to navigate and harder to survive.

Not somewhere rogue elves end up by accident or for amusement.

It means that the pesky two-foot-high menaces are working for someone. It means that Holly has gotten herself into more than she realizes. And it means that someone is targeting Willow Creek—and that this is a bigger problem than I thought it was.

The coven's only just started to settle here. Things are working. My brethren have found their footing and Willow Creek has found a way to live with us. It's a fragile arrangement, whether anyone admits it or not.

And I've seen how quickly that sort of balance can unravel. One wrong incident, one convenient scapegoat, and suddenly everything we've built becomes the problem.

I have no intention of letting that happen here.

Which means I need to find out exactly who is behind this—and stop them before anyone leaps to the conclusion it was a vampire.

It looks like Ronan will get his battle after all.

I surreptitiously glance at Holly as the town's warm glow welcomes us back. Windows fog softly. Garlands bead the lampposts. Someone in a doorway is shaking powdered sugar over a tray of rugelach. She doesn't seem comforted by any of it. Her nose is red from the cold, and her brows are furrowed as she wrestles with the problem at hand.

Now also doesn't feel like the time to tell her things just got worse.

Her lips press into a thin line as we push open the diner door. A bell tings. The smell of pancakes rolls over us. A pie case glows like stained glass, all apple and pecan and mince. Warmth and chatter spill out as a ripple smooths itself against one of the coffee pots.

People turn to look. I'm used to it. Holly isn't. She stiffens at the attention, holding herself tight, like she's bracing for impact.

I guide her to a quiet booth at the back, only to find it already occupied.

By Frank.

The town mayor. And, more importantly, a Cupid.

They're not twelve-inch cherubs. Hollywood directors and Renaissance artists did their best with the legends, but most Cupids resemble ordinary humans. This one favors the shape of a solid middle-aged man with a handlebar mustache and a perpetual cigar stub. He's currently finishing off what looks like several plates of French fries and when he sees Holly approach, his face breaks into a delighted smile.

"My favorite event planner!" His voice is warm, gruff, and booming as he heaves himself from the booth and wraps her in a crushing embrace.

Holly pats his back, a futile attempt at returning the hug before he releases her and turns to me with a grunt. "Draven."

"Cupe."

His mustache twitches. "It's Frank, round these parts. You know that."

I let it go, sensing Holly's disapproval. "Apologies, Frank. Mind if we sit?"

"Sit, sit." He shoves some plates aside, and Holly and I slide in across from him. Our thighs press together. I pretend not to notice. It's really very distracting.

Frank eyes us with amusement, and it makes me wonder what he's up to. Cupids are powerful, and Frank is stronger than most. They are also, by nature, meddlesome in the benevolent way that moves seating charts and lives.

"Didn't expect this when your mom recommended you to me. Certainly not you and the town's most eligible vampire."

"We're not together," Holly says. "He's...helping me. With the tree problem."

"Nasty business." Frank leans back, stretching his arms over the seatback. "Rogue elves, I hear?"

Holly hesitates, looking at the floor.

I don't like her nervousness, and a strange ripple of protectiveness surges through me. It appears I've returned from our trip to Mímir with more than a riddle to solve, if the sudden urge to throw my coat over Holly and growl at anyone who looks at her sideways is any indication of what I've brought back.

"Yes, Frank. Draven chased them off."

"Easy work?" Frank winks at me.

"Nothing to it."

The leather of the seats creaks as Holly shuffles uncomfortably. I don't like it. It's a small thing, but it irritates me. Like an itch under my skin. Frank shouldn't be making her feel worse.

Before I can say anything noble and reckless, we're interrupted by a young man. He's barely twenty, and he shuffles up to the booth, hands deep in his pockets as he hunches all the way over. He looks like he has a bad case of acne and love sickness, and neither bodes well.

"Mayor Frank?" He glances around nervously.

Frank nods. "Casey. Good to see you, son. What can I do for you?"

Casey runs a hand through his greasy hair. "I was hoping you could...help. With a problem."

Frank sighs, apparently already knowing where this is going. "What's on your mind?"

"I'd rather say in private." Casey looks around and drops his voice. "It's about Sarah Waterson."

Frank's expression softens, but he shakes his head. "I don't do that sort of thing here. You know that."

"I know, but I thought—"

"She's not for you, lad."

His voice isn't loud. It doesn't have to be.

I can feel the waves of power emanating from him, and the diner hushes by a degree. Frank has the kind of magic that reroutes crushes, eases old knots, and prevents very bad poems from being written—and Casey doesn't stand a chance. Not against a display of divine intervention dressed as heartbreak, like the world's most passive-aggressive Valentine's Day card.

The diner's background noise softens. The air seems to steady. Frank's power ripples through the room, subtle but undeniable. It is not empire-toppling power, at least not tonight. It is the sort that gently turns a heart toward a better path and saves a barista from a sonnet.

Casey flinches but tries again. "I just thought—"

Frank repeats himself, voice like iron wrapped in velvet. "She's not for you. Listen to me. Move on. Let her move on."

There's another faint pulse of energy, barely perceptible. Casey's shoulder slumps further. He mumbles a thanks and slinks away.

I exhale slowly, grateful for the reminder of who Frank really is. He may play the role of the affable mayor, but it's a game. Just as I play the humble bar owner. Both are ruses, designed to mask what lies underneath. The power beneath Frank's aw-shucks exterior is raw and absolute. If it came to a fight, the outcome would not be clear-cut. I'd probably win if Ronan turned up, provided he brought his axe and left Crinkshaw at home.

Thankfully, the moment passes. Frank smiles, the weight of his power gone as if it was never there. Holly studies her menu, oblivious to the cosmic-scale romantic smackdown that was almost unleashed around her.

"Mayor Frank, about the tree?"

"I know you'll handle this, Holly," he says, beaming at her. "Your mom swears you're the best."

Frank's voice is warm and buttery, the kind of voice that soothes children to sleep and convinces adults to do the sensible thing. But right now, it's also a voice that makes Holly sit up straighter, her fingers tightening around the edge of the table like it's the only thing keeping her from bolting.

There's something about the way he says it that makes my teeth clench. It's not quite a suggestion. Not even a command. Worse than that. It's an expectation. He doesn't say *if* she fixes the problem. He says *when*.

Holly swallows hard. "I'm trying. I really am. I don't know how to yet. I'm working on it."

Frank waves a hand. "Oh, I have every faith in you. The whole town does." He leans back, all casual magnanimity, as if he hasn't dumped a snowstorm's worth of pressure on her shoulders. "Celeste doesn't recommend people lightly."

Holly nods stiffly. I can practically hear the internal screaming.

"Celeste?" I ask.

"My mom," Holly shrugs, trying for casual and not quite getting there. "She's based in Los Angeles. Event planning. Big event."

"My last event planner moved on after I helped bring Willow Creek together and launched the Winter Wonderland Gala. Celeste called. Put in a very strong word. And when Celeste Frost calls, you pay attention. She said Holly was ready. That she understood how to take something important and make it unforgettable. I knew I had to give her daughter a chance. But without the Winter Wonderland and its Christmas tree, Willow Creek is just another supernatural town with too many gift shops."

Holly's expression turns into something between confusion and concern, like she's trying to do math in her head and all the numbers are made of fairies. I, meanwhile, feel my irritation rise by the second. Why is he talking like the tree is some sacred artifact? Is it? Does it grant immortality? Is it powered by collective goodwill and the town choir's better harmonies? Why is everyone being so weird about a damn tree? I need to get more information.

"Right." I sit forward, giving Frank a long look. "And by important, you mean...?"

"Well, Willow Creek has always been a special, magical place." Frank's voice turns proud, and I realize I'm in for a story. "It's a place where goodness can exist, unironically. A place where neighbors still know each other's names. Where everyone is welcome, whether they're vampires, or humans, or anything else. The Winter Wonderland is a reminder of that."

"It's more than that though, isn't it?" It might be a stab in the dark, but several lifetimes spent in darkness have made my aim unusually good. Unsurprisingly, this hits its mark and Frank slowly nods.

I glance at Holly, and she looks sick.

It's possible I feel sick. For her.

And then Frank winks. He winks, like this is all just a fun little puzzle we're supposed to solve.

"You'll see."

I stare at him. Holly stares at him. There's no need to look at her to know she's about three seconds away from a small festive detonation.

"Frank," I say, doing my best impression of a reasonable man, which is becoming increasingly difficult, given my vampiric tendencies and proximity to Holly. "If this tree is such a big deal, why not just tell us why?"

Frank shoves a fry into his mouth, and his power starts to gather around us. He's talking to both of us, but the message lands differently for me. He lets the words out slowly.

"I told you it matters."

Holly looks like she wants to bang her head against the table. Personally, the idea of introducing Frank's head to the concept of gentle honesty has a strong appeal. Repeatedly. Maybe then he'd stop being so damn cryptic.

And only now does it occur to me that this is about more than protecting our place in Willow Creek. That was the sensible reason. The one I could admit to. I've been telling myself I'm doing this to make sure the coven stays settled and we weren't blamed when things went wrong.

I'm doing this because Holly needs me.

Whether she knows it or not, this needs to be handled.

All of which is, quite frankly, concerning—because it suggests caring is involved.

And caring is the first step down a slippery slope that ends in feelings. And I don't do feelings. Or launching myself into oblivion like some ski jumper hurtling down toward disaster. I do brooding. Smirking. Ominous lurking in shadowed doorways. But apparently, Holly Frost has single-handedly started to dismantle my carefully cultivated persona, and it remains unclear how I feel about that.

Probably best to pretend it's not happening.

This strategy has never failed me, except when it has.

"I'll let you two work out the details," Frank says, abruptly back to the cheerful mayor. "You have it under control, Holly. I know you do. I would hate to step in if you cannot get this done. That would be very disappointing."

Holly nods automatically, but her hands are clenched in her lap, and when Frank turns away, she exhales like she's been holding her breath for an hour.

I watch him go, still trying to decide whether it would be worth the paperwork to escort him outside for a brisk chat in an alley. Eventually, I turn back to Holly.

"You okay?"

She huffs out something like a laugh. "Oh, I'm peachy. Love a good impossible task with zero context. Really gets the blood pumping."

The server appears with two hot chocolates, unasked, each crowned with whipped cream and a dusting of cinnamon. Holly wraps both hands around one as if it might argue.

There's a tension in her voice, an exhaustion she's trying to hide under humor, and it makes something in my chest tighten. I *hate* that Frank put this all on her without so much as an explanation. I hate that she's just *taking* it, like she doesn't have a choice.

I drum my fingers against the table. "Well, there's nothing we can do about it tonight. But I do know a place that serves a very strong drink."

Her brows lift. "You mean Hemoglow?"

"The very same." I flash my best smile. "C'mon, Frosty. Let's get you a civilized drink. Tonight's on me."

She sighs, but there's the tiniest curve to her lips, like she's trying not to smile. "I've never been to Hemoglow. I'm not sure I approve of a blood bar."

I adjust my shirt and put on my most charming six-out-of-ten smile.

"Even better. That means if you enjoy yourself, you'll have to admit I was right."

She gives me a long, considering look, then finally stands. "Fine. One drink. But if you try to sell me a membership package, I will deploy a candy cane in a manner you won't enjoy."

"Fair enough," I say, offering my arm.

She gives me a stare that suggests I'm already on thin ice, but takes my arm anyway, and I decide not to be thrilled. I fail. Immediately.

I was supposed to be using all of this to protect my coven. Right now, I don't care about that.

Right now, I want to make Holly Frost smile.

And that's more dangerous than whatever Frank's not telling us.

Probably.

Chapter Seven

HOLLY

Nick leads me out of the diner, and everyone's watching. It makes me feel awkward, conscious that every slight mistake will be noticed. He gives the waitress a wink as he opens the door, and the wink lands. I wish he'd stop doing that. Or at least save it for people who are not working.

The pressure is staggering. We should be brainstorming ways to find the Hollow of Mischief. I should be out looking for that stupid tree. But right now, it feels like I've had the wind knocked out of me, and I'm too tired to keep fighting.

Outside, the wreaths along Main Street tilt toward the fairy lights. Snow lifts in little swirls. The evening air is cold and kind. Shop windows glow. Somewhere, a brass trio attempts *Good King Wenceslas* with enthusiasm if not precision. Hank and Marvin, the Folder twins, are practicing knot-tying with red licorice ropes, and then eating the evidence.

The world outside seems stuck in some kind of limbo, just like me. My thoughts drift as we walk toward Hemoglow with the snow falling gently around us, their dazzling display helping to clear the noise in my head. The town lights twinkle against the backdrop of the dark sky, and the cozy cheer settles in enough that I can breathe again.

Nick slows at each icy patch, and I'm quite grateful his arm is there to steady me.

"You good?" he asks, leaning forward with a genuine, unguarded look.

I try to muster up some enthusiasm, but it's hard when everything feels like it's teetering on the edge of disaster. We're one carol away from a catastrophe, and it's going to take more than a Christmas miracle to fix this one. I would kill for a manageable amount of catastrophe, like the town sliding into a yawning chasm of infinite despair or finding out the nativity scene is carnivorous.

"Yeah. Just thinking."

Nick doesn't say anything for a moment, probably sensing something is off through whatever sixth sense vampires possess. "Willing to let me in on what you're thinking about?"

A sharp retort rises in my mouth, but it gets swallowed back before it can leap out. I'm on edge, and even though Draven irritates me, none of this is his fault. Not specifically.

"I'm fine," I lie, and by the look on his face, he clearly knows I'm fibbing. "I'm mostly fine. Closer, anyway."

"Settle down, Indigo Girls," he teases. "Halfway?"

"Making progress towards it. This is a lot to take in. Elves. Weird, talking heads. Commerce was my favorite class in school, and none of these topics were really covered in any detail."

"It's a lot," he says. "More than I expected."

"Why are you really helping, Draven? I doubt it is a sudden love of carols. What do you get out of this?"

He doesn't flinch at my tone. Instead, he gives me a small, sheepish shrug. It's almost adorable. Almost boyish. And I decide I do not like the way it makes me want to like him.

"The pleasure of your company?"

A small scoff escapes my lips. "Sure. I believe you."

He rubs the back of his neck, self-consciously. "I know this might look a bit opportunistic. But it's not about taking advantage of your situation or making the vampires into something we're not." He glances toward the square, his eyes glinting with something darker than humor. "My coven likes it here. Willow Creek works. And when things start to go wrong, people tend to look for someone to blame, and I'd rather we weren't the obvious suspect when they do."

I shake my head. "I don't need you turning this into...whatever this is for you."

The square should be brimming with holiday cheer, but it's as deflated as the snowman that one of the town's residents is trying to patch up with black electrical tape. Faint traces of garland still hang from the lamp posts, but they're half-fallen, as though the town's Christmas spirit has been abandoned with the missing tree. The space feels hollow, the empty patch of snow where it should stand only highlighting the chaos that's been left behind.

Nick watches my clenched jaw for a moment, then speaks in a lower voice. "Holly—"

I cut him off, not wanting to hear whatever sympathetic words he's about to offer. "Don't. I know Frank's trying to *help,* but my mom's said the same thing before. It's not like I can fix it all at once."

Nick rolls his shoulders, visibly uncomfortable for the first time ever. "Look, I don't know your family dynamics, but I know you're putting way too much pressure on yourself. That's why you're acting like this. And it's not good for you."

I'm about to argue, but the words die on my lips. For the first time, I actually think about what he's saying. Maybe he's right. Maybe this has been too much, too fast—because, for all my bravado, the gala matters. The town matters. And doing this alone isn't working.

The silence stretches, and his gaze softens as he watches me, his face still relaxed but there's a hint of concern creeping through. It's strange, this shift. Nick's usually so wrapped up in himself and the other vampires that it's easy to forget he's capable of *caring* about something more than his blood bar and the chaos he brings.

I let out a long, steadying breath, rubbing at my temple. "I don't know where to start. Everything feels like it's slipping out of my hands, and I can't catch up."

Nick locks his eyes with mine, and for once, there's nothing hidden there. Their silver isn't clouding anything, and he isn't trying to charm me. He's just being Nick, and he's just standing here. Listening. Trying to help.

"You don't have to do this alone, you know. I get that you're trying to hold it all together, but you've got people who want to help. Me included."

"So, what now?"

"We figure it out," he says. "Do you know where the real power in being a vampire comes from?"

The question takes me by surprise. "Anne Rice? Or, do you have, like, a vampire God or something? I don't know."

"It's the coven. The group of individuals we travel with, the ones who support us through our endless passage through time. The fact that we're never alone." He slides his sleeve so it brushes mine, then stills. "Let us be your coven, Holly. We can help."

The sincerity of the offer catches me by surprise, and I'm flustered. I can deal with sarcastic vampires and arrogant vampires, but genuine vampires are a bit much.

"Is there a membership fee? Or do you have to eat me?"

He doesn't say anything; he only stares at me. As the seconds pass, I realize the exact words that just left my mouth, and my face heats with embarrassment. Draven leaves me to flounder in my moment for a few more uncomfortable seconds before jumping in.

With a theatrical cough, he says, "Let's leave that part out for now."

Nick stays silent as we walk to the blood bar, occasionally

offering me his elbow to lean on as I skirt around the half-frozen puddles. Reflexively, I type out a message to Mr. Patel, who likes to know when patches appear. We carry on past the shopfronts with their Christmas displays, each cheerfully trying to outdo the next. Mrs. Christie, proprietor of Sugar Me Timbers, is out front locking up. She's a delightful grandmother who wields her authority with the rolling pin that rarely leaves her side, and as we go by, she gives me a sly grin and lifts it in salute.

Ahead, the neon sign of Nick's blood bar shines like an oasis in the dark.

Hemoglow looks like a tavern that grew up into a speakeasy and then made friends with a holiday market. The sign is a soft red script with a single teardrop for the O, casting a soft blush over the pavement. Frosted windows wear etched snowflakes and veined leaves, velvet curtains parted just enough to show the candlelight beyond. Beneath a low timber lintel, a wreath of black green holly hangs on the door, its glass berries a deep garnet, and a chalkboard advertises a Warm Winter Flight with clove mulled O, spiced AB with orange peel, and a cranberry tonic chaser. The brass handle gleams, polished by a thousand late-night arrivals.

We reach the door, and Nick holds it open for me, his usual swagger firmly back in place. The warmth hits me immediately, the sound of laughter and clinking glasses wrapping around us as we step inside. The place smells of dark wood, cloves, and a hint of something mineral that reads more library than laboratory. It's a scent I've started associating with Nick more than I care to admit, and worse, I've started to like it.

The bar is nothing like I expected.

Warm light glows from beeswax sconces and old glass pendants, casting honey across polished wood and deep red velvet. Behind the bar, bottles gleam like liquid jewels. A fireplace crackles in the corner, lending a cozy note that feels almost out of place against the elegance. Paper snowflakes drift overhead, and a chalkboard near the door reads *House Rules: be kind. Consent is required. Hydrate between drinks. Free rides home after ten.*

The crowd isn't what I imagined, either. I expected broody vampires nursing crimson cocktails or maybe a few terrified humans hoping to be glamoured into oblivion. Instead, it's oddly normal. A mix of humans and vampires chatting, laughing, and even clinking glasses over what looks suspiciously like mulled wine. A small spruce twinkles in the corner, all mismatched ornaments and a paper star that lists the staff cookie swap schedule.

Nick watches me take it all in, a smirk tugging at his lips. "Not bad, huh?"

"It's nicer than I thought it would be."

He places a hand over his heart, feigning a wound. "Your faith in me is overwhelming, Frost."

We take a seat by the bar, and I'm about to fire back a retort when a sharp-dressed bartender in suspenders with a sprig of holly on his lapel interrupts me. His dark brown hair is immaculately combed, and there's a devilish glint in his eyes. He's tall, muscular, and seems to be the kind of man who's used to having women fawn over him, and he looks like he knows every regular's order and their dog's name.

"Evening, Nick. Your usual?"

Nick nods but gestures toward me. "And whatever she's having."

The bartender arches an eyebrow at me, clearly amused. "First-time? Welcome to Hemoglow. Hot toddy with rosemary honey, or our mulled cranberry spritz?"

"Either," I reply, feeling strangely out of my element.

Nick leans against the bar, his focus shifting to a pair of women across the room. They're clearly human, their faces flushed from one too many drinks, giggling as they make their way toward us. One of them, a blonde in a glittery dress that screams holiday party reject, zeroes in on Nick like a child who's spotted the biggest present under the tree.

"Nick!" she exclaims, her voice high-pitched and slurred. "There you are! We were hoping we could tempt you to join us!"

Her friend, equally tipsy but marginally more restrained, giggles behind her. "You can't leave us to fend for ourselves, you know. It's dangerous. Anything could happen to us with all these *vicious* vampires around."

I brace for Nick's ego to inflate, ready to roll my eyes at whatever smug comeback he'll deliver. But to my surprise, he doesn't take the bait. Instead, he stiffens and puts a hand on the blonde's arm, stopping her from falling over before he eases her back to rest against the bar.

"Ladies," he says smoothly but with a touch of firmness. "I'm glad you've enjoyed your evening. Sounds like you might be close to the end of it."

The blonde pouts, leaning heavily on the bar, practically thrusting her cleavage at Nick. "But we're having fun—"

"And you'll thank me tomorrow when you're not dealing with a hangover," Nick replies, his tone light but insistent.

The blonde lets out an exaggerated sigh, leaning closer to Nick until she's practically draped over him, her glittery dress catching the light like a disco ball.

"You're no fun," she purrs, her voice slurring as she places a hand on his chest. "Come on, Nick. Dance with me. Just one dance. Or something more private." She winks, the kind of dramatic, over-the-top gesture only someone three drinks past their limit can pull off. "I'll let you bite me wherever you like..."

I expect Nick to make some smug comment or, worse, encourage her, but instead, he gently removes her hand and takes a small step back, creating space between them.

"Jenna, you've had enough excitement for one night," he says, his voice calm but firm. He's surprisingly gentle, and the polite, polished smile never leaves his face. "Let's get you and your friend home. No more drinks, no more bad decisions. Wes, can you get them some water and call them a car?"

The friend, who's been leaning against the bar, giggling into her glass, finally speaks up. "He's right, Jenna. Let's call it a night." She tugs at Jenna's arm, pulling her away from Nick with surprising efficiency.

Nick waits until Wes places glasses of water in front of them, making sure the women are settled at a nearby booth, before returning to his spot at the bar. He slides back into his usual relaxed stance, but there's no trace of smugness in his expression. Just quiet satisfaction.

I raise an eyebrow at him. "Not what I expected."

"What, you think I let people stumble out of here into the night with no help?" he asks, his smirk returning. "I've got standards, Holly. It's nice to know you have such a low opinion of me."

I glance toward the women, who are now sipping water and laughing quietly as they wait. "I thought you'd be more...arrogant about it. You seem to enjoy reveling in attention."

Nick shrugs, his expression unusually subdued. "Look, I get it. People think vampires are all blood and seduction and bad decisions. And sure, we lean into it sometimes. But we have rules. We keep people safe. That's the point of Hemoglow."

Wes sets our drinks in front of us, and Nick picks up his glass, swirling the dark red liquid inside. He takes a sip, and his eyes meet mine, and yet again, he isn't trying to charm me. Or hide anything from me. He's leveling with me over a glass of blood in a bar full of questionable decisions.

"You've got this idea of me in your head, Frost, but it's only part of the story. Spend a little more time looking at the rest."

An answer evades me. It's disarming seeing him like this. This version of Nick, the one who isn't all smirk and scheme, is different. The possibility of being wrong about him sits in my chest like an ornament that doesn't match the others and somehow matters more because of it.

I sip the toddy, and it's ridiculously good. Warmth spreads. The room is still warm and a little hush-hush, like a library that decided to learn carols. Someone by the hearth starts a quiet chorus of In the Bleak Midwinter and the room hums along, off-key and wholehearted. It feels right. Intentional, like Nick has created a place where people, human or not, can feel at ease.

Maybe he isn't all bad.

Maybe he's more than I thought he was.

Not that I'm going to tell him that.

Chapter Eight

NICK

Watching Holly emerge from her shell is delightful. There's still a tightly wound core that never fully relaxes, but her guarded tension has dropped, and she seems to be enjoying herself. I make her laugh with a story about Henry II of England, and if that's not a Christmas miracle, then I don't know what is.

"I can safely say that the invention of the shower was the greatest contribution to humanity's future of anything else," I finish. "I had to breathe through my mouth during most of the early centuries."

Her laugh is wonderful, and it sounds like joy. Paper snowflakes spin lazily in the draft from the door. Somewhere near the hearth, someone attempts harmony and nearly finds it. I can't help but smile when I look at Holly.

"What's it like?" She finishes the last of her mulled wine. "Immortality, that is."

"It's...fine, I suppose. You get perspective. After the first century, you learn about how temporary everything is. Everything comes and everything goes. You learn not to get too connected to anything."

"It sounds lonely."

Wes sets down a plate of sugared shortbread between us, as if loneliness is best handled with biscuits. He isn't wrong.

I shrug, trying to brush off my emotions as she hits the nail on the head. "That's why a coven is so important. It's a thing of permanence in an ocean of impermanence."

"And that's why you started the bar here?"

"It lets us be a part of Willow Creek." My eyes go distant. "The hardest thing for humans to understand is how unbelievably long a century is. It's the longest possible thing you can imagine, and I mean that literally. Human brains aren't very good at large scales. By the third century, it becomes hard to keep going. You've done everything you've ever dreamed of. You've had just about every experience there is to have."

"You give them purpose." She places her hand on my arm, and my skin tingles with the contact. We share a look, a real one, and some of that glimmer I've been working so hard on expands. She leans forward. "Who gives you purpose, Niklaus Draven?"

My entire body reacts, a flush of electricity jolting through me. Holly's asked a real question, and more than that, she's looking at me like it matters. Like she's worried I'm sad. Or lonely. If I had blood, there'd probably be blushing involved, possibly combustion. Instead, the entirely unhelpful urge to kiss her until the room forgets its carols surges through me.

It's exhilarating.

It's too soon, so with a profound force of willpower, I force a nonchalant smile onto my face.

"Oh. This and that."

My answer, my reaction, all of it is too casual for the moment, and the glimmer in her eyes vanishes. The wall snaps back into place. She moves away. The moment breaks.

I blew it.

There were only so many ways that could have gone. I was unprepared for my feelings, and she caught me by surprise. Startling, really, and yet another thing that hasn't happened in a very long time.

"Why don't you tell me about the Hollow of Mischief?" she asks.

This isn't a conversation I want to have. Not now. I want to recapture our moment, that shared whisper of intimacy we experienced just now. Wanting that moment back more than I've wanted anything in centuries is...inconvenient.

God, wanting *her* more than anything in centuries is worse.

"Tomorrow," I say.

"Now," she counters, and business Holly reappears. A sigh arrives with that realization, and I lean forward. Winning Holly's affection is clearly a long game. Fine. Time isn't exactly a constraint. First, I'm a vampire. Second, I'm a vampire, and we're on a mission to save Christmas together. That means she's stuck with me. And third, I'm a vampire. I'm awesome. My experience gives me a few advantages.

"There's not much to say," I shrug, attempting understatement. "It's a pocket dimension of unspeakable evil. It's a terrible place of endless sadness and misery. There's always jazz playing, for reasons no one has successfully explained."

"I can't tell if you're joking."

"I *never* joke about jazz. That's how Isaac Newton almost destroyed Cambridge."

"Why would they have taken my tree to an evil pocket dimension?"

"Who knows why rogue elves do anything? They're elves."

She's right to ask, and I wonder if I should tell her the truth. The real answer is that they wouldn't, not without direction. They're definitely working for someone else, but with no clear suspect, speculation feels premature. Suspicions are one thing, but without proof, they're the kind of thing that will worry her, and so my thoughts remain mine. For now.

"How are we supposed to get it back?"

"I'll bring my coven. They'll help. It should be fine."

"What should I expect? Goblins? Goblins with swords? Fire Goblins with swords who go around saying, "How about this heat?" What can I do to prepare?"

"You're staying home," I say, aiming for heroic and landing somewhere near concerned. "I'm not bringing you into the Hollow of Mischief."

"Says you," she snaps, veering off script. "I'm going. This is my Winter Wonderland, Draven, and in this little movie miracle you're imagining, you're the sidekick."

I laugh and raise my hands in mock surrender, delighted with how easily she's able to run through all my defenses. Holly Frost is blade-sharp, and there's no getting anything past her. The sooner I realize that, the better.

"You're stunningly insufferable; do you know that?"

She gives me a flat look. "It's been said. So tomorrow, then? You organizc your coven tonight, and tomorrow we'll get the tree back?"

"That's the plan. Some more of my more magically inclined brethren can prepare some guarding spells, at least enough so you don't die the instant that you set foot inside."

"Yay," she says weakly.

Her skin goes a bit pale as the reality of what we're about to do sinks in. She's either brave or crazy, and probably a combination of both, but spending time with her is the most fun I've had in ages. I want more of it, and I'm going to make sure I get it.

We finish our drinks and bundle up, readying ourselves to go back into the chill night. It's been a long day, and she's tired. More snow is falling, and the flakes twinkle in the lamplight, making everything look like a snow globe. Window boxes wear neat hats of snow. A wreath on the bakery door breathes cinnamon into the street. Outside, I pause and tilt my head towards the sky, closing my eyes and letting each snowflake hit me like a kiss.

"Are we going?" Holly nudges me in the arm.

"Ah," I shake myself from my reverie. "Of course. Shall we?" I offer her my arm, which she snorts at before trudging down Main

Street, leaving me behind. Hurrying to catch up, I fall into step beside her. Hopefully, she finds it charming.

Despite the lightly falling snow, the sky is clear, and the wind is crisp enough to give the skin a wonderful nip, but not enough to burn. The streets are completely empty, and most everyone is still inside the shops or has gone home for the night.

Main Street is well-decorated for the festival, with holly and garlands dripping from everything. It's all quite delightful, really, and I wonder if there's a much longer future for us here.

"Did you do all this?" I gesture at the decorations.

"Yes. I start planning for the festival in the spring. The work takes most of the year. Logistics, orders, catering, waste disposal, events, hotels, all of it. Each year there's something new."

"It's incredible. I wouldn't have thought organizing an annual event involving several thousand people would be quite so much work, and now that I say that sentence out loud, it seems absurd."

This line gets a genuine laugh from her, and I try to be as present in the moment as I can. Her head tilts forward and she covers her mouth as she laughs into her glove. Snow falls around her, leaving traces behind on her eyelashes. Unable to help myself, I step forward and take her by the arm.

"Holly—"

Before I can get further, a screeching animal launches itself at her and they both tumble to the pavement. I'm forced to stumble back, surprised, as another creature thumps into me from the side, knocking me to the ground hard.

At first, it looks like a stray dog or something, but then several more shapes dart in and out of the shadows, and a better look reveals what's happening. It's not dogs.

It's elves.

Rogue elves.

Scrambling to my feet, I look for Holly. I'm firmly past the point of irritation and have moved all the way to annoyance. Rogue elves?

Really? Here I am, trying to be a nice guy—a gentleman even—and this is my reward? Being accosted by these creatures?

Holly is being pinned down—quite possibly tickled—while muffled sounds of battle and frustrated giggling emerge from the pile of bodies. I move to help, but another elf blocks my path, snarling and brandishing a candy-cane shaped staff. It swings at me, and I fold my arms. The staff shatters against my frame, exploding into shards of candy. The elf is left holding a jagged stump of cane, and he frowns at it.

"That was never going to work," I say, before punting him neatly into a snowdrift, where he lands with an offended squeak. I make a note of his position so that I can tell Ronan. Or perhaps not. This is easily the stupidest battle I've ever been involved in, and a possessed goose once fought me for half a ham sandwich.

But I need to impress Holly, so this must be taken seriously.

To my surprise, she's managed to push the elves off and has already armed herself with a wreath and a stick of garland. She uses the wreath as a shield and begins poking at the elves with her garland stick. One gets too close and she slams it against the side of the head. It vanishes in a puff of tinsel.

She pauses as tinsel floats through the air, settling on her shoulders. "They explode into Christmas? Did we know that?"

"Yes."

I explode an elf myself with a well-aimed punch.

Faintly, Christmas carols sound. *Deck the Halls. Tra la la la la.*

"And I knew about the carols too," I add.

There is no end to the layers this woman possesses. Not only is she a magic-themed event planner, but she's also a seemingly gifted elf-fighter. Her beanie has been knocked clean off her head during the fracas and she plops it back on.

"Did you see that?" she asks, breathless and breathtaking.

"Wonderful," I murmur. "But we should get out of here. There might be more of them, and this isn't the time for heroics. These little gremlins are on a sugar-fueled rampage, and there's no telling what—"

"Ha!" she cries and flashes a triumphant smirk as she punches another elf and more tinsel blooms around her. "Season's beatings!"

A stray elf slams a candy cane against her upper thigh. She hollers in pain and falls into a nearby snowbank. I cry out and lunge to help, but suddenly there are elves everywhere. Another group leaps on top of her and this time they act as if they're going to carry her away. Her cries have gone from frustration to genuine terror. She's in trouble.

Enough of this.

There are lines, and these creatures have skipped merrily past all of them.

They've hurt someone under my protection, and that alone is sufficient for them to know my wrath. Yet something colder settles into place. Something older. Far less inclined to tolerate this nonsense.

No more snowballs. No more games.

Reputation matters. Precision matters. And I am very, very good at resolving problems. Especially the sort that come gift-wrapped in trouble and poor decisions.

These rogue elves are about to discover how unfortunate their choices have been.

All of them.

I attack.

Time slows as I move from one elf to another. One takes a punch to the head and explodes into tinsel. Another barely manages a befuddled groan before I hammer it in the chest.

I am fully in the midst of them, and it is a Christmas extravaganza. My hands become tidy little snowplows, my speed a festive blur. They fall before me as easily as a child might blow over a dandelion, and I'm soon covered in tinsel. And streamers. And something that looks suspiciously like glitter.

Crinkshaw will have to work to get my outfit suitably pristine again.

The fight takes mere moments, and as the last elf scampers off, cackling and screaming something about Rudolph and stampedes, I rush to Holly's side to check she's okay. She's completely immersed in a snowbank, with only her arms and legs visible, and they flail comically. I pull her out, chuckling at the sight but also nearly limp with relief that she's okay. Her eyes are wide with shock and something else. Is that glimmer back? I help her to her feet and brush snow from her sweater.

"That was..." she gasps. "You were..."

"Did you yell Season's beatings?"

It's impossible to tell if the blush is a lingering effect of the fight or embarrassment from her terrible line. All I'm aware of is the heat of her, the closeness of her body, the way she trembles under my touch.

She goes to put weight on her legs. They're unable to support her and she stumbles.

"You're hurt." I rush to put my arm around her.

"It's nothing," she says.

"It's something."

Our eyes lock and, for a moment, it looks like she's going to argue.

"I don't understand you, Draven."

"What's to understand?" I give her my megawatt smile. "I am, broadly speaking, delightful."

She snorts and once again tries to put weight on her leg, but it's not going to hold. I bend over to inspect the damage.

"It doesn't look broken, but you can't walk on that. You need hot water, a compress, and an unreasonable amount of cocoa."

"It's fine. I don't need your help."

She's too stubborn for her own good, and she needs a firm hand.

"You're not limping through the snow, Frost. Martyrdom's for Easter, not Christmas. You're coming with me."

Before she can object, I scoop her into my arms. On instinct, she reaches to clasp around my neck, and it's striking how perfectly she fits. This could become a habit. I may never let her go.

"You're enjoying this, aren't you?" she asks.

Her face is buried in my chest and her breath tickles against my skin, but she doesn't tell me to put her down. I'll be damned if she doesn't like this too, and even though there's no need for me to breathe, my chest puffs out a little.

"This isn't what I'd imagined working with you would be like," she whispers.

Her low laugh hums through me, almost intoxicating. This absurd adventure is becoming something remarkable. It's been centuries since anything made me feel this alive, and I'm beginning to care, far too much, about what happens to Holly and, by extension, to her Winter Wonderland Festival. That is as spectacular as it is surprising.

With a touch of vampire-assisted speed, I carry her toward the coven, glitter absolutely everywhere, and the puzzle of Holly Frost light in my arms.

Chapter Nine

HOLLY

Morning light blares through the curtains, and I groan. I screw my eyes shut and dive under the thick, warm covers, trying to forget about being dunked in a snowdrift by rogue elves. A twinge of pain catches in my thigh as I stretch out, while my cheeks burn from the humiliation of remembering my arms and legs flailing uselessly in the snow. Right in front of Nick 'Tall, Dark, and Infuriating' Draven, and as if it wasn't already embarrassing enough, the vampire carried me to his mansion like he was some knight in shining armor.

By the time we arrived, the agony in my leg was horrible, and delirium hovered at the edges of my consciousness from both exhaustion and pain. I remember being whisked through the mansion to this room, where Nick bandaged my leg and handed me some generic pajamas. Sleep arrived almost immediately after that.

How very, *very* mortifying.

I inhale, trying to calm myself, and catch the smell of cinnamon, cloves, and something else. Something like warm sugar cookies. It's not at all what I expected from a vampire's mansion. Shouldn't there be dust and despair? Gloom? Instead, the room is downright cozy—if a little over-the-top.

The sleigh bed curls at head and foot and is dressed in winter-white linen with a soft cream quilt, an ice-blue knit throw that spills across the end, and pillows stitched with tiny snowflakes. A crackling fire fills the room with flickering light, garlands wrapping around the carved wooden beams of the ceiling. I blink, sitting up slowly, wincing as my leg twinges again. The bandage there reminds me that while the surface events are absurd, the danger is real.

Elves. Rogue elves. *Seriously?*

I groan once more, pushing the covers back, only to find them embroidered with poinsettias. Of course they are. The whole room looks like Santa's workshop collided with a gothic estate. It's strange and surreal and completely right. It shouldn't work, and yet it does.

There's a gentle knock at the door, and after an appropriate pause, Nick walks in.

"Ah, Sleeping Beauty is awake," he says, holding a steaming mug in one hand and an entirely too smug expression in the other.

"Where am I?" I ask, swinging my feet on the fur-like rug.

"One of the spare rooms in my home," he says, like it's obvious. "And before you get any ideas, there's no need to thank me for carrying you here last night. Yes, it was heroic. No, I don't expect anything in return, though if you'd like to bake me a fruitcake, I wouldn't say no. The coven is particularly fond of it at this time of year."

"You're impossible," I mutter, standing up carefully. "Why does your mansion look like the North Pole exploded in it?"

Nick glances around, as if seeing it for the first time. "You don't like it? Our resident ghoul's display usually pleases everyone, and he went all out this year. Personally, I thought the life-sized nutcrackers were a bit much, but he has a vision, and it wasn't my place to deny him."

I follow his gaze to the doorway, where, sure enough, two wooden nutcrackers stand guard, their painted faces somehow managing to look both festive and faintly menacing.

"I don't even know what to say."

"How about 'thank you for not leaving me in a snowbank to be rogue elf bait?'"

"Fine," I grumble. "Thank you for not leaving me in a snowbank to be rogue elf bait. Happy?"

"Ecstatic."

He hands me the mug, and I sniff it cautiously. Hot coffee, bitter-smelling with hazelnut and frothy milk. The first sip hits, and it's scandalously perfect.

"I have some bad news, I'm afraid." He frowns. "I had a few people head back into town after the attack. It was a diversion. While we were busy fighting them off, they made off with some more of your Christmas bits and pieces."

I take in the news with a sigh and stare at the cup, wondering how bad the damage is going to be. I'm already up against it with the mystery of the missing Christmas tree, and having to tackle another problem feels like it might just break me.

"They ransacked the cookies and Christmas goodies you'd had stored in one of the barns. They're either gone or turned to crumbs now, Holly."

This is a disaster.

The Christmas tree is important, but it's the Christmas treats that make the gala really stand out. Everyone in Willow Creek looks forward to it. Mrs. Christie has spent hours rolling spice-dark dough, hand-piping cuffs on every gingerbread sleeve, tucking orange-scented mincemeat beneath neat lattices, and sugaring the stollen until it looks like fresh snowfall. She even shaped a tray of marzipan fruit—pretty enough for the shop window and guaranteed to divide opinion.

My bottom lip quivers. "The catering?"

Nick nods slowly. "But don't worry."

That's easy for him to say.

"We've put Crinkshaw on it." Nick crosses his arms and leans against one of the posts of my bed. "He's roped in a couple of the other vampires and they're cooking in batches. He's turned the kitchens into a culinary production line."

"What is a Crinkshaw?"

"A who. Not an *it.* He's the five-hundred-year-old ghoul who happens to be the coven's steward. He's also an exceptional cook."

My mouth forms a small but perfect circle, and I'm lost for words.

Nick just grins and I swear his chest puffs out a little as he watches me shift in the bed. "Well, I'll let you get up. There are some clean clothes in the bathroom. Just catch up with me when you're ready. Head down the stairs and then towards the back. We'll be in the central kitchen."

"Central?" I ask. "How many kitchens do you have?"

"I dunno. Six?"

He leaves and I edge my way out of bed, easing my weight onto my injured leg. It's just a sprain, but I doubt I'd have made it home without considerable difficulty and as much as it pains me to admit it, Nick did me more than one favor last night.

I wash and dress, surprised that the bathroom's stocked with more than enough toiletries to keep even the fussiest girl happy. What's even worse is that the clothes fit perfectly, almost like the vampire knew my exact size and had them bought for me. I cast away the awkward thought that he arranged this just for me and drift out of the room, keen to explore the mansion he calls home.

And it is quite a mansion.

The hallways are a riot of Christmas, so lavish it's hard to tell whether the decorations or the paintings they're covering are more impressive. Nick wasn't kidding about this 'Crinkshaw' going all out. Every banister is wrapped in garlands and twinkling lights. Wreaths hang from every door, their ribbons tied in perfect bows. Even the chandeliers have been decked with ornaments dangling from the crystal.

It's like Christmas exploded and then tidied up after itself.

Downstairs, the ostentation only escalates. An actual Degas

hangs on the wall. I'm almost certain there's a Rodin on a marble plinth by the doorway. Even the Dowager Countess would pause at the threshold, purse her lips, and say, very softly, that this is 'a bit much.'

I find the kitchen around the back of the winding staircase, just as Nick said. Broad double doors open into a room large and well-equipped enough to host cooking shows. A chalkboard by the pantry reads *Kitchen Rules: Be Kind. Ask before borrowing spices. Label your blood bags and your biscotti*.

Nick is sitting at an island the size of my entire living room. He waves and smiles awkwardly, showing me a grin I haven't seen before. His hands wring when he walks over, and he looks strangely unsure of himself as he hands me another hot drink.

"You know," he says, "if you're impressed now, wait until you see the blood fountain. We dyed it green for the season. Very festive."

I choke on my hazelnut latte. "You're joking?"

"Am I?"

His smile widens, and I can't tell if he's serious or just messing with me.

A side door swings open to reveal a gentle burble of chocolate tinted with matcha. Tiny gingerbread men skate the rim on toothpick skates. A placard reads: *Not Blood. Please stop asking*.

Before I can say anything, he takes me by the elbow and guides me to another doorway at the far end of the kitchen. We enter a large dining room where two people are sitting at an elaborately set table. One is a tall, attractive, broad-shouldered redhead who radiates a kind of quiet menace that makes me instantly uneasy.

The other is an actual zombie, and I scream.

"What is that!?"

"Holly," Nick says, gesturing to them, "meet Crinkshaw and Ronan. Crinkshaw is the coven's steward and my...assistant. Ronan handles security."

It's impolite to stare, but I can't stop myself from looking at a very real zombie. Crinkshaw's face is a hollow, sunken skull with just enough skin stretched over it to be unsettling. He grumbles something that sounds like a curse muttered under his breath, while Ronan gives me a polite nod that still feels intimidating.

"Uh, hi," I say, clutching my mug a little tighter.

This is somehow worse than the severed head in the forest.

"Don't mind Crinkshaw," Nick says. "He's upset because I vetoed his all-vampire caroling troupe. Undead harmonies are, generally speaking, an acquired taste."

"I won't be lectured on taste by someone who believes solid black represents the height of fashion." Crinkshaw's voice sounds like parchment turning at midnight, and I shudder involuntarily. Nick sends him a look that would make most mortals wish they were dead.

"Oh, be pleasant, Crinkshaw. Holly was just saying how much she likes the decorations," he says in a tone as smooth as eggnog. "She might even need an assistant next year."

At this, the half-dead gargoyle comes to life and starts rambling about the decorations and the hours he's spent decorating the mansion. Apparently, he insists on a mix of festive cheer and vampiric flair, meticulously curating every detail. The tree in the kitchen, for example. The glass ornaments are shaped like bats and the icicles hanging around us gleam faintly red at the tips, as if dipped in blood.

My eyes lock onto the topper of the tree. Looking away might be possible, but it would take real effort. The plastic, googly-eyed bat wearing a lopsided Santa hat, clutching a candy cane like a tiny festive vampire is not something I ever expected to witness.

"Is that really what you put on the top of your tree?"

Crinkshaw scoffs. "What else would the lady expect at Bloodmas?"

"Bloodmas?" I repeat, raising an eyebrow.

"Don't look at me like that," Nick says, leaning back in his chair. "Sure, the name is a little dramatic, but we try to do our part. Festivities, gift-giving, the whole thing. Just, you know, with a bit more blood and a lot less mistletoe."

Ronan lets out a low chuckle. "It's a little loophole. Vampires had a historical disagreement with a certain person in charge of Christmas, so we are politely excluded from partaking in the magic. But they can't stop us from having our own festival, at exactly the same time of year, with vampire-themed decorations."

Crinkshaw laughs and it's unpleasant. His long and bony fingers tap against each other and I can't decide if he's trying to be merry or kill off the conversation. His features turn even more gruesome as he tries to smile and then recites story after story about the good old days, when mortals found the traditions vampires keep over Christmas unsettling. Eventually, he grinds to a halt and sniffs indignantly, oozing the opposite of festive cheer.

"One does not slap a wreath on a door and call it Bloodmas, Sire. There's an art. Balance. Elegance. Decorum."

"One that required skull-shaped baubles and nutcracker sentinels?" I ask, pointing to the decorations.

"And bats," Crinkshaw says, missing the sarcasm entirely.

Nick retrieves a leather tube from the sideboard and eases out a vellum map dusted with cinnamon sugar. I glance around the room, at the gleaming decorations and twinkling lights, and now the winter wonderland made of old sheets of paper. It's bizarre, but it fits in a weird, twisted way. Vampires embracing Christmas with an over-the-top flair feels oddly appropriate.

He spreads the map out on the table, pointing to a shaded area on the outskirts of town. "This is where we think the Hollow of Mischief is. Because it's a pocket dimension of sorts, it's accessible only at certain times and under certain conditions."

"But it won't be easy to get in," Ronan says, his voice low and measured. "The Hollow of Mischief is temperamental."

"Temperamental how?"

"Think of it like a Christmas snow globe," Nick says. "Shake, and the inside decides to rearrange you instead."

"That doesn't make me feel better."

"It shouldn't," Ronan grumbles. "It would be better if the lass stayed here."

Nick and I shake our heads in unison and although we're agreeing, it's clearly for different reasons. I'm determined to go, whereas Nick's resigned to it. Neither Ronan nor Crinkshaw pushes the idea of me staying behind, though Ronan's disapproving gaze flickers between us as Nick begins laying out a plan.

The Hollow of Mischief, as it turns out, isn't just temperamental —it's downright malicious. It shifts its entrance like a trick door in a haunted house. We'll need to wait for the right time, and finding it will require navigating through an area that will likely be defended by legions of rogue elves.

The map sprawled across the table is littered with notes and markings, each one a reminder of how little control we'll have once we step inside. There are traps, both physical and magical, and if the vampires are right, it's a twisted, backward place. Nick traces a path with his finger, explaining potential entry points, while Crinkshaw jots down a list of supplies we'll need and fetches hot cocoa whenever I need it. Trays appear with warm banana bread, sugared cranberries, and something labeled experimental stollen, which tastes like a hug.

There's a practicality to the planning that I didn't expect. For all Nick's bravado, he doesn't cut corners. He's meticulous, considering every angle, and it's clear that this isn't just a job for him—it's personal. As someone whose most enduring relationship in the past fourteen months has been with her clipboard, this aspect of him is strangely compelling.

I watch, trying to reconcile the vampire I thought he was with the one standing here now. Last night, he carried me through the snow without a word of complaint, and this morning, he'd made sure I was comfortable before diving into this mission. Even now, as he talks about rogue elves and magical traps, there's a quiet determination about him that feels genuine.

I'm less worried about failing because he's helping me, and I think I rather like it. It's been a long time since anyone made me feel like this, but it's impossible to deny that Nick makes me feel better and like I can do anything I want to. He's not the smug opportunist I thought he was—not entirely, anyway. There's more to him, something deeper beneath the layers of sarcasm and charm.

The plan comes together in pieces, each step carefully considered. When Nick finally rolls up the map, the room falls quiet, the weight of what's ahead settling over us like the first snowfall of the season.

"You ready for this, Frost?"

"Born ready," I say with a bravado I don't feel. "The question is, are you? I heard rogue elves are particularly vicious toward vampires with inflated egos."

He smirks, unbothered. "Good thing mine's perfectly proportioned."

Ronan and Crinkshaw both choke on cocoa in perfect unison while they stare at Nick like he's just suggested they decorate a coffin for Christmas. And even though part of me is terrified about what lies before us in the Hollow of Mischief, I am genuinely enjoying teasing Nick.

"Keep telling yourself that," I lean back, brushing imaginary dust off my clothes. "Just don't expect me to carry *you* home if things go sideways."

Nick chuckles, adjusting his perfectly cut shirt with an exaggerated flourish. "Please, Frost. If anyone's doing the rescuing, it'll be me—again. You're falling quite a bit short on your side of the ledger."

"Short?" I scoff, slurping my drink for dramatic effect. "Keep dreaming, Draven. The only thing coming up short is your memory."

Nick throws his head back and laughs as I sip the last of my cocoa, letting the warmth steady me. Maybe, just maybe, Nick Draven isn't the vampire I thought he was. And maybe that's not such a bad thing.

Chapter Ten

NICK

Both Crinkshaw and Ronan insist on coming with us, and although I'll never reveal any sort of weakness to the coven, I'm glad to have them by my side. I debated bringing more with me, but the Hollow of Mischief can react poorly to undead energy, and this might be one of those cases where less is more.

Against my wishes, Ronan insists on strapping his enormous battle axe to his back. Its name is Sally.

"Why not simply announce to the entire town that we're striding into a mystery dimension?" I huff, folding my arms in irritation.

"Why, Mr. Draven," Holly purrs, looking every inch the satisfied cat. "I don't believe I've ever seen you flustered before."

"I'm not flustered. This isn't decorous."

Ronan scoffs. "Decorum when we're marching into a maze of mischief packed with elves?" His voice goes to a mocking falsetto. "Should we make tea, or bring a bottle of red? Crinkshaw, do you have any biscuits we could bring? Someone look up what Miss Manners says is an appropriate *cadeau d'hôte* for entering a dimension of pure evil. Nuts?"

"Alright, alright." I shush him and glance at Crinkshaw. "What do you have ready for us?"

Crinkshaw lifts a tin. “Shortbread, mince pies, and a thermos. Also, hand warmers.”

“I meant for Holly.”

“Oh. That.” Crinkshaw produces a bracelet and locks it around her wrist. “This will protect the young lady from any of the dimension’s more aggressive effects on humans.”

“Perfect. We’ll head to where the Hollow of Mischief should appear. Then we’ll capture it and answer the riddle. It shouldn’t be a problem.”

“Wait,” Holly holds up her hand. “Riddle? There’s a riddle?”

“There’s almost always a riddle when dealing with elves. They’re obsessed with them.” Ronan tests the blade of his axe with his thumb.

“What happens if we get the riddle wrong?” she asks.

“Don’t worry about that,” he shrugs.

“Ronan,” she repeats firmly. “What happens if we get the riddle wrong?”

“Tinsel tendrils of unspeakable festive malice will—” Crinkshaw starts, but I interrupt him with a clap of my hands.

“Great talk, everyone. Let’s get going.”

Unsatisfied, Holly pesters me about the riddle as we walk to the garage, but it’s honestly for the best that she doesn’t learn any more. It’s not like we can do anything if we get it wrong. We’ll be almost immediately destroyed, our very molecules being tossed to the cosmic winds like confetti. At least it will be quick.

We make our way through the grounds, and it affords Holly a new opportunity to tease me. That, more than anything else, distracts her from her questions. Lucky me.

“What kind of cars do vampires drive?” she asks playfully. “A hearse seems too on the nose. A stagecoach of some kind? Or, I know, some deathly sleek sports car?”

“Not quite,” I say.

The garage is home to a fleet of cars, each acquired by different members of my coven. I throw open the broad, double doors and flick on the overhead lights. They click on one at a time, chasing away the cavernous darkness. The garage is the size of a small soccer field and full of all sorts of cars. I click the fob in my pocket, and we all hear the cheerful chirp-chirp.

"Please be a Porsche. Please be a Porsche." Holly is crossing her fingers and bouncing on her toes like a toddler who's had too many candy canes. We walk past a row of Mercedes before coming to a stop in front of my car.

"Here we are."

"This is a Toyota Camry." Holly's voice is flat and unimpressed.

"It's economical," I shrug.

"You are the most complicated vampire ever. I've met very few vampires and yet I feel very comfortable in saying that."

We pile into the car. Or at least, we attempt to. Ronan loads his giant, preposterous axe in the trunk. Holly's disapproval lingers, and, annoyingly, it matters to me more than it should.

"No offense," Holly says as we try to configure ourselves, "but why is Crinkshaw coming?"

"What is the inoffensive version of that sentence?" Crinkshaw asks.

"We'll need him."

Everyone seems to be entertaining themselves by second-guessing me, and my patience is beginning to wear thin. After some grunts and seat shifting, we manage to get everyone situated, and I warily pull out and take us to the road that leads to the outskirts of town. Blinkers on. Complete stops. Not risky maneuvers. Holly taps her fingers impatiently as we drive.

"If we went any slower, we'd be walking," Holly notes.

"No one wins when you play games with traffic safety."

I lean forward, making sure no cars are coming before inching out onto the road from the last intersection. Technically, sweating isn't an option, but this is close enough. So I rub my hands on the steering wheel.

"This is absurd. At least go the speed limit."

"Your odds of survival improve ten percent for every ten miles per hour you do not go."

No one verifies this statistic.

"You're immortal," she huffs. "I'm the only one who might die if we crash, and I'm completely fine with going faster."

I check my blind spot for the third time. There are no cars on the road, but you never know. The odometer shows we're doing a dangerous, reckless speed. A frantic forty miles an hour. I pump the brakes a little.

"Oh my god," Holly says. Her eyes are sparkling with humor, and even though it's me she's targeting, I like the way she teases me. "You're afraid of driving, aren't you?"

There's no point saying anything. Besides, I don't like to talk and drive. Concentration is important. Particularly when Holly's sitting next to me.

"You are." She laughs and claps her hands. "You're afraid of driving."

"Don't be preposterous."

"Crinkshaw?" Holly turns around to look. "Is he afraid of driving?"

"Oh, now you're happy to have me on the trip?"

"It's more accurate to say he's afraid of cars," Ronan interjects.

"They just don't make any sense," I huff. "Things the size of wagons shouldn't move without horses. It's indecent."

"Every immortal has some modern invention that unsettles them," Ronan says. "It's a consequence of living across the ages."

"What's yours?" Holly asks.

"Bread makers," he says without pause. "The machine accepts flour and eggs, hums ominously, and manifests bread. There is no difference between what they do and a warlock summoning a demon."

Holly laughs, light and musical. "And you, Crinkshaw?"

"Postage stamps," he says. "Miniaturized paintings with adhesive backs that enslave men to carry paper. Civilization shouldn't hinge on glue and faith."

Holly pokes me in the chest. "You're an undead creature of the dark who drinks blood to live and hangs out with ghouls and monsters, and you think a car is unnatural?"

"It's complicated." I adjust the rearview mirror, feigning indignation. "You're inside and outside at the same time, moving while staying still, trapped in this metal rolling box powered by explosions and dinosaur blood. Somehow, a free-floating steering rudder gives you control. It's nonsense. With horses, you point them and they mostly go."

"Steering rudder?"

"That's not at all true," Ronan pipes in from the back, presumably in an effort to be as unhelpful as possible. "Steering a horse-drawn wagon is impossibly complicated. He just hates cars."

"Moving boxes of madness," I mutter.

Holly is laughing so hard she can hardly breathe, and she's lucky I find it so enchanting. If she were any of my coven, I'd be tempted to turn her into a bat.

It's strange and a little wonderful how perfectly she fits in with our dynamic. Crinkshaw and Ronan can be a bit much for outsiders, but Holly is giving it back as good as she's getting it. And I know my coven; they're both enjoying themselves enormously. I don't adore being the topic of the jokes, but she's having such a good time that it doesn't seem to bother me very much at all.

We approach a windswept field, and I cautiously pull the car over. A quick check of the GPS confirms it. This is the place. It's the definition of nowhere: an open, grassy plain broken only by the occasional pile of rocks and boulders. I get out, happy to stretch my legs.

"Are we lost?" Holly asks. "Did we run out of gas?"

Everyone else piles out of the car, and Ronan retrieves his axe from the trunk.

"Nope."

Gracefully, I leap over the low wooden fence that marks the edge of the field and move through the snow-covered grass. The portal is close. I can practically taste the magic. Burnt syrup and peppermint. It has to be here. Where—

"Here, Sire." Crinkshaw points like he's rising from a crypt.

"I don't see anything." Holly hugs herself and hops from one foot to the other. Right. Humans feel the cold. Best to hurry.

Now that Crinkshaw has me facing the right direction, the outline of the portal comes into view.

"Exactly where I'd predicted it would be, give or take a few feet," I say over my shoulder, giving her a winning grin. Four out of ten.

She blows into her hands.

My grin falters. I release a whisper of vampire power.

The portal to the Hollow of Mischief appears.

Holly screams.

It's not the reaction I was hoping for.

To be fair, the portal is horrifying. It's several stories tall, slick with rime and shadow, and emanates waves of monstrous evil. Twenty-four shuttered windows line its height, each marked with a number, like a row of dark, watchful eyes glaring down at us. With malevolence. One hangs half-open, and something red flutters from its edge—velvet, trimmed with pale fur, snapping softly in the wind like a warning.

It's also quite an unflattering shade of peppermint green.

"It's the world's worst advent calendar," she gasps, craning her head to peer at the monstrosity before us.

"It's not great," I agree. "But if we solve the riddle, we can get inside."

"What happens if we don't solve the riddle correctly?" Holly asks.

"Garden gnomes will materialize to pelt you with hard candy and—" Crinkshaw starts to say, but a hand over his mouth cuts him off. I beam maniacally at Holly.

"Nothing!" Slowly, carefully, I remove my hand from his mouth, ready to clap it back down if needed. "It doesn't matter because we'll get the riddle right. We always get the riddle right. Or at least he does. That's why we brought him. Crinkshaw is fiendishly clever at riddles."

"And decorating and cooking," Holly says flatly.

"Yes. Those too."

"I'm a Renaissance zombie," Crinkshaw deadpans.

He steps forward and squints at some markings on the side of the structure. He reads aloud:

Think on the Holly's Eve of cheer,

Two digits open, drawing mayhem near.

"What does that mean?" Holly whispers. "Why does this door know my name? I don't want a giant nightmare calendar to know my name. This is worse than when an ex likes your posts."

I shrug. "It's how magic works. Crinkshaw, you have the answer?"

"Twenty-four. Christmas Eve. Eve of cheer."

"There was an S," Holly says, backing away from the calendar. "Digits. More than one."

"Two and four, that's two digits," Ronan says triumphantly.

Holly frowns. "No, it isn't. Do you know how numbers work?"

"It will be fine," I soothe, certain that it will be anything but.

I wave a thread of magic toward the window marked twenty-four. The structure flares to life, glowing white, and Holly immediately buries her face in the back of my coat. I lift a hand to shield my eyes against the brightness, which rather unfortunately prevents me from properly appreciating this moment.

When the light finally fades and the air clears, the calendar is gone. In its place stands a frost-covered archway, filled with a glimmering nimbus of multicolored light. Bells tinkle softly in the background. Something dangles from the entranceway, and I reach forward to cup it in my hand.

"Look," I say. "Mistletoe."

I waggle my eyebrows at Holly and deploy every last ounce of charm I possess, letting the silver of my eyes catch the light reflecting off the snow as I lean in. Slowly. Agonizingly slowly. At a pace that makes women swoon.

It hardly registers. She's too busy clutching her chest and breathing deeply.

"I hate magic so much," she says. "So very, very much. None of this was covered in Event Planning School."

"There's an entire school for that?"

"It's a series of online courses."

I laugh and rub her arm because there's nothing else to be done.

"We'll be in and out before anyone notices. Ronan, be so kind as to lead the way. Let us enter the Hollow of Mischief."

Chapter Eleven

HOLLY

We step through the portal, and the world twists around us in a dizzying swirl of red and white, like the stripy spiral of a Christmas lollipop. The colors blur together, streaking past in a hypnotic whirl, their sugary brightness edged with cracked peppermint—festive on purpose, but with a prickle of oddness underneath. The air is thick with the scent of candy canes and frost, sweet, cloying, and my stomach churns as the swirling slows, depositing us into the Hollow of Mischief with all the grace of a snow globe shattered on the floor.

This place is a Christmas fable gone wrong. Like if Willow Creek's gala were designed by a madman who thinks 'chaos' is a type of tinsel. The ground beneath our feet is springy, felted snow—like a carpet underlay—over something that refuses identification. Twisted, blackened trees lean in closer with every step, their branches creaking like they're trying to whisper secrets left behind. There's not a single animal noise. Sound itself feels muted. Above, through a web of branches, the sky shows its sickly pink stripes—an unsettling reminder that we're no longer in Willow Creek.

My spine shudders, and I decide a joke might help me feel better. Gallows humor feels appropriate when I'm surrounded by vampires.

I open my mouth to say something witty, but to my surprise, I scream.

Crinkshaw and Ronan stare at me, eyes narrowed and eyebrows arched. Nick looks at me like I've lost all composure.

"I said it would be better if the lass didn't come," Ronan sighs.

"That's not terribly gentlemanly of you," Nick replies, that usual, annoying smug grin he always wears lighting his face. "Now we know that Holly has excellent projection."

I turn a shade of crimson appropriate for the season and immediately wish the ground would open and swallow me. Of course, Nick would say something like that. Of course, he would.

"I'm having a perfectly normal, completely justified reaction to seeing this nightmare version of Christmas," I mutter, brushing off the awkwardness like snowflakes on a coat. "And I'm not a screamer."

Nick laughs, a deep rumble that cuts through the Hollow of Mischief's eeriness. "Sure, Frost. Keep telling yourself that."

We make our way further into the grove of trees. There's not a path exactly, but rather a slight thinning of the trees that we follow. Nick leads the way like he's been here before, and I'm learning that with Nick Draven, it's impossible to separate unearned confidence from actual knowledge.

We march in silence, an awkward parade through this snowy madness, trying not to draw any attention. Crinkshaw produces a thermos and presses it into my hands.

"Cocoa. Calming," he rasps.

I take a sip, and it's flawless. Nick winks at me, and I wonder about the relationship between vampires and their not-incorrect belief that hot chocolate solves nearly everything.

And then Ronan speaks, in his default voice, which is a bellow.

"I'm not sure why we're even bothering to sneak around," he rumbles, entirely unconcerned with alerting anyone. "Battle is the way to solve this. Whoever's behind this will have to face Sally."

Nick's expression shifts from amused to serious in an instant.

"Easy, Ronan. The goal is to get the tree while escaping notice. And Holly," he adds, glancing at me, "if you've got any more screams left in you, I suggest you keep them to yourself. We're about to need all our wits about us. Stay sharp."

"Thanks for the advice, Draven." I swallow against the terror rising in my chest.

The air thickens around me, and an ominous buzz rings in my ears. Nick's right. This place is more than a puzzle—its magic bites at nerves and fusses with courage. The trees groan and their twisted branches reach toward us like claws. There's something darker here than rogue elves, and it's been brewing in this perverted place for centuries.

There's more to this than a few mischievous elves, and whatever's happening with Willow Creek's gala is more than a prank. It's been planned. Someone's pulling some strings. And that means they've made my naughty list.

"Nick," I murmur, my voice low. "This place is worse than I expected. What if this is a setup? Maybe we should tape fifteen smaller trees together and hope that does the trick. Quantity over quality."

It sounded better in my head.

Nick doesn't respond right away, but there's slight tension in his shoulders now. He knows this is bad, and he knew it before we walked in here.

And just as the gravity of that realization hits, the ground beneath our feet trembles slightly. There's a soft creak and the sound of sugar-crunching underfoot, and it makes the hairs on the nape of my neck stand on end. I stumble forward and prepare myself as best I can for the unexpected.

We emerge from the nave of trees—to find an enormous gingerbread house looming in a clearing. The icing roof sparkles in the sinister Hollow light. At first, the giant hut seems like a harmless, whimsical decoration. Something out of a Christmas fairy tale. Almost pretty. Covered in candies, it even has soot-stained footprints leading to the front door. It reminds me of the ones I used to make as a child, and it seems innocent. Innocuous even.

Then the door opens.

A gingerbread man steps out.

I blink twice, sure I'm seeing things. But no. There it is. He is. A gingerbread man. Larger than life, with candy eyes glowing red. He raises his arm, and I swear I hear the faintest rustle of crumbling cookie. He notices us and growls. Menacingly.

"Uh, Nick?" I duck behind the vampires.

The door of the gingerbread house slams open, and more creatures pour out—a generous handful of gingerbread sentries with licorice ties and oversized candy-cane batons. They approach us like rejects from *West Side Story*, fanning out to surround us.

This is insane. And yet, it's actually happening.

We've solved the riddle of the world's worst advent calendar, gone through a lollipop portal and found a life-sized gingerbread house, and now we're fighting a small army of gingerbread men armed with candy.

I'm pretty sure my health insurance doesn't cover this.

"Guess we're fighting cookies now," Nick mutters, his smirk not quite reaching his eyes. "Ronan, you take point. Crinkshaw and Holly, stay at the back. Let us handle this."

Before I can blink, we're swarmed.

Nick and Ronan jump into the fray, creating a distraction. Nick punches one, and it explodes into a mound of crumbled confectionery while Ronan barrels into a group. Some still manage to get past and rush toward Crinkshaw and me.

I stumble, steadying myself with a jagged tree branch sticking out of the snow. It comes up loose. On impulse, I douse it with hot cocoa from the thermos as a three-foot-tall gingerbread monster wobbles towards me, wearing an unhinged, icing-slick grin.

I swing my cocoa stick.

The cookie monster's head caves in with a soft crack, and it collapses into crumbs, coating me in a fine dusting of cookie. Four more rush in to take its place, and just like that, I'm in the middle of a battle.

Ronan's axe cuts a devastating path through the chaos. I never thought I'd find myself saying this, but I'm very glad he brought it with him. He cleaves through gingerbread people like they're nothing, roaring with glee as they crumble around him. And Crinkshaw's hovering at the edges, contributing in his own way—lobbing the occasional stick with surprising accuracy.

"Is this what you meant by unspeakable horror?" I yell.

"Pretty much." Nick strikes another blow, destroying another gingerbread attacker. The creature falls apart in a shower of sugar, but more keep coming. This is like a Christmas parade that will not end. Not how I imagined dying, but festive nonetheless.

I narrowly avoid a sugary fist aimed straight at my face.

"How do we stop this?" I ask.

"Keep breaking them apart," Nick calls over his shoulder, moving with an effortless grace. "There aren't many left."

And to my surprise, he's right. We've actually beaten most of them. The ground is covered in cookie crumbs.

"See?" He grins. "It's just sugar and magic. It can't get much worse—"

I glare at him. He gives me a sheepish look.

He's broken the cardinal rule. The one that everyone who's ever watched a movie knows. You do not, ever, under any circumstances, tempt fate.

Now things are about to get very, very much worse.

The ground shudders again. The gingerbread house trembles, then groans as its walls bow outward, as if something inside is forcing its way out. Its sugar-sculpted windows crack and splinter.

Something far worse than sentient cookies is inside that house.

I do not know how I will explain this moment to my future therapist.

In a move that doesn't just defy physics but openly mocks it, the structure swells to four times its size. The door slams open.

A creature bursts out and roars.

It's a dragon.

Not a normal dragon—another phrase I never thought I'd use—but a gingerbread one. Complete with chocolate horns and a jaw full of caramel teeth. It's impressive, and I wish that it wasn't. It opens its wings in a clearly threatening gesture and flashes a grin laced with every ounce of candy-based badness that my mom tried to warn me away from. I shudder, and I wonder if the dragon should visit a dental hygienist.

"This is ridiculous," I mutter. "Now we've got dragons made of cookies."

"I was wondering when things would get fun," Nick says, dashing forward.

Ronan charges after him, roaring louder than the gingerbread dragon, which thrashes its massive candy cane tail in retaliation. It swings toward Ronan, narrowly missing him as he ducks and rolls. The dragon snarls, its caramel teeth glinting, but it doesn't stop. The scent of burned sugar fills the air, thick and cloying, as it lunges again, its wings flapping with a sickening crunch.

I'm scrambling to keep up with the chaos and dodging flying candy shards when Nick lands a solid hit to the creature's underbelly. The gingerbread dragon stumbles back, a jagged crack splitting its once-perfect sugary exterior.

"You're just an overgrown cookie," Nick yells, rolling his shoulders like this is a sparring match instead of a battle for survival. "Just crumble already."

Crinkshaw flicks cocoa across the wing joints; the icing softens and begins to sag. Ronan follows with Sally—less berserker now, more baker—tapping at the seams until whole sheets of gingerbread shear loose, sliding off like badly laid tiles.

The dragon screeches, thrashing as more gingerbread pieces fall from it in a glittering avalanche of sugar and caramel. It is like watching an overbaked biscuit surrender to a polite dunking.

Nick steps in to finish—one swift, decisive stroke to the creature's heart-shaped gingerbread chest.

The dragon collapses with a final, sugary hiss.

I stand there, wiping caramel off my cheek and taking in the scene.

"I've faced tougher biscotti."

Nick's laugh is wild. "Told you it'd be a blast, Frost."

The air settles for a moment, the last remnants of the gingerbread dragon falling to the ground like crumbs from a shattered holiday treat. But the victory feels empty because it doesn't change the fact that we're still deep in the Hollow of Mischief. And we still haven't found what we came for. Meanwhile, Ronan is cleaning cookie dough off his axe, whispering to his blade in tones that would make the heroine in a romance novel blush.

"We're not done yet," Nick says, his eyes narrowing as he glances toward the gingerbread house. "Let's move before this whole place decides to serve us up as dessert."

The four of us warily approach the gingerbread house. The door swings open as though inviting us in. A wave of stale, sweet air washes over us, and my stomach turns. It smells like whiskey and mince pies. I'm more than ready to be done with this sugar-coated nightmare.

"This place is wrong," I say under my breath, wiping more frosting from my sleeve. "We're walking into a gingerbread death trap."

Nick's jaw tightens, but his eyes are sharp. "It's not a trap. Not yet."

"Not yet?" I repeat, half-laughing in disbelief. "You've got to be kidding me. What do you think that dragon was?"

"A message."

We step inside and everything is made of candy. Chocolate bricks line the walls. Lollipops rise as pillars. Candy canes twist into warped arches overhead. The floor is a gloopy, sugary mess, and my boots make an unpleasant squelching sound at every step. I give the sagging sacks that line the walls a wide berth, and I don't pick up any of the parcels that have spilled loose from them. The air is wrong too. It presses in, like the place is holding its breath.

It's as if the whole place is watching us.

"Don't eat any of this," Nick says.

"I wasn't going to," I say, surprised Nick felt the need to warn us, but then I catch Ronan stopping himself in mid-lick of the walls. He coughs and reddens.

I peer over Nick's shoulder, and my breath catches.

An object sits on the table in the middle of the room. It's a faintly glowing snow globe, and at the center is a Christmas tree.

Technically, this is a tree.

It just isn't the tree we're looking for.

It's a garnished monstrosity of swirling glitter and cheap plastic. The lopsided tree inside the globe leans slightly to the left, its tiny ornaments painted in clashing colors. Every time I look at it, the faux snow churns unnaturally, catching the gaudy string of blinking lights inside the globe. The effect is both chaotic and nauseating, and it takes every ounce of my self-control not to sweep it off the table and smash it into tiny pieces.

Instead, I throw my head back and scream in frustration, stamping my feet on the ground in protest.

"That's...not fair," I cry.

Nick moves toward it, his eyes scanning the strange snow globe with a frown. "This is weird," he mutters, almost to himself. "What could you possibly want from a tacky snow globe with a wonky Christmas tree in it?"

We circle around it, trying to make sense of what we're seeing when something catches my eye—a small piece of parchment tucked under the base of the festive ornament. I reach out, plucking the snow globe from its place. The paper is old, the ink smudged, but the message written on it is clear:

Drain the magic and holiday current. Christmas still too powerful. Siphon the cheer. Re-route wonder. Begin the new era.

I read it twice, my mind racing. Something about it is deeply wrong, and my heart drops into my stomach. The Hollow of Mischief isn't just a twisted Christmas trap.

This is all part of someone's plan.

"Nick," I whisper, my voice unsteady as I hand him the note. "The stupid magic head said the tree is in the Hollow. This isn't our tree. What's going on?"

He scans the note, and for the first time since we entered the Hollow, I see something serious hit him. The ease drops away, replaced by a quiet, dawning understanding. He hands the paper to Ronan without a word.

Ronan reads, his brows furrowing deeply. The change in him is subtler, but no less real—his expression hardens as his stoic demeanor cracks ever so slightly. Eventually, his gaze lifts from the paper to the tree, and then back to us. Colder now. There's no confusion in it. Only an unspoken understanding of how dangerous this is.

"Well, this is great," Ronan says, his voice tinged with an unseasonal bitterness. "Rogue elves. The Hollow of Mischief. What's next, Krampus with a clipboard?"

The words hang in the air, a reminder of the escalating absurdity —and danger—of our situation. The note crinkles in his hand as he folds it deliberately, his gaze locking onto the hideous snow globe with its wonky tree. The faint swirl of snow inside the twisted creation stirs again, flurrying enough to mock us in a swirl of sparkling glitter and twinkling light.

Nick's gaze flicks between the tree and the note, the tension in his jaw revealing the thoughts brewing beneath his usually smug composure. He reaches for the snow globe and studies it, as if daring it to do anything other than mock him. The glitter slows, then stills, the tiny Christmas tree inside listing further as its blinking lights sputter and fade, as if even the ornament has given up. With a frustrated shrug, he stuffs it in his pocket.

"Siphon the cheer. Whoever's behind this...I think their plan is bigger than some minor festive disruption. Someone wants to drain the holiday magic, and they're not stopping with the tree."

"It's bad enough that we don't get Christmas," Ronan says quietly. "We're not letting someone take it from everyone else."

Nick's hands clench, and his fangs seem a little longer than they were moments ago.

"Come on, Frost. We'll find out who's behind this and toast their plans like chestnuts roasting on an open fire. They've got my full attention now—and they're going to regret it."

The fury sparking in his silver eyes makes it clear he isn't speaking metaphorically.

Chapter Twelve

NICK

Holly insists on driving back to town, and I'm happy enough to let her, so I can stew in my thoughts. They're a bitter flavor, and nothing seems to sweeten them. Even sitting next to her doesn't make this better.

Outside, snow taps against the windshield; inside, the heater sighs while the dash throws a soft amber glow over Holly's scarf and my currently thawing boots.

Almost everything about this little adventure has turned sour. We didn't find the missing tree, except for the tacky snow globe, with its garish plastic and awkwardly swirling glitter. This cheap holiday curio is very clearly hiding something unpleasant.

Then there was the gingerbread dragon.

There's no way rogue elves could organize enough to secure the support of a dragon. That takes serious, heavy-hitting power, and for the tenth time, I wonder what is truly going on in Willow Creek. This has the markings of a more sinister scheme, presumably from 'he of the crooked crown,' whatever that meant.

A familiar pattern nags at the back of my mind. I've seen this kind of thing before—the careful layering, the misdirection, the way every thread pulls toward something larger. A particular kind of mind works like this. Old. Patient. Delighted by spectacle.

I sink deeper into the passenger seat, watching fairy lights blur into soft constellations along Main Street, the way they do when a town is trying its best. Time is slipping through my hands. The festival is only days away.

“Easy there, speedster,” I snap at Holly as she careens around a gentle bend at a terrifying twenty miles an hour.

“Stop sulking,” she barks back.

I sit up straighter. “I am the Lord of Tomorrow, the Arrow of Vengeance, the Feast That Rises Before Dawn.”

“Here we go,” mutters Crinkshaw from the back seat.

“I am the Last Breath of the Night. Mortals cower in my presence. I do not sulk.”

Holly keeps her eyes on the road. Her knuckles are white on the wheel, sugared with a dusting of portal grit. The smell of burnt caramel lingers in her hair. I am performing for the cheap seats when she needs a plan.

“I didn’t know you were a theater major,” she says, her voice light in the way glass is light before it shatters. “When do tickets go on sale?”

“Ha,” Ronan laughs and even dour old Crinkshaw rearranges his mouth into a curve that might be a smile, if seen from a distance and given generous lighting.

Silence settles in like heavy snow. The car smells of damp wool and burnt ginger. A gingerbread button is welded to the dashboard by caramel and stubbornness. The wipers squeak. Holly’s jaw works once, as if she’s chewing on a thought she cannot swallow.

“It is not over,” she says to the windshield more than to us. “We’ve still got time, right?”

It takes all my considerable vampiric powers to provide her with a nod that resembles reassurance. She is one splinter away from bleeding. Sugar glass glints in her hair. There is icing on her sleeve that used to be a dragon's eye. None of us wants to say Christmas might be broken. None of us wants to say there's too little to salvage.

A singular image enters my brain, of Holly and me laughing together in bed. It's late at night, and her hair is up, and she's wearing a mud mask. I'm wearing reading glasses and doing my sudoku puzzles, an affectation I don't require to perform an activity I don't enjoy. *Will and Grace* is playing on the giant TV at the foot of the bed. There is a cat. And fluffy slippers.

I shake my head to clear the idea.

What's wrong with me? I shouldn't be daydreaming of soft domestic idiocy. And I shouldn't be fantasizing about kissing her neck, her wrists, her ears, putting my hands on her—

"We're here," Holly says as she brings the car to a stop, and I blink. We're in front of the coven, and I have no memory of passing through the iron gates. The heater hums. The gingerbread button lets go and drops into the cup holder with a soft, defeated click.

"What's next?" Her eyes stay on the door.

"Plans," I say, scrambling to give my brain time to keep up. "The next step is planning. Huge, firm plans. Ronan and Crinkshaw will bring the coven up to speed while you and I have dinner."

"We will?" Ronan asks.

"How does dinner help us?" Holly squints at me.

"Can't plan on an empty stomach. Napoleon swore by it." I lean in, lowering my voice. "Close friend, in case you were wondering. Terrible height. Threw excellent parties."

"Fine," she says, staring grimly out the window. "We'll get a quick bite at the diner." She swallows. "Then we plan."

I sputter out a half-hearted protest, once again thrown off course by Holly's inexhaustible ability to befuddle me. In the back seat, Ronan nudges Crinkshaw, and I glare daggers at both of them. As they get out of the car, I take the snow globe from my pocket and toss it to Ronan.

After they leave, Holly drives us to town. The diner is once again full, and we once again retreat to the cubicle in the back that I'm coming to think of as 'our' booth. The young server—Tessa—is still there, and she giggles at me while Holly studies the menu. I'm strangely piqued that her attention has drifted away from me. I defeated a gingerbread dragon for her, and I expected her to be at least a third of the way to fawning.

"I'll have steak," I say. "Blood rare with cinnamon butter on top, just to keep it festive."

"Bold choice," Tessa giggles. "And you?"

"Caesar salad." Holly shuts the menu, and I raise my eyebrows at her. She exhales sharply. "Fine. With cranberries on the side. Good enough?"

We sit in silence, each lost in our own thoughts. The snow is falling yet again, and Holly's face looks lost and desolate in the reflection of the glass. There's nothing of me to see because I don't cast a reflection, and that makes me think about how different she and I are.

Not as much as she thinks, and more than I'd like.

"We should call Frank," Holly says. Her shoulders are hunched, and she's chewing on her bottom lip. I'm shocked to see a hint of moisture in her eyes. "I don't think I can do this. Maybe he can magic up another tree. This is obviously too much for me. He never should have trusted me with this."

"Hey," I reach across the table and rest my hand on hers. She looks up, her big eyes shining at me. "You're doing great, okay? Willow Creek still looks wonderful, and that's in huge part thanks to you. Even if we don't get the tree, we can find another, and there's still enough going on to make the gala special. You still have Meribel and the Christmas Carol Choir, don't you?"

"Yuh," she sniffles.

"And the eggnog river with the marshmallow waterfall is still running?"

"It is." She sits up a bit straighter.

"And the chocolate maze is open for business?"

"You know a lot about the Winter Wonderland Festival."

I offer her a warm smile. "I fear cars, not Google."

She laughs and wipes her eyes, digging into her purse for a tissue. I'm surprised to realize that what I want more than anything isn't to solve this for her, but to give her as much support as possible so she can solve this. I know she can do this. She can do anything she wants to. She's that kind of woman.

Why can't I just tell her that?

"You've got this," I stumble on my words, tongue-tied for the first time in centuries.

"We've got this," she says, emphasizing the 'we'. Our gazes dance together for a single beat before she coughs, seemingly embarrassed, and pulls her hand away.

The moment breaks, and just like that, we're back to business.

"Okay, think, Draven," she says. "What clues do we have? We know the crooked crown person is behind the rogue elves. We know they left a tacky ornament behind. Think. There must be something we can use in that."

"It's not enough." I tap my fingers on the table. "I've got fragments of clues, at best. There's something there, but I can't quite place it."

"Can we go back to Mímir?"

"Not for a week. He's full after a reading and it'll be some time before he wakes up."

"What if we shake the snow globe? Or we could take it apart and see if there's something inside it we can use?"

"We can try. The worst-case scenario is that it explodes and kills us and the entire town."

Holly pales alarmingly. "Is that an actual possibility?"

"Technically, everything is a possibility. But I don't know. It's a magic snow globe we found in a pocket dimension protected by cookie monsters and a gingerbread dragon. For all we know, it's not even a real snow globe—it could be anything."

Because she is biting her lip and my speech isn't helping her distress, I flash her a very good smile. Probably a six. She doesn't swoon, not even a little bit.

"You're the most unhelpful vampire I've ever met."

"That can't be right. You've met Ronan."

"I stand by my assessment."

"I destroyed a gingerbread dragon."

She takes a deep breath, presumably to give it to me with both barrels, when I feel a vibration in my chest, starting all the way from my feet. It's deep and thrumming and wrong, and from the look on her face, Holly feels it too.

"Draven?" she says. "What is that?"

"I don't know, Frost. An earthquake?"

"Oh god," she groans. "What now?"

I run to the front door. Other patrons have felt the rumbling as well, and a few of them are also standing. We're about to have a riot in here if I don't do something.

"Everyone, be calm." I raise my voice and add a touch of vampire charm to sweeten my speech. Dozens of eyes turn toward me. "Holly and I are professionals. We'll take care of whatever's going on. Trust in us. Good will be our star in these dark times. In the meantime, have a round of eggnog on me. Be reckless and add nutmeg. Huzzah!"

The smitten server swoons, and the assembled patrons provide some scattered applause. I bow a few times, waving in case anyone is filming. My *saluts finaux* are rudely interrupted by Holly elbowing me in the ribs.

"Draven," she hisses. "The rumbling?"

"Right. Sorry. Let's go see what it is."

We pour out onto the street, hunting for the source of the disturbance. It's close to empty. Just a few stragglers looking for a last-minute hot chocolate and some patrons from the diner who've wandered out despite my magnificent speech. Everyone's as confused as we are, looking everywhere, trying to work out what's causing the commotion.

Dropping to my knees, I put my ear to the ground. Gravel jitters and bounces like popcorn in a pan. With my vampire-enhanced sight, I squint down one end of the street. As bad as I'm starting to believe this is, part of me screams I'm being overly pessimistic.

But there's something there—

I can make out the edges of it. Something large and rolling and coming towards us like a freight train out of control. As the thrumming grows more intense and a low rumble fills the air, the details of the shape heading towards us become clear.

I gasp.

"Everyone inside," I croak.

No one moves.

I raise my voice to a yell. "Everyone back inside! Now!"

Holly looks at me with terror in her eyes and grabs me by the collar. It's dramatic and worthy of a romance movie. Maybe even Hallmark.

"What is it, Draven? What did you see?"

Bells. Lots of bells. Wreaths. And...antlers...

My jaw clenches, as is appropriate for this moment.

"Reindeer. Stampede."

Chapter Thirteen

HOLLY

Nick pushes me back into the diner, closing the door as he steps back outside. My mouth falls open in disbelief at the sheer nerve of the vampire, watching his brooding silhouette disappear into the snowy night. He thinks he's playing the hero, but I refuse to be a damsel in distress.

I storm back outside. Nick is nowhere to be seen. The rumbling has stopped and the cold nips as snow flurries across Main Street; fairy lights bead the eaves like frost, and the café's windows glow butter-warm behind me. Somewhere, a cinnamon bun is achieving sainthood. The streets are quiet except for the soft crunch of my boots on the snow and the faint jingling of distant Christmas music drifting from a nearby shop.

That's when I hear it again.

Another rumble.

It spreads through my chest and crescendos as a wall of gray dust materializes at the far end of Main Street. A rolling wave of debris kicked up by whatever's inside. I squint, trying to make out the dark shapes inside—antlers, fur, and a blur of chaos barreling toward me at a speed that should not belong to anything associated with Christmas.

Reindeer.

A herd of reindeer.

An *exceptionally large* herd of reindeer.

Blitzen and bother. Nick was right.

I yelp and dive into a forgiving snowbank. Cold goes down my collar; my dignity goes up in smoke. The reindeer thunder past, hooves striking sparks against the cobblestones, their bells jingling wildly. They're huge—draft horse huge—and they're not prancing or dancing. They're charging.

I drag myself out of yet another snowbank and scramble to my feet, brushing snow off me as I watch reindeer wreak havoc on Main Street. They've splintered off into groups, filling the streets like water from a burst dam. One crashes into a lamp post, sending garlands and lights cascading to the ground. Another snags its antlers on a string of Christmas lights, dragging them like some kind of unhinged holiday banner.

"Is this happening?" I ask the night. The night, unhelpfully, jingles.

But I know this is real, because like everything else that's happened in the past few days, it is ridiculous and completely out of my control. Willow Creek's Christmas gala has become an unmitigated disaster, and instead of organizing the festival of the decade, I'm presiding over a catastrophe that could ruin this town.

Reindeer scatter, some darting into alleys while others charge into shop windows, leaving cracked glass and startled patrons in their wake. One particularly massive buck stops in the middle of the square, snorting and pawing at the ground like it's preparing to challenge Santa to a duel. Another smaller buck emerges from a bakery before running away from the larger male, taking its antlers and the stolen holiday cookies with him.

Marcy barrels out of the Knit and Kettle, clutching a paper bag full of holiday beignets, staring at the scene like she's walked into the wrong Hallmark movie. When she spots me, her face lights up.

"Holly! What on earth is going on?" she yells over the uproar.

"Reindeer," I say, still trying to process the absurdity of the situation. "Stampede. Christmas chaos. You know, normal middle-of-the-week stuff in the run-up to the gala."

Marcy scampers across the road, dodging a reindeer before she skids to my side, panting. "Are things okay with Nick? Did he *summon* them? Because this feels like the kind of prank you'd pull if you were someone who wanted to get one over on you."

"No, Nick didn't send them. Why would he—?"

I stop myself because, honestly, it *does* feel like something he might do. But no. Even he isn't this dramatic. Or ridiculous.

"Are you sure?" she presses. "You two have been spending so much time together lately. I mean, you're practically inseparable now. Maybe this is his way of keeping you on your toes? Or livening things up?"

"Are you suggesting that the standard repertoire of vampire skills includes hippiatry? What's next? Softball?" I snort so hard that the snow considers changing direction. "Now isn't the time for whatever this is."

She shrugs and gestures toward the mess. "Well, what are we supposed to do about that?"

The reindeer buck lets out a loud bellow—do reindeer even bellow?—and charges toward the gazebo in the center of the square, splintering one of its wooden posts. The roof stays up somehow, an act of structural defiance that no one saw coming.

Marcy and I stare at the gazebo, its garlands now hanging limply as the buck continues its assault, antlers smashing through the decorations with wild abandon. Around us, the reindeer scatter through the square like furry missiles, upending trash cans, and snagging lights.

I've frozen. Too shocked to know how to react.

This is insane. Ridiculous.

And it's ruining my Christmas gala.

"Well, we can't just let them keep…doing this," Marcy says,

gesturing vaguely to the carnage as another reindeer crashes into a snowman, sending its carrot nose flying.

"Oh, really? I thought we'd stand here and wait for them to finish before offering them a rubdown and some oats," I snap, dodging a rogue reindeer that streaks past, jingling like it's auditioning for the world's loudest carol. "Any brilliant ideas, Marcy? Other than knitting them an apology scarf?"

"Have you tried singing *Silent Night*? Or calling Nick?"

I groan, dodging a rogue wreath that one of the reindeer has managed to fling off its antlers. The thing bounces off a stack of nearby presents, and I hear a soft squeal as it knocks into a stack of mistletoe. A jingle bell somehow detaches mid-flight, twirling through the air like a missile. Flying holiday decorations are the very last thing I need today, and I watch the metal bell arc through the air and roll down the street after it lands with a thump.

"Could you stop talking about Nick and start helping me stop this?"

Marcy shrugs. "I'm just saying, Holly. You two have been awfully cozy lately. He'd probably come running if you called."

I don't dignify that with a response, mostly because my focus is on the reindeer now trying to eat the town's nativity display. And where, precisely, is Nick? I duck into the diner for five seconds. Did he use me as a festive diversion?

"Now? Now, Marcy? Is this really the best time to discuss Nick?" I pantomime picking up a phone. "Hey, Marcy, phone call for you. It's the cast of the musical, *Stomp*. They'd like their timing back."

"Let's see if they need a snack," she says, rummaging in her shopping bag. "Who doesn't love a good gingerbread bribe?"

Before I can point out how dangerous gingerbread can be, she tosses a cookie toward one of the smaller reindeer. To my astonishment, it pauses, sniffs the snow-dusted treat, and then snatches it up and starts chewing noisily.

"See? Brilliance!" Marcy declares, tossing another cookie toward another reindeer.

"You got enough to feed the whole herd?"

I grab a handful of gingerbread, flinging pieces toward a cluster of reindeer. A few more stop their rampage, and I start to think we might be onto something.

"Scatter them far apart," I say. "We're luring them in. Not baiting a buffet."

It's working. I allow myself a single breath of relief before the realization that it's working too well dawns on me. The massive buck —the one that's been terrorizing the gazebo—snorts loudly as he clocks the cookie economy and declares inflation. He charges toward us, scattering the smaller reindeer like skittles in a bowling alley.

"Uh, Holly?" Marcy squeaks, backing up as the buck closes in, its antlers glinting menacingly in the faint Christmas lights.

"Run!" I shout, grabbing her arm and dragging her behind me as we sprint toward the nearest side street.

We don't make it far before a blur of black and red streaks past us, cutting off the buck's charge with a sharp, almost lazy, movement. The reindeer skids to a halt, its hooves digging into the snow, as Nick steps into view, looking infuriatingly calm despite the chaos surrounding him.

"Always a pleasure, ladies," he says, flashing his signature smile. "Delighted to see you have everything under control."

"Don't just stand there. Do something," I demand, panting as I glare at him. "This isn't under control."

He's still insufferable. Still annoyingly tall, dark, and handsome. Still looking at me like he wants something, and I still can't figure out what that is.

Nick shrugs, flexing his fingers against the cold.

"I've corralled most of the herd in the children's playground. A buck that looks suspiciously like Rudolph seems to have taken a liking to the merry-go-round. It's really quite amusing." He pauses for dramatic effect, and Marcy swoons like a woman who's read *The Vampire Lestat* and taken it far too seriously. "I thought I'd check you hadn't gotten trampled. Looks like I was just in time."

The buck snorts again, pawing at the ground, and Nick turns to it with an arched brow.

"Easy there, big fella," he says, his voice low and smooth. "No need to make this personal."

The reindeer hesitates, its ears flicking back as though considering whether to listen.

"Is there anything he can't charm?" Marcy whispers, staring at Nick like he's a reindeer whisperer. "At this point, I'd let him talk me into alphabetizing his wine fridge."

I can't help but be grudgingly impressed as Nick steps forward and gently guides the buck away from both us and the wreckage of the gazebo. The darn thing follows his instructions, its large antlers dipping low as if in shame. Nick's hand rests on its snout, and the reindeer, despite its previous apparent rage, settles under his touch. I watch, feeling a mix of awe and irritation.

"How does he do that?" I mumble under my breath.

Nick shoots me a glance over his shoulder, that same smirk tugging at the corner of his mouth. "Years of practice. And maybe a little charm. I could show you sometime—"

I scoff and plant my hands on my hips. Nick, meanwhile, rounds up a few more stray reindeer and guides them into a neat line, their hooves skidding slightly on the icy ground.

"The trick, Frost, is to ask nicely."

Nick clicks his tongue once—soft, certain—and the buck's ears tip like sails catching wind. He pats the reindeer on its neck and gives it a sharp tap on its flank. It jumps and then trots off, with the rest of the reindeer following behind in an orderly procession. I watch, silently impressed, as the chaos vanishes like it was never there.

"You're welcome, by the way," he calls out as he walks over.

"Yes. Thank you for saving us from the Christmas apocalypse."

Nick's expression softens just enough to catch me off guard. "Anytime. Whatever you need."

Marcy giggles and nudges me with her elbow. I make a point of ignoring her, although I can't suppress the small smile tugging at the corner of my mouth. Nick's offer hangs in the air like a promise, and I can't help but wonder what else he's willing to do—*or* what he's hiding behind that devil-may-care grin.

When I glance up, Nick is already looking at me. For a fleeting second, his eyes glimmer. His usual cocky smirk falters, replaced by something quieter. Warmer. Something that feels like it's only for me.

It's a look that makes my chest tighten in a way I can't explain. Heat creeps up my neck all of a sudden, while my face flushes, inconveniently.

"Really," Nick says, his voice gentler than before, "it's no problem. You make it very easy to want to help."

I try to hide my reaction, but it's useless. Nick watches me for a beat longer, his expression shifting, as if he's caught in the strange moment, too. And for a brief, wonderful second, it's just us, standing in the quiet aftermath of chaos, the world fading away as I forget about everything except the way his words settle in my chest.

My mouth opens to say something—anything—but before the words come out, Marcy's voice cuts through the quiet, bright and cheery as ever.

"You know, there's a reindeer farm a few miles outside of town. North Star Reindeer," she says, glancing between us with that knowing smile of hers. "I bet the stampede started there. Nick should probably make sure they get home safe, and there might be more clues about who stole the Christmas tree. These events must be related. This can't be a coincidence."

I blink, the moment shattered, and glance back at Nick.

His eyes glint with amusement, that signature smirk returning. "Not a bad idea. How about it, Frost? You think you can endure another trek through the woods with me?"

I nod, wondering about my decision to go into event-planning as a career.

"Great! I'll grab my hat and gloves. Back in a second," Marcy says, clearly pleased with herself. She doesn't wait for us to respond before she's off, practically skipping towards her flat above the chocolate shop she owns.

"Grab hand warmers," I yell at her. "And the good scarves. We're doing this politely."

Nick exhales and watches his breath fog in the air. "Guess we're going on another adventure."

A small smile sneaks onto my face. This is ridiculous. It's with him. And somehow, I'm committed to it.

"Guess so."

As Marcy's footsteps crunch through the snow ahead, I find myself wishing it wasn't the three of us going. If it were just Nick and me, maybe that strange, quiet moment from earlier would have stretched a little longer. Maybe I wouldn't be quite so flustered now, wondering if he'd seen the way my cheeks flushed—or if he'd felt that weird pull like gravity bending between us.

Nick adjusts his scarf and slips his hands into his pockets.

"You cold?" he asks, his voice softer now, more like it was a minute ago when it was just us.

"No. I'm fine."

I shake my head quickly, but the thoughtfulness in his tone makes me warm all over again. We fall into step together, the quiet stretch of snow between us feeling heavier than it should. For just a second, I wish the night were ours alone, without interruptions or reindeer to round up.

Chapter Fourteen

NICK

The drive to the North Star Reindeer farm takes about twenty minutes. Marcy supplies cheerful road trip chatter about laundry triumphs, cocoa rations, and something called 'the great scarf debate.' Neither Holly nor I engage in it deeply, but we try the best we can. I can't pull my thoughts away from that brief moment we shared. They're arriving more frequently, those brief moments, and I wonder about how I might make them last longer.

Before we left, I saw the real Holly, the determined and resilient event planner, on full display. She contacted half the town—her army of assistants—by group text, assigning them tasks before signing off with three snowflakes and a candy-cane emoji. Someone's rebuilding the gazebo. Someone else is making sure the power grid isn't damaged. Others are cleaning up the destruction on Main Street. Truly, she makes logistics look easy.

I sigh and look out the window, letting Marcy's chatter wash over me. I barely catch the last of what she's saying.

"I took three loads before I was done."

"I'm sorry?" I blink myself back to attention. "I missed the start of that."

"Marcy's been telling us about her laundry adventures," Holly says. "It's thrilling."

"I'm just saying, a visit to a reindeer farm is more exciting than what I had planned for this evening."

"Brakes!"

I clutch the side of the car as Marcy rolls through an intersection without coming to a complete stop. She didn't even look in both directions. Holly shoots me a long-suffering look but then undermines it completely with a smile.

"He's afraid of cars," she stage-whispers to Marcy. "You should drive slower."

"I maintain a healthy suspicion about cars," I counter.

Marcy steers this absurd death vehicle down a dirt road, and just like that, we find ourselves at the reindeer farm at the edge of Willow Creek. North Star Reindeer is a perfectly charming place, complete with a cheerful cottage at the end of a winding dirt road, lit with dozens of lanterns that cut through the darkness. A hand-painted sign hangs crookedly from a spruce bough. Warm barn light spills like butter. It even has some perfectly placed pine trees decorated with some scattered red ribbons to add festive cheer.

"Look at this," Holly says as she exits the car. She's bent down and pointing to the torn-up dirt driveway. "You can see the path the reindeer took. It goes all the way around to the back."

Marcy turns on the light on her phone and angles it at the ground. The moon casts long shadows as we follow the skid-scuffed hoofprints and trail of shredded red ribbon. Behind the house, the fence hangs wide open, and the door to the small hut beside the enclosure bangs in the wind. We hurry inside, and I'm relieved Holly won't freeze, but disappointed there's no socially acceptable reason to stand scandalously close.

The interior is a mess. There's obviously been a struggle. A table lies overturned, and the chairs are scattered. And in the middle of it all stands a face I haven't seen in...let's call it 'a while' for everyone's comfort. Long enough that it should have stayed that way.

The person in the middle of the ruin is older, with a deep, gray beard that runs down to his chest. A huge, painful-looking welt is rising on his perfectly bald head. As we enter, he's groaning and using a chair to pull himself off the floor. He grabs his head as he slumps down into the chairs. Holly and Marcy rush to his side.

"Jackson," Marcy breathes. "Are you okay? I was worried something bad had happened when we saw the reindeer stampeding."

"My head," the man says miserably.

I lean against the doorframe, trying to hang back, wondering how I should handle this. This...person isn't named Jackson. He's not a humble reindeer farmer, and he certainly isn't all sweet and innocent. I know exactly who he is, and if I had been aware he was living here, this would been the first place I came looking for answers when all this madness started.

All the pieces fall into place. I knew this was too familiar. Too calculated. Far too vicious for a mere prank. Something truly evil is at work here—and it's not just Willow Creek that's in trouble.

Now I know who's behind this.

Who's been pulling the strings.

I know exactly what I'm dealing with, and I am not pleased about it.

While Marcy and Holly fuss over him, I turn my collar up and get to work tidying the place up. I re-right the table and pull up a few chairs up. 'Jackson,' meanwhile, is preening under the attention, telling them what happened.

"I was getting ready to feed them when I heard a noise. Next thing I knew, someone clonked me on the head. That's all I remember. You say my reindeer were in town?"

They both nod their heads, looking worried. Holly is genuinely concerned, and this farce has to come to an end.

"All right, Jackson—let's skip the performance."

Marcy gasps at my rudeness, and Holly gives me a nasty glare, but my eyes are pinned on this so-called Jackson. He lifts his head, and his eyes widen when he sees me. For a moment, I think he's going to try to bluff his way out of this.

Instead, he sighs and waves his hand.

A tinselly draft lifts, bells chime like a drawer of teaspoons, and with a pulse of magic, the room rights itself. Items levitate back onto shelves, and a broom whisks its way across the floor. Marcy and Holly watch, and I'll begrudgingly concede that the tinkling bells are a nice touch. Even the welt on 'Jackson's' head vanishes, and in seconds, everything is put back together, pristine and perfect. Four mugs of steaming hot cocoa have appeared on the table, and he gestures towards them.

"Didn't know you were involved, Draven. Why don't we all take a seat and not do anything crazy?"

"Does everyone else in Willow Creek have magical powers except us?" Holly asks.

"You know each other?" Marcy asks.

"He and I go back a few years," I say as I pull a chair up to the table. "Hello, 'Jackson.' Or, should I say...Jingle?"

I wait for impressed gasps or other demonstrations of awe from Marcy and Holly. Marcy sips her drink politely. Holly chews her lip.

"Jingle? Santa's second-in-command, logistics elf, bell enthusiast? If Christmas ran on clipboards, he'd be the clipboard."

Humans always get the lore wrong. It's all 'vampires are dark and brooding and vicious', and 'elves are cute and cuddly and would gift you presents every day of the year if they could.' It's a long way from the truth, and I'm going to have to set a few records straight before this Christmas carol is finished.

"You expect us to know the ins and outs of Santa's operation?" Holly asks. She turns to Jingle. "Wait, you're an elf? How do you know Nick?"

"Small world," Jingle shrugs. "Draven knows everyone."

I step close and let my fangs drop an inch. Just one.

My hands curl into fists and the urge to slam Jingle into the nearest wall slams through me. It hums, old and violent. But Holly's somewhere behind my shoulder. Watching.

"Santa," I say, as the last pieces fall into place. "Santa is behind this, isn't he?"

Jingle goes very still. His gaze flicks to my fists, then my fangs, then back to my fists. He lifts his hands slowly, palm out, like I'm something that might bite. Which, to be fair—

"Easy, Draven. I'm not in the middle of this. The big guy sent me here to watch, that's all. That's all I've done."

"Tell us everything. Now. And maybe I won't send you back to the North Pole wrapped in return-to-sender tinsel with a strongly worded card. I'm sure the snowman look would be good on you. I've heard it's coming back into fashion."

Jingle pales because he knows I'm capable of that and more.

I glance back at Holly. Her mouth is set too tight. Her fingers are curled into the sleeves of her coat like she's bracing herself. She looks between Jingle and me, her gaze lingering a fraction too long on my teeth before snapping away.

A cold edge settles in my chest.

She hasn't seen this side of me before.

And for the first time, I'm not sure what she sees.

"You're saying Santa is behind all of this?" Holly shifts, like she's trying to square the idea with reality. "*The* Santa? The jolly fat man with the beard?"

"He's not jolly," I say. "Why don't you tell them, Jingle?"

My fingers drum on the table, each tap sharper than the last. Heat crawls up the back of my neck. This should have been obvious. It would have been—if my attention hadn't been elsewhere. On Holly. On the swing of her chestnut curls, catching the light as she bounces through the snow.

A distraction.

One that stopped me from helping her.

"It's not like that, Draven. It's not what you think."

"I think Santa is intentionally trying to sabotage Holly's festival for his usual, devious purposes."

Jingle blinks. "Fine. It's exactly what you think."

Holly puts her mug down. "Santa wants to ruin the Willow Creek Christmas festival? Why?"

"He's taken over Sulphur Ridge," Jingle says.

Both Marcy and Holly gasp. They look surprised. Shocked. I'd already guessed, and the only reaction I give is the look of unbridled threat that I shoot Jingle for upsetting the woman I'm becoming very, very attached to.

Sulphur Ridge sits a short drive away from Willow Creek, and the difference is immediate. Where Willow Creek leans into warmth and goodwill, Sulphur Ridge runs on something darker. Demons, mostly. It's like a supernatural Las Vegas—flashy, excessive, and built on very questionable morals, which I suppose makes it not all that different from the real thing.

It's not a place you go looking for anything good.

It's exactly the sort of place you'd base an operation like this. Loud enough to hide in plain sight. Corrupt enough not to care what's being drained or who it hurts.

"This makes no sense," Holly says.

"Of course it does," I say. "The songs tried to warn you. Humans never listen. *He watches you while you sleep*, Holly. It's practically the tagline for a horror movie. He's got a naughty-or-nice list, an omniscient info network, and unrestricted chimney access to every house on Earth, and you people leave him snacks."

Everything in me tightens, coiling in a way I don't enjoy. It takes a deliberate breath to ease it loose. A sip of cocoa buys me a second. The chocolate's rich, sweet, and entirely unhelpful because it immediately conjures the idea that Holly would taste the same.

Not now. Focus.

She's looking up at me with wide green eyes, glistening with tears and far too much hope—like I'm meant to fix this. Like I can.

I am so screwed.

"Tell them everything," I say to Jingle. "The truth. All of it."

Jingle sighs and runs a hand over his bald head. "It's like this. Santa hates Christmas. Always has. Always will. He didn't take on the holiday by choice. He was forced into it."

"Forced?" Marcy asks.

"Santa was the spirit of winter. Originally. A wind sprite. Made of pure elemental impulse. He'd blow through towns, bring ice and sleet and cold, like summer spirits bring heat and sun and life. People didn't pay much attention to wind sprites, because they're just there. They come, they go, the end. They also smell horrible, so no one misses them when they've gone."

"Santa was different. He wasn't content with blowing ice around," I add, keeping my tone even. "He decided winter shouldn't end. Not for anyone. If everything froze, time would hold still. A world locked in winter where he was in charge."

I pause for a beat.

"That's how the first ice age started."

"You're kidding," Holly breathes, pressing a hand to her temple. "Santa caused the first ice age?"

"Yup," Jingle says, far too pleased with himself. "Took ages to unwind it. The powers that be didn't appreciate the mess." He shrugs. "So they rewrote his job description. No more storms. No more endless winters. Just joy. Gifts. Cheer. Eternal servitude at the North Pole."

Holly and Marcy go very still. Too still.

Jingle slurps his cocoa, milking the moment.

I've heard this story before. He really needs to get to the point.

"Anyway," he continues, tone turning flippant in a way that doesn't quite hide the edge beneath it. "Santa hates Christmas. He does the job because he's bound to it. But he's been looking for a way out for centuries."

His gaze flicks between us.

"He heard about Willow Creek. The biggest celebration of Christmas the world has ever seen. All that joy. All that belief." His mouth curls. "You don't build something like that without attracting attention. Especially not his."

"I can think of dozens of reasons why not," Holly says.

Jingle ignores her.

"He bought Sulphur Ridge. Started building his own version of things. Less of a celebration. More of an inversion. Strip the joy out, leave everything else behind. He calls it Crapmas. Which is either a joke or a warning." He tilts his head. "When he realized what your tree does...well, that was the turning point. All that negativity, carefully gathered, neatly contained—all ready to be redirected. Not dispersed. Just used."

"Wait," I cut in. "What do you mean the tree takes all the negative energy?"

"It's not a decoration," Jingle says. "It's a conduit. Frank built it to draw the worst out of people. Quietly. Gently. So no one would notice. By Christmas, it's saturated." He taps the table lightly. "All that anger. Grief. Resentment. Stored up in one place."

"Why would Frank do this?" Holly asks, aghast.

Jingle gives a thin smile. "Because he meddles. That's what he does. People, relationships, entire towns if he thinks it'll improve things. Like most cupids, Frank doesn't see the harm in smoothing the edges off problems."

"And the rest," I ask. "The stampede? The rogue elf attacks?"

Jingle shrugs. "That's a bit of mischief. Santa likes a bit of havoc."

I don't like where this is going.

"He's tried this before," I add, my voice flat. "In the thirteenth century. It took the vampires to stop him then. That's why we're banned from Christmas. He doesn't forget losses. Doesn't forgive them either."

My jaw tightens.

"I doubt he expected us to get around his ban with Bloodmas."

Jingle flinches a little, and I know my instincts are bang on.

"What do we do with this?" I ask, pulling the tacky snow globe from my pocket. I set it on the table, and glitter whips into motion like it's trying to escape.

"A snow globe?" Jingle scratches his chin. "I don't know. Looks like something my aunt would keep next to a porcelain shepherdess."

"We found it in the Hollow of Mischief."

"Then I definitely don't know," he says with a shrug. "Santa dropped me off here to keep an eye on things. He's not big on sharing."

"Can you at least call off the elf attacks?"

"Outside my remit." Another shrug. "They're...enthusiastic."

Of course they are.

The urge to vault the table and rearrange his smug little face rises fast and furious. It would be easy. Satisfying, even. A clear message that no one messes with Willow Creek's Winter Wonderland.

But Holly is here.

And this—whatever this is becoming—doesn't feel like something I want to curdle. Not after she looked at me the way she did earlier.

Is this what growth looks like?

"This is a waste of time." I rise slowly, letting the chair scrape. My gaze settles on Jingle. Eleven out of ten on the glare scale. "Willow Creek is under my protection. If you see Santa, you can pass that along."

"You're not the boss of me," Jingle mutters, though his voice holds little conviction.

I send him a final look—sharp enough to linger—and then I turn away.

Outside, the cold has teeth. The wind cuts across the pasture, dragging the scent of pine and frost with it. The sky is strung with stars. The holiday is closing in. You can feel it in the air. In the way everything looks a lot like Christmas.

"We're no further along than when we started," Holly says once we're back in the car, her voice worn thin. "And now it's even worse. If we don't fix this..." She trails off and swallows. "He gets all of it. Everything the tree's holding. What does he even do with that?"

The answer comes uninvited.

Nothing good.

"Then we don't let him have it," I say, keeping my tone steady. "We've been pushing hard. Let's regroup. Eat. Sleep. Then we outplay him."

She nods, but it isn't in agreement. It's surrender dressed up as patience.

It lands somewhere unpleasant.

That look doesn't belong on her. Not when she still believes in Willow Creek. Not when she's built her gala out of nothing but stubbornness and good intentions. And not when she's starting to believe she might not be enough.

That will not stand.

"Willow Creek is getting its Christmas back. You're going to get your gala exactly the way you imagined it—lights, laughter, and those ridiculous mince pies no one likes."

Even if I have to break a few Christmas baubles to deliver it to her.

Holly's hands tighten on the wheel as we turn onto Main Street. "I don't know if I can fix this. This is bigger than a missing tree. I don't even understand what we're dealing with anymore."

"It's not falling apart," I reply. "Not while I'm here."

She huffs out a breath. "You can't promise that."

"I can promise that you're not doing this alone. You have me, the coven, and I'll throw everything I have at this until your gala happens exactly as you want it to."

"That's a big promise, Draven."

"I'm a big vampire."

Marcy sighs softly in the back, clearly enjoying herself.

Holly shakes her head, but there's a hint of something lighter there. "You're ridiculous."

"And yet," I say, settling back, "I'm still your best option."

She doesn't argue.

I let the quiet sit while my plan settles into place.

All I need is a way in.

One rogue elf.

And a little bit of unpleasantness.

Chapter Fifteen

HOLLY

I fiddle with the key in the lock of my front door, grateful for the little porch roof shielding me from the wind. Snowflakes swirl under the warm glow of the porch light, catching on the wreath ribbon and the brass bell like confetti that forgot the party was over. It would feel like stepping into a Christmas card if only my brain weren't full of rogue elves and glitter with an attitude.

With a final twist, the door unlocks. I push inside and let the familiar scent of pine and cinnamon wrap around me like a comforting hug before kicking off my boots by the door.

The living room is small, with a tartan couch that's seen too many movie nights and a fireplace I rarely use because it smokes more than it warms. Fairy lights frame the windows, and my slightly crooked Christmas tree stands proudly in the corner, decked out in mismatched ornaments collected over the years.

This house isn't much, but it's home.

Its normally welcoming quiet feels too still after the day I've had.

I let out a long sigh and collapse onto the couch. My legs ache from running around all day. My thigh still stings where that elf hit me, but my mind is far worse. It's a chaotic swirl of reindeer stampedes, naff Christmas decorations, rogue elves, and—most frustratingly—vampires with dark hair and silver eyes.

Nick Draven is a problem. More than usual. He'd said nice things on the way home—sweet, even—but apparently my traitorous brain wanted more. Like hand-holding. Or that steady, reassuring weight of his hand on my thigh as I drove.

A knock at the door makes my stomach flip. The last time someone knocked on my door unexpectedly, Nick had shown up with some sarcastic quip and a load of trouble. It couldn't possibly be more rogue elves. Surely not? They don't seem the type to knock before attacking, but I suppose you never know. So to be safe, I grab a magazine from the coffee table and roll it up.

"Who is it?" I ask, pressing my ear to the door.

"It's me, Holly."

My shoulders slump as I recognize Frank's voice.

I hesitate for a moment before pulling the door open. He's standing on the porch, his cheeks ruddy from the cold and a thermos clutched in his hands. Snow clings to the brim of his knitted hat, and he gives me a sheepish smile. The thermos hisses gently, promising cocoa; his snowman gloves glimmer with tiny sewn-in fairy sequins as if they're pleased to see me.

I don't usually get visitors this late, but this week hasn't exactly been normal. I brace for bad news, but Frank just smiles. Easy. Unworried. Like he's not here on official business.

"Frank?" I step aside, holding the door open. "What are you doing here?"

"I figured you might need someone to talk to," he says, stepping inside and closing the door behind him. "And I need to check in about the Winter Wonderland."

"Those feel like two very different conversations."

Frank walks into the living room, taking in the cozy chaos of my decorations as he shrugs off his thick winter coat. The penguins on his novelty sweater earn him a small smile before he sets the thermos on the coffee table and twists the lid open, filling the air with spiced brandy and its nutmeg and orange.

"I came prepared," he adds, producing two enamel mugs from his coat pocket like a magician who knows his audience.

"At least someone is."

I drop onto the armchair as he pours us both a generous measure.

"We cleaned up after the reindeer stampede," he says. "And I heard about the Hollow of Mischief. And...well, Nick."

I groan. "Please don't start."

Frank chuckles, but there's a knowing glint in his eye. "I'm just saying, it's not every day a Draven vampire takes an interest in a human. It's unusual, but not unheard of."

I curl my fingers around the mug, staring into the steam.

"There was a Draven in the 1600s who fell for a baker's daughter," he says. "The poor girl used to sneak loaves of garlic bread to him. Neither of them knew he was allergic. Broke out in hives every time they kissed. The town diagnosed 'mystery bakery hives' and thought her beignets were fatal."

I huff out a laugh. "That's tragic."

"They figured it out eventually," he says. "Lived happily ever after. Less garlic."

My smile doesn't quite stick, and Frank notices.

"Holly," he says, his voice softer now, "you don't have to handle all of this on your own."

"I'm not—"

"You are," he cuts in gently. "You came to Willow Creek to prove something. To yourself, to your mom...to everyone really."

I look away, finding the photo of my mom on the mantle. It's not just the ache. It's the standards. The kind that turns 'good' into failure if it isn't perfect.

"This job matters," I say quietly. "If I pull this off—if the Winter Wonderland is spectacular—then it's not luck, or connections, or..." I shrug. "It means I've actually earned it."

Frank nods. "I know it does."

He pauses, long enough that I know he's choosing his next words carefully.

"And I do need you to pull this off," he adds. "The tree, the gala, the whole festival. Willow Creek's counting on you."

My stomach knots.

"But," he continues, steady, "I asked you to give this town something special. I didn't ask you to be your mom. There's a difference."

"It doesn't feel like there is."

"That's because you've set the bar somewhere in the stratosphere," he says. "And now you're trying to reach it on your own."

I don't answer.

"You don't get extra credit for making this harder than it needs to be, Holly. And you don't have to prove you belong here by burning yourself out."

A short, sharp breath escapes me. "I only got this job because my mom put a word in for me. And you've been very clear you want the best Winter Wonderland Willow Creek's ever seen."

He doesn't flinch.

"That's true," he says. "I do."

I look at him.

"But I didn't say it had to look like one of Celeste's events," he continues. "And I didn't say you had to do it all yourself to prove you deserved the job. There's a difference between high standards and impossible ones. You've blurred the line."

"I just want people to feel like it matters," I say, my voice quieter now. "Like it's... more than decorations and mulled wine and hoping for the best. Everyone thinks event planning is just logistics. But it's more than that. It's a feeling. It's looking at what you've created and seeing the joy people find in it. In knowing the work you did made the world a little better, even if it's only for a night."

Frank watches me while I pick at the couch upholstery.

"That's stupid, isn't it?"

"You're talking to someone who shoots people with arrows to

make them fall in love," he says. "Which is not even remotely how arrows work. My bar for stupid is a lot higher than yours."

I laugh, blowing on my mug before taking a sip. It burns all the way down, and I gasp. "How much of this is pure liquor?"

"Probably eighty percent. Figured you might need something stronger."

He knocks back his own drink with practiced ease. "You're good at this," he adds. "You make people care. That's half the job."

"And the other half?"

"Not running yourself into the ground trying to prove it."

I let out a breath, not quite a laugh.

He sets his mug down and reaches for his coat, like the conversation has already moved on in his head.

"Frank," I say, before he can fully shrug it on. "Were you ever going to tell me what the tree actually does?"

He stills, one hand caught in his sleeve.

For a second, I think he might dodge it.

Instead, he exhales and finishes pulling the coat into place.

"No," he says simply. "It wouldn't have changed anything you needed to do. And I didn't want you worrying about things you can't control."

"It would have been nice to know what I'm trying to fix."

"You already knew the important part. That it matters."

"That's not the same thing."

"No," he agrees. "It isn't."

He hesitates, then relents a fraction.

"Around here, when we talk about the magic of Christmas, we're not always being metaphorical," he says. "The tree...keeps things running the way they're supposed to. The festival, the town—people show up expecting something, and the tree helps make sure they find it."

The room feels a little too still.

"And now it's gone."

"Yes."

The rim of the mug is no longer warm as my thumb drags along it. "You should have told me."

"Maybe," he says. "But it wouldn't have changed the plan."

"And the plan is?"

"You and Draven get the tree back," he says. "You get the gala back on track and deal with the rogue elves."

"So everything."

"Yup. That's the gig, kiddo. If events were all sunshine and order, we wouldn't need event planners, would we?"

"I can't tell if that's profound or idiocy."

"That's how you know it's right."

The grin he flashes me would make Nick jealous.

I look up at him. "No more surprises?"

"No more unnecessary ones."

I let that sit, then nod once. It's not perfect, but it's something.

"Why can't you fix it?" I ask. "You know—" I make a vague circling motion with my hand.

"Because magic has a habit of attracting more of itself," he says. "And not always the kind you want. If I step in directly, there's a good chance I make things worse, not better."

"That feels like a fundamental flaw."

"It's a feature," he says mildly.

"Great."

He picks up his scarf from the back of the couch and wraps it loosely around his neck.

"You're doing exactly what you need to be doing," he says. "Even if you don't like how it feels."

"That's not reassuring."

"It's not meant to be."

Frank opens the door and cold air slips into the room. Then he pauses, glancing back at me.

"And Holly?"

I look up.

"Try doing this your way," he says. "If I wanted Celeste, I'd have hired Celeste."

He steps out into the night, and the door closes softly behind him.

I lean against it for a moment, letting the quiet settle. The living room is cast in the soft glow of the fairy lights strung from the bookcases, their light catching in the frost on the windowpanes. The air feels heavier than it should, like the house is waiting for something to shift. My crooked little Christmas tree stands in the corner, its mismatched ornaments glinting in the faint light, but even it seems weary, as if it knows the weight of the season has fallen squarely on my shoulders.

The throw blanket catches under my fingers as I drag my hand along the arm of my couch and let the frayed edge ground me. My sitting room now feels crowded with half-finished things—the presents waiting on the coffee table, the empty stocking, the photographs on the mantle.

Mom's smile is bright and certain. Dad's softer, steadier. Together, they look like they already know how everything turns out.

I look away first.

The room gets smaller as I stand here, like it's closing in on all sides.

My keys are in my hands before I've quite decided to move. Before I can stop myself, I've headed out, searching for clarity or distraction, or maybe a little more space. The drive to Nick's is quick, the streets empty save for the occasional shimmer of Christmas lights reflecting off the snow.

My brain lists all the perfectly reasonable excuses it can think of for this trip. I can ask about Ronan. About Crinkshaw. About whatever's happening next. We're working together—this is practical. Necessary.

The tight pull in my stomach is definitely the brandy. The heat in the car explains the sweat on my palms.

Nothing else.

His outrageously oversized house comes into view, its warm glow spilling from it like a beacon against the cold. I park in the wash of light from the living room window and decide not to go straight to the front door. Instead, I walk across the drive to the window, drawn by the idea of catching Nick doing something I can tease him about later. Like brooding in a way that suggested he'd done extensive research into proper brooding techniques.

I peer through glass that's quilted with frost ferns. My breath blooms in the night air, then fades.

I freeze.

Nick stands in the middle of the room, his dark figure hunched over something—or someone. The low, eerie light catches the edge of his fangs as he shifts, and something dark glistens at his mouth.

My stomach drops as the shape in his grip resolves into a rogue elf, limp but still twitching.

The elf jerks weakly, limbs dragging against the floor. There's nothing willing about it. Nothing controlled or careful. It's messy. Violent. Nothing like the careful lines he outlined for me in Hemoglow.

He promised Frank. Promised that the vampires wouldn't feed on anyone in Willow Creek without consent.

For a heartbeat, the polished gentleman blurs—and the predator steps into focus.

My heart judders. I don't notice I've moved until my mitten brushes against the glass with a soft squeak, the sound far too high pitched for my liking. My hand flies to my mouth as my feet step back too quickly.

My boot skids on the ice.

The world tilts—and Nick's head snaps toward the window.

I don't wait to find out if he's seen me.

I barely catch my balance before I turn and run, the cold air burning my lungs as I fumble for the car door. The handle slips once in my grip before I wrench it open and shove the key home.

The engine roars too loudly in the quiet street.

I pull away too fast, my tires skid on the snow, but the car doesn't slow down. All I can see is the dark smear at his mouth—and the sickening thought that whatever Frank nudged me toward, it wasn't safety. It was the edge of something I don't understand.

Chapter Sixteen

NICK

I spit into a porcelain bowl Crinkshaw holds at my side. The rogue elf slumps onto the couch, and Crinkshaw lurches forward with a glass of red wine as if this is the sort of thing that belongs on a checklist. Alcohol doesn't make me drunk, but nothing washes the taste of tainted blood from my mouth like an Australian red. He follows it with a peppermint-clove rinse, all with the solemn air of a maître d' at a tiny funeral.

"Someone's really messed with that elf." I wipe my mouth with a towel as Crinkshaw tilts the elf's head with a quiet precision.

"He'll be out for some time, Sire." Crinkshaw drapes a tartan throw over the elf and sets a snowflake compress on its forehead. "How much did you take?"

"Only a mouthful, but it went everywhere, and it tasted foul. He's been drugged. Santa's been giving them something to make them more malleable."

"Boozy eggnog?"

"Almost certainly."

Elves are lunatics for boozy eggnog. They'll do just about anything for it, which explains how Santa's been getting them to play along. Honestly, this whole thing feels like a holiday-themed pyramid scheme, but with more sugar and less plausible deniability.

"Were you able to get anything else, Sire?"

I nod. Crinkshaw knows blood carries more than nutrients. Older vampires can sometimes pull something back if they're good. Fragments. Impressions. Not much, and not often, but I've been at this longer than most.

I'm good at a lot of things, actually.

Things that might appeal to Holly. I'm handy with flatpack furniture and navigating tight spaces without making a sound. I make a mean hot chocolate. Marshmallows included. Then there's my decorum. Charm. Finesse. The sort that might make Holly's eyes soften—for entirely professional reasons, of course.

Crinkshaw taps his bony fingers against the side table. A small shake of my head snaps whatever that was back into place. I force a cough, assuming he'll think my state is due to the rogue elf blood. At least vampires can't blush.

"A little. Mostly scattered images with a few flashes of chaotic rage. This elf doesn't know what he's doing, or why. There was a factory, too. Could be anywhere. Conveyor belts, red-and-white smokestacks like candy canes, and a sign in bad cursive: *Naughty Intake*. Nothing definitive, but it smells like Santa's logistics."

Ronan bursts into the room—his preferred method of using doors—looking more worried than usual. His hair is unreasonably disheveled, and there's a bright, battle-ready glint in his eyes. He's even donned his tartan kilt, which suggests I'll soon be revisiting the topic of appropriate attire for the modern age.

"You've got to see this." He thrusts a laptop at me, a video paused on screen. It's grainy, indistinct—until it isn't.

"Why are you showing me security footage of our house?"

"Watch." He leans in to press play, and I find myself leaning forward with him.

The footage shows the exterior, zooming in on the giant bay window of this very sitting room. A flicker of movement in the corner draws my eye—someone creeping toward the glass with the subtlety of a penguin on roller skates.

Holly Frost.

With her cute little crinkled-up nose and a glare that's like she's personally offended by the weather, she looks like she marched straight out of a Christmas card—one that's had its edges frayed from being thrown across the room too many times.

A slow unease settles in as she stumbles back from the window, her hand flying to her mouth. Even grainy and soundless, the hurt reaches right through the screen.

The video ends with her running.

I close the laptop.

She saw.

"Well," I say, and hand the laptop back to Ronan. "That's unfortunate."

Neither Ronan nor Crinkshaw says anything as I walk to the window, my hands clasped loosely behind my back, watching snow drift past thc glass.

"You should talk to her, Sire," Crinkshaw says. There's a hesitation in it, like he'd rather be doing anything else—including wrestling a yeti.

I don't look at him. "I'm aware."

"Sooner rather than later," he adds.

"Yes, Crinkshaw. I gathered that."

The pause is uncomfortable.

"You're not very good at apologies," Ronan offers, entirely unhelpfully.

"I'm not apologizing."

Crinkshaw makes a small, diplomatic sound that suggests he absolutely disagrees.

I exhale. "I don't even know what I'd be apologizing for."

Before I can reconsider, my coat is being settled onto my shoulders and a scarf looped firmly into place.

"Sire—"

"I'm going," I mutter.

"So I see."

The door opens before I can argue further, and a moment later I'm outside, the night wrapped in that peculiar, muffled quiet that only comes with fresh snow and too many Christmas lights.

The scarf smells faintly of clove and starch. Somewhere down the street, a string of lights flickers in uneven rhythm, casting soft red and gold across the frost. By the time I reach Holly's, I haven't managed a single useful thought.

Her porch light glows like a star, which feels aggressively on-brand for Holly Frost. Of course she'd have a porch light that looks like it belongs on a Christmas card. Of course it would make this worse.

I knock, sharper than intended, and immediately regret it.

There's no plan. No clever lines. No carefully constructed explanation. Just the increasingly unhelpful urge to fix something I may have already broken beyond repair.

The door flies open, and I realize how much trouble I'm in.

Color climbs Holly's throat and settles high in her cheeks, and her mouth does that small, precise thing it does when she's decided she won't be persuaded by anything short of divine intervention. This isn't the Holly who laughs like sleigh bells or scowls like thunder. This is the other Holly. The one who's reached a conclusion and barred the gates behind it.

"Holly," I say, but she cuts me off before I can get any further.

"What do you want, Nick?"

Her voice is sharp enough to cut glass. She stands square in her doorway, one hand on the edge of the door as though she's already half considering the pleasure of slamming it in my face.

"I—"

Brilliant. For a man who has talked bishops into bad ideas, kings into worse ones, and entire rooms into agreement they never should have offered, this is an astonishing failure of basic speech. My words snag in my throat like tinsel caught on a branch, glittering there uselessly.

Holly lifts one eyebrow. "Either say it or get off my porch before I freeze you solid."

"That seems excessive."

"Then work quickly."

There it is. That spark. The impossible, fire under her frost. Familiar enough that, for one ridiculous second, my chest forgets it is here to hurt.

I have lived through plagues, revolutions, and three deeply regrettable styles of cravat. In all my centuries, I've never met anyone remotely like her. Even Eleanor of Aquitaine wasn't as interesting as Holly Frost.

"I need to talk to you," I manage at last. "About what you saw."

"Oh, I saw plenty," she says. "I did wonder if there'd be a follow-up performance."

"Holly—"

"Don't do that."

"Do what?"

"That thing where you say my name like it's a substitute for an explanation."

"It's not like that. I was trying to help."

She lets out a laugh that has no joy in it at all. "By feeding on a defenseless elf?"

"That's not..." I stop, because apparently even my excuses need reorganizing. "Sometimes we pick things up when we feed. Memories. Impressions. I thought it might tell us something useful."

"Oh, good," she says. "So only a little violation of bodily autonomy, with festive mind theft on the side. Very seasonal."

"It's not stealing," I say, hearing the edge in it too late. "It's not deliberate."

"It looked pretty deliberate from where I was standing."

"That's not fair."

Her face changes at that. Not softer. This is far worse. She's offended, yes, but beneath that she's wounded in a way that makes me want to grab my sentences back out of the air and throttle them before they reach her.

"Not fair?" she repeats. "You want to talk to me about fair?"

"Holly, I didn't hurt him."

"I can't believe I trusted you." Her voice is low and clean, stripped of heat in a way that means that the heat has already done its damage. "You stood there and told me you wanted to help. That the vampires wanted to be part of Willow Creek. You told Frank you understood the rules."

"I do."

"Really?" she asks. "Because from where I was standing, what I saw was a man who heard the rules, nodded solemnly, and then decided they were for other people."

"I didn't break my word to Frank."

The silence could draw blood or make a lesser man start confessing to unrelated crimes.

"No one in Willow Creek gets touched without consent," I continue. "Not like that. The elf isn't from Willow Creek."

The look on her face is not encouraging.

She blinks at me once, very slowly. "Congratulations. You found a loophole."

"That's not what this is."

"No?" She leans a little more on the door. "Then what is it, Nick? Go on. I'm fascinated."

I hesitate. Which is new and unpleasant. I don't hesitate. I advance, retreat, devastate, charm, and occasionally dance. I do not stand on winter porches like a boy in a bad ballad trying to remember how nouns work.

"It's me trying to fix a problem. One that's affecting you."

"I didn't ask you to fix it like this."

"Is that what this is? You're worried that you're implicated?"

"No," she says. "I'm worried about my integrity."

Porch light and frost gather between us, along with the distinct sense that I am making an already poor evening more ambitious. And because I am apparently already committed to making this night memorable for all the wrong reasons, I decide to keep going.

"I was trying to help you."

Her mouth tightens. "Right. Because that's what this is about."

"It is."

"No," she says. "It's what you're calling it. That's not the same thing."

I open my mouth and close it again.

She goes on before I can risk another sentence. "Do you know what the worst thing is? It's that you're standing here trying to explain why it doesn't count."

"It does count."

"Then stop talking like it doesn't."

That lands.

"I didn't hurt the damn elf," I say, and now the words are coming from a lower, rougher place. "He was sedated. I took a thimbleful. He is alive, on my couch, with Crinkshaw tending to him as if he's a visiting aunt with a chill. It was for information, not hunger."

Holly's gaze doesn't move from mine. "I saw you."

"Yes."

"The poor thing was in agony."

"He was drugged," I say. "Santa's been dosing them, making them pliable. I needed to know what he's seen, where he'd been, what they're doing with the tree."

Her head tilts. "So because Santa is doing monstrous things, you think it's fine to do a slightly more tasteful version?"

"That's not what I said."

"It's exactly what you said."

"What I meant was that we are running out of time, and I chose the expedient option. To get you your gala, your tree, your impossible miracle of a Winter Wonderland."

The words hang there like damp washing: unpleasant, undeniable, and very much mine.

For the first time since I arrived, she does not interrupt me immediately. She just looks at me, and in that silence, I can almost hear the final boards going over some interior window.

"I see," she says quietly. "So this is my fault?"

"That's not fair."

"No, Nick. It isn't." She draws in a breath that trembles only once before she gets a grip on it. "Do you know what I have been doing since I got here? Trying to hold this whole thing together with ribbon, bluff, and a frankly unreasonable amount of battery-operated fairy lights. I have one chance to pull this off. One. I need this festival to work. I need that tree back, and I need this town not to fall apart while I'm standing in the middle of it. And through all of that, I still understood that there were lines."

"If you'd just let me explain—"

"No, you listen." Her voice is no louder than before, but it reaches much further. "You promised Frank the vampires would not feed on people without their consent. You promised Willow Creek you weren't here to make trouble. You promised me you were helping. Not that you were helping right up until it became inconvenient. Not that you'd be good until you found a technicality. Helping."

Every word arrives exactly where it ought to, which is unfortunately all over me.

"I know what I promised."

"Then why are you standing on my porch arguing definitions?"

I should tell her it's because I'm losing her. That I am frightened. That there is something particularly humiliating about finding the one person whose opinion matters and then failing exactly where she can see it.

Instead, I say, "An elf is not a townsperson."

The instant the sentence leaves my mouth, I despise it.

Holly stares at me as if she can hardly believe I've made myself worse voluntarily.

"That," she says, "is exactly what I mean."

I rake a hand through my hair. “I know how it sounds.”

“You should. You’re the one saying it.”

“I am not trying to make this smaller than it is.”

“You already have.”

That does it.

That.

I have been called a monster by people with torches, priests, kings, widows, magistrates, and one unforgettable opera singer with a knife. None of them has ever managed to make the word feel as possible as Holly Frost does without using it at all.

“I was trying to get something useful,” I say, and my voice sounds tired now, stripped of all the polish I usually keep on it. “Something that could help us.”

“Us?” she says, and there’s the bitter edge again. “When exactly did you decide there was an us?”

I do not have an answer that sounds sensible.

“A while ago,” I say.

Something passes over her face. Just once. Not well, not safely, and not in any way that improves my circumstances, but enough to tell me the words found their mark.

Then she shakes her head.

“I don’t know if I can trust you anymore,” she says.

There is no dramatic thunderclap. No heavenly choir. No poetic collapse of the porch roof. Just a simple sentence, spoken quietly by a woman in a winter doorway.

It is devastating.

“Holly,” I say, and hear the plea in it too late. “I am sorry. Not the polished version. Not the one that comes with an argument attached. I am actually sorry.”

She looks at me for a long moment, and I see the exact instant she chooses herself over the possibility of believing me.

Sensible and catastrophic.

Then she says, “I hope you get the tree back, Nick. I hope you save the festival. I hope you help fix all of it. But right now I don’t want you on my porch telling me that breaking your word was somehow for the greater good."

I take a breath that feels lined with needles. "Give me a chance to fix this."

Her hand tightens on the door.

"That's just it," she says. "You already had one."

Then the door closes.

Not a slam. Holly is too precise for that. Just a firm, final click, the kind that says she has considered the matter and reached a conclusion I do not enjoy.

Snow begins again as I stand there, fine as sifted sugar, settling on the porch rail and the steps and my shoulders. It falls with the innocent industry of something that has never once broken a promise in its life.

I stay where I am for a moment longer, with my apology cooling uselessly in the air and no clever thing left to say to it.

Chapter Seventeen

HOLLY

The last thing I need right now is silence.

Silence leaves too much room for replaying things, and my brain has latched onto last night like it's a terrier that's got a personal vendetta and a trouser leg. Nick on my porch. Nick in his sitting room. Nick with dark on his mouth and excuses lined up behind his fangs, waiting for their cue.

I lasted exactly forty-three minutes alone in my house before deciding I'd done enough character building for one day.

Willow Creek has woken up and is already putting itself back together.

I cut past the playground on my way to The Knit and Kettle and catch just enough to register how much progress has been made. The fencing's upright again. The slide has been persuaded to resemble a slide. The merry-go-round is no longer trying to reinvent itself as modern art. A cluster of volunteers is still at it, wrapped in scarves and grim determination as they negotiate with the aftermath of several hundred reindeer who clearly did not believe in civic planning.

The south fence will need checking later. Preferably by someone who isn't me and is enthusiastic about fences. There are a dozen things still broken in this town. My phone hasn't stopped buzzing all night. I've signed permits. Ordered lumber. Created groups and appointed team leaders. There are still a million things to be done.

Coffee comes first.

I push through the door of The Knit and Kettle, trailing cold air and a mood that could curdle dairy, with the bell above the door giving its usual cheerful little jingle as if I am not one frayed nerve away from strangling a decorative garland.

The place is warm, crowded, and smells aggressively of cinnamon. Someone has draped knitted snowflakes across the chalkboard menu. The big armchair in the corner is wearing a festive cushion cover, this one featuring a robin with the haunted expression of a bird that has seen too much. At the back, the espresso machine hisses —even the appliances are judging my choices.

Marcy is already here, of course. She is tucked into our usual table by the window with a mug the size of a soup tureen and the expression of a woman who knows she is about to receive an emotional unburdening disguised as gossip.

"Oh no," she says. "That's not your regular festival crisis face. That's your 'I have seen something deeply troubling and possibly extremely handsome' face."

I sink into the seat opposite her and peel off my gloves one finger at a time.

"You're deeply annoying."

"You don't believe that," she says, sliding a mug toward me. "You're friends with me because I'm right and because I keep emergency cinnamon buns on hand for personal disasters. Start talking."

I wrap both hands around the mug, more for the anchoring than the heat.

"I think I might have made a terrible mistake."

Marcy brightens like someone's announced an ice-skating accident and a scandal in the same sentence.

"Excellent," she says. "Those are always the best stories."

"They're not," I say. "They're stressful, humiliating, and usually involve me wanting to move to another country and change my name."

"Mm," Marcy says, entirely unbothered. "Still entertaining for me. Go on."

I stare into my drink like it might rearrange itself into answers if I give it enough time.

It doesn't.

Rude.

"I went to his house last night," I say finally.

"Oh, really?" She purrs and leans forward.

"Not like that. He didn't know I was there."

Marcy doesn't react immediately, which is suspicious. Marcy always reacts immediately.

Then, very carefully, she says, "And when you say 'So this was less of a socially acceptable visit, and more of a creeping-around-outside-his-window kind of thing?'"

"...I don't like your tone."

"That's because my tone is accurate."

"I wasn't creeping," I say. "I was...observing."

"From outside the window."

"Yes."

"In the dark."

"It's winter," I snap. "It's dark at four in the afternoon. That's not my fault."

Marcy hums into her mug. "Mm. Continue your completely normal and not at all concerning behavior."

I take a sip of my gingerbread latte, mostly so I don't have to look at her.

"I saw him," I say. "Feeding."

Marcy stills.

Not dramatically or a gasp or a clutch at her chest. Just...still, like a thought has decided to sit down and take its hiking boots off.

"Okay," she says after a moment. "Define feeding."

"I don't think that needs defining."

"I'm asking anyway."

"He had a rogue elf," I say. "And he was—" I gesture vaguely now that my vocabulary has packed up and left "—doing the vampire thing."

"Drinking blood."

"Yes."

"Right." She nods slowly. "And this is upsetting because...?"

"Because—Marcy—he was drinking someone's blood."

"Yes," she says patiently. "He is a vampire. That is very much their whole thing. It's in the brochure."

"That's not—" I stop, aware I sound ridiculous, even to myself. "It's not that simple."

"It might be," she says. "Walk me through it."

I exhale, long and slow, and try again.

"He promised," I say. "To Frank. To the town. To me. That they wouldn't feed on anyone except in Hemoglow and only with consent."

Marcy nods. "Okay."

"And then I see him. Feeding," I say. "He said it was for information. That vampires can sometimes pull memories when they feed. He was trying to find out what Santa's doing with the tree."

"That tracks," Marcy says.

"That's not helpful."

"I'm not trying to be helpful yet," she says. "I'm trying to understand why you look like you're about to either cry or commit a small but meaningful crime."

I give her the sort of look that ought to come with weather warnings.

"I am not going to cry," I say.

"That's good," she says. "Means we're in the crime zone. Are we talking felonies or misdemeanors?"

"I'm serious, Marcy."

"So am I." She leans forward slightly. "You saw him do something vampires do, for a reason that—annoyingly—makes sense.

The elf is fine. The town is still standing. So why are you this upset?"

"I just told you—"

"No," she says, gently but firmly. "You told me what happened. That's not the same thing."

I open my mouth.

Close it again.

"I trusted him," I say finally.

"There we go," she says softly. "That's the one."

My attention drops to the latte foam, which has arranged itself into the sort of meaningless swirl people in expensive wellness retreats probably call an answer.

"I trusted him," I repeat, quieter now. "He stood there and told me he wanted to help. That he wanted the vampires to be part of Willow Creek. That he understood the rules."

"And then you saw him...bend them."

"Break them."

"Bend them. *For you*," she says. "Important distinction."

"It's not," I say. "He found a loophole."

Marcy tilts her head. "And that's the problem?"

"Yes."

"No," she says. "That's not *his* problem. That's *your* problem."

I frown at her. "They're the same thing."

"They are absolutely not the same thing." She takes a sip of her drink, entirely too calm about this. "The problem is that he made you feel safe enough to believe him. The thing you're struggling with is that it's made you think that maybe you shouldn't have."

"I don't—" I start, then stop, because I don't actually know how to finish that sentence.

"You don't like that he made a choice you wouldn't have made," she says. "And then stood there and explained it like it was reasonable."

"Yes," I say, too quickly.

"And you don't like that part of you understands why he did it."

I hesitate.

Which is answer enough.

Marcy smiles, small and knowing. "There it is."

"I don't like any of this," I mutter.

"No," she agrees. "It's messy. And you like things to be..." she gestures vaguely and then continues, "less messy. What a shock that professional event planners happen to be type A personalities."

"I run events, Marcy. My entire job is making things not messy."

"Shame your emotions disagree with you."

A cinnamon bun comes apart under my fingers in sticky spirals, shedding onto the plate like evidence. Across from me, Marcy twirls one dark curl around her finger and waits with the patience of someone who already knows the ending and is enjoying my slower route to it.

"I just—" I stop, trying to get the shape of it right. "If he'd just... told me. If he'd said, 'this is what I'm going to do, and you might not like it, but I think it's necessary.' I still wouldn't have liked it, but at least it would have been honest."

"Instead, he did it and then explained it afterwards."

"Yes."

"Like a man who thinks the explanation is the important part."

"Exactly."

Marcy leans back in her chair, considering me over a drift of milk foam dusted with nutmeg like it's a particularly festive interrogation.

"So you're not upset that he's a vampire. It's that he acted like one in a way that didn't match what he'd told you he'd be."

"Yes."

"And then he tried to logic his way out of it."

"Yes."

She taps her spoon twice against the side of her mug, a small, decisive punctuation mark. "Okay. That's fair."

Something in me unclenches enough to be noticeable. "Thank you."

"But," she adds, pointing a piece of cinnamon bun at me with the grave authority of a woman about to ruin my afternoon, "you also need to decide what you actually want from him."

The thought catches in my head like a scarf on a nail. "What?"

"You're mad," she says. "That part's clear. But what do you want him to do? Do you want him to apologize? To never do it again? Or do you want him to be something that he isn't?"

"I don't—" I stop. "I want him to mean what he says."

Marcy smiles, soft this time. "That's a good answer."

"See. It's perfectly reasonable."

"Yes," she says slowly. "But it's also a hard thing to ask because it requires him to never make a mistake and people are consistently bad at that."

"He's not people," I say. "He's—"

"A vampire," she finishes. "Which, ironically, simply means he's had longer to practice getting things wrong."

I press my lips together hard enough to qualify as a decision.

"This is a disaster."

"This is a crush," she corrects.

"It is not a crush."

"You went all cat burglar on him to stare at him through a window."

"I did not—"

"You crept up on him," she says, sweetly. "From outside. Through glass."

"I hate you."

"You love me," she says. "And you're deflecting."

My hand goes over my face on instinct, as if one good palmful of skin might cancel the conversation.

"I've got to focus," I say. "On the festival. On the tree. On fixing this."

"And you will," she says. "You're very good at fixing things."

"Not this," I mutter.

Marcy gives me the sort of look usually reserved for crossword clues and people about to make avoidable mistakes.

"Maybe not yet," she says. "But you don't have to solve everything today."

"I do," I say. "Christmas is in—" I stop, because I don't actually want to count the days out loud. "Soon."

Marcy drums her fingers against the table in a syncopated little rhythm that suggests she is enjoying this far more than she should. "Yes, that famously unspecific deadline of Christmas."

"Exactly."

"Okay," she says, pushing her empty mug aside. "Then here's your plan."

"Since when do you make plans?"

"I always have a plan," she says. "Step one: finish your coffee. Step two: you go home and do something that does not involve spiraling. Step three: you decide what you actually want him to say when you're not actively furious. If you survive steps one through three, step four is having a conversation with him without exploding."

"I am not spiraling."

"You absolutely are spiraling."

"I am processing."

"With dramatic flair."

"That is my brand."

Marcy grins. "Finish your coffee, Holly."

I look down at the mug in my hands. It's gone lukewarm, which feels, irrationally, like I've failed at coffee as a concept.

"Fine," I say, and drain it with the sullen obstinacy usually reserved for teenagers. "Happy?"

"Ecstatic."

I shove my gloves back on with more force than the situation strictly requires, which is satisfying in the limited way small acts of aggression usually are. She leans in and bumps her shoulder against mine on the way past. "Go home. Do not spiral. Do not lurk outside any Gothic architecture. Do not commit crimes."

"I'll do my best."

"That," Marcy says over her shoulder, "is exactly what people say before I end up having to bring them bail money and a muffin."

I pull open the door before she can keep going. The cold hits me all at once, bitter and needling, and the bell above the shop gives its little jingle again, unbearably pleased with itself.

Behind me, Marcy calls, "Text me when you get home."

I glance back. "You hate texts."

"I hate waiting more."

The walk back is short, which is rude. I would have appreciated more time to become a different person. Willow Creek is still busy in that determined, woolly way small towns have when something awful has happened and everyone has decided the correct response is casseroles, practical footwear, and mild martyrdom. Two teenagers are sweeping up splintered wood beside the park in matching Santa hats. Mr. Patel is rehanging garlands. Mrs. Lee is on a stepladder retying a bow the size of a small yacht.

I answer a few dozen texts and by the time I reach my street, the sky has turned a pale pewter that makes the town look both expensive and slightly doomed. My house sits where I left it, small and familiar beneath its dusting of snow, the porch light still glowing with the smug sincerity of a nativity tea towel.

And there, pinned dead center to the front door with a candy-cane striped drawing pin, is an envelope.

I stop.

It's cream, thick, and expensive-looking, which suggests either money or menace. Possibly both. My name is written across the front in a curling hand dramatic enough to deserve its own entrance music.

Holly Frost.

For one ridiculous second, I wonder whether Marcy has beaten me home and decided to escalate from emotional support to theatrical intervention.

The envelope is scented with peppermint and woodsmoke,

which is not a smell I trust in correspondence. The seal is still intact: dark red wax stamped with the shape of a sleigh.

I glance up and down the street, although I have no idea what I expect to see. A messenger in a velvet cape? A fleeing elf? Nick pretending he's not lurking behind Mrs. Abernathy's holly bush?

Nothing.

Just Willow Creek, carrying on around me in all its festive delusion, as if people do not regularly leave ominous stationery on one another's front doors.

I ease the envelope off the door. Turn it over in my hands—once, twice—and let the wax seal catch the light.

I should get Nick.

The thought arrives fully formed, sensible, strategic, and unwanted. This is exactly the sort of thing he's good at. Suspicious letters. Questionable decisions. Situations that feel like the beginning of a bad idea.

Then I think last night. About promises and loopholes and the look on his face when he decided those were the same thing.

"Right," I say.

And instead of calling Nick, I break the seal.

Chapter Eighteen

NICK

"Another," I say to Wes, gesturing at the bottle behind him.

Wes, ever unflappable, raises his eyebrow at me. "You sure? That's a lot, even for you."

"I can't get drunk, Wes."

"I know. But since we're both going through the hackneyed routine of 'sad man at bar,' I felt I should play my part of a reluctant bartender. Drink the bottle if you like—just leave enough to dye the fountain green."

It's late afternoon, and I've retreated to Hemoglow to lick my wounds. Twinkle lights loop the back bar like fairy-laced ivy, while garlands of spruce—not pine—and dried orange slices scent the air. Candy-cane swizzle sticks lean in a cut-glass tumbler, and someone's got a jazzy *Carol of the Bells* low on the speakers. The bar is lightly populated at this time of day, and it's as good a place as any to feel sorry for myself. If gloom must be endured, it may as well be festive. It's not like I can go home.

My coven, bless their undead hearts, can be staggeringly efficient when it comes to things that are none of their business. By the time I'd left the house, it was already common knowledge that Holly and I had argued. Not discussed. Not disagreed. Argued. With feeling. Possibly with subtext.

Crinkshaw chose the moment I was putting on my coat to murmur, "I did mention, Sire, that you are not especially adept in such circumstances."

I chose not to respond, largely because I did not have one that wasn't either inaccurate or undignified. Ronan, meanwhile, looked delighted. As if he'd been handed emotional drama and intended to treat it as a spectator sport.

I left before either of them attempted to improve the situation further.

Which is how I ended up here, drinking something that cannot numb the pain, surrounded by people I don't know, in a bar decorated like Christmas has developed a personality and that personality is based entirely on thrifting.

The look I send Wes is enough to send him retreating to the opposite side of the bar, where a group of twentysomething women are already competing for his attention. He goes easily, of course. Wes is a fresh vampire—barely seventy—and still firmly in the phase where physical dalliances are the highlight of existence.

Not that they're without their merits. It's just that after a few centuries, the novelty fades. There are more interesting pursuits than a taste and a tickle.

Was Holly right? Did I go too far?

Frank had been perfectly clear about the terms of our stay in Willow Creek. No feeding on residents unless it was with their consent. That was the line—bright, immovable, and it ran right through Hemoglow. Not open to interpretation.

A rogue elf, however, is not a resident.

After a solid ten minutes of semi-productive rumination, Wes reappears at my elbow, having abandoned his admirers with the casual cruelty of someone who expects them to remain exactly where he left them.

"You're looking grim, boss. Ready to talk yet?"

I take a measured sip of Cabernet Sauvignon. "Holly is under the impression I've done something unforgivable."

"And have you?"

"No," I say, with dignity. "I have been misinterpreted."

Wes leans one hip against the bar. "Ah. Technically correct. The least adored of all the corrects."

"I wasn't aware there were scales."

"There are five." He counts on his fingers. "Actually correct, technically correct, correct but wrong, incorrect, and not even close to correct."

"How can you be correct but wrong?"

"Enjoying the music of the Eagles, for example. You're correct inasmuch as you are the owner of your own taste, but you're incorrect because they're a terrible band and you should feel bad for liking them."

"I'm actually correct, then. The agreement was very clear. No feeding on residents of Willow Creek and elves do not live in Willow Creek."

"Mm."

"Rogue elves, in particular, live at the North Pole. With Santa. This is not controversial information."

Wes watches me for a moment. "So your defense is geography."

"My defense," I say, "is accuracy."

"Right," he says. "And Holly called that what?"

"A technicality," I say, annoyed. "Which is an entirely unfair characterization. It's a distinction. A meaningful one."

"I doubt Holly saw it that way," Wes says. "Remind me of the last time you managed to win a person over with semantic arguments? Has that ever happened?"

"That's not fair," I say finally. It sounded more convincing in my head.

Wes brightens. "I see we've reached the sulking stage."

"I am not sulking." I straighten and adjust my collar.

"You're at a bar, drinking enough alcohol to keep a small

Christmas market operational, complaining about a woman who's angry with you. That is the textbook definition of sulking."

I don't dignify it with a response.

"There are plenty more Hollys out there, you know," he adds.

That earns him a look.

"That's the problem. There aren't, Wes. It's been..." I pause, as if I'm counting the years, when in fact there's no need. "It's been a long time since I met a Holly. Or anyone who comes close."

"Even easier, then."

"How is that easier? She's impossible. She's stubborn, obnoxious, aggressively convinced she's right—and infuriatingly often is."

"You say that like it's a complaint."

I look at him. He doesn't even flinch.

Apparently, we've stopped respecting our elders.

In this coven, rules matter. So do the distinctions that keep them from being unbearable—the kind that mean we have Bloodmas instead of Christmas. Holly may have dismissed them as a technicality, but it was the only thing standing between me and breaking my word...and the only way I had to save her gala from what Santa is doing.

"Don't you have somewhere else to be?" I ask.

"Nope." He winks at me again and I realize how annoying it is. "The way I see it, this is all pretty simple, and you're being a bit ridiculous. One might even say juvenile, if one had a poor sense of self-preservation."

"Oh, do tell. Please unburden your decades of wisdom on me." I put my head in my hands and flutter my eyelashes at him. "Do enlighten me. I'm sure it will be brief."

"Do you like her?"

"It's not that simple."

"It's *exactly* that simple." Wes flashes me that grin again. I'm downgrading his to seven for its annoyance. "And you still haven't answered."

I mumble something into my glass.

"Sorry, that sounded like cowardice."

"I said she's not without her charms," I snap. "Infuriating, yes. Narrow-minded, occasionally. She smells of blood oranges and cinnamon, which is an absurd combination. And she scrunches her nose up when she's thinking. Bites her thumb when she's worried. I haven't decided if that's adorable or irritating."

"Nick." He leans in. "Yes or no?"

I make a face like I've been presented with a moral dilemma involving fire. It has been a long time since I've let this happen. Relationships are unwise at the best of times. Worse when one of you can die.

Holly makes none of this matter.

She gets under my skin. Quietly. Persistently. Like a problem I can't charm or outmaneuver. She's sharp. Unimpressed. The sort of person who expects you to be better and then stands there until you are.

And I was not.

The memory of last night sits badly.

I chose expedience. She saw something else.

I don't like the version of me that makes her look at me like that.

"Yes," I admit.

Wes spreads his hands like he's a magician revealing a card trick. "There it is."

"There is what?"

"The problem. And the solution."

"How is that the solution?"

"Nick," he says, leaning in again, "you like her. That's the whole thing."

"She's mad at me, Wes. She says I broke her trust."

He doesn't answer immediately, picking up a glass and holding it to the light like it might confess under pressure.

"Yeah," he says. "That'll do it."

"But I didn't—"

"No," he cuts in. "She's not angry with you because you're a vampire. She's upset with you because she started believing you weren't going to let her down when it mattered."

A pause.

"And then you did," he adds, not unkindly.

I look back at my drink. It offers no defense.

Wes takes his time polishing a glass, dragging the moment out until the crystal all but hums. I note his insolence while filing this technique away for later use.

"You older guys make everything so complicated. There are two options. You sit here and feel sorry for yourself... or you get up and do something about it."

"It might not work." I dislike how that sounds.

"No," Wes agrees easily. "It might not. But if you stay here, it definitely won't."

I blink.

"Go say sorry. Properly. No loopholes or speeches. Just...mean it." He jerks his chin toward the other end of the bar. "Now, if you'll excuse me, I have an audience that still thinks I'm interesting."

I watch him go, reflecting briefly on how irritating it is when other people are right.

Sitting here isn't helping.

Holly is not the sort of person who waits around for things to fix themselves.

Which leaves me with exactly one option.

I drain my glass and stand.

I'm still assembling something resembling an apology when Ronan bursts through the door hard enough to suggest it has personally offended him. It slams against the wall. A few people gasp. I count backwards from five and briefly wonder what our annual expenditure on door replacements looks like. I make a note to ask Crinkshaw—who, as ever, is following a step behind the chaos.

"Betrayal!" Ronan roars, face flushed and eyes blazing. "Betrayal most foul, Lord!"

He barrels toward me, clutching a piece of paper like it might escape if not properly supervised. It rustles, ominously. I remind myself that my second-in-command is a warrior who once won the Battle of Bognor Hill single-handedly, and not, in fact, an unusually dramatic courier.

"What now, Ronan?" I sigh, my patience for theatrics at an all-time low. "Have they removed *My So-Called Life* from cable?"

"Claire Danes is a triumph," he says, deeply offended. "But no. That's not it. Look at this."

He thrusts the paper into my hand.

It's written in ornate, archaic script, and reads:

Holly,

The heart of the season lies where roots run deep,

Where branches bear secrets and shadows creep.

Find the place where the tree holds truth and lies,

Wrapped in dusty ribbons, beneath cold, watchful layers.

This isn't good. It's the same paper as the note beneath the snow globe—ancient, expensive, and reeking of caramelized mildew and bad decisions.

"What am I looking at?" I ask. "And where did you find it?"

"When Sire slunk out of the house in a mood," Crinkshaw says, carefully, "we thought it prudent to check in on Miss Frost. Ronan was worried. I was not."

"I did not slink."

"No, Sire. My Lord was profoundly dignified in your exit."

I look at Ronan. "The note."

"Pinned to her door," he says, not quite meeting my gaze. "An envelope—wax seal, proper presentation. And a stake left nearby. Not for her, I think. Subtle was not the goal."

A knot tightens in my gut. "Why?"

"To lure her," he says. "The old Christmas decoration factory."

"You're certain?"

Ronan points to the page. "First line. 'Heart of the season.' The place is called Season's Heart Factory. As I said, not subtle."

I close my eyes briefly. "Let me guess, it's on the outskirts of town?"

"On the border between Willow Creek and Sulphur Ridge," Crinkshaw says. "Practically apologizing for existing."

Naturally. A half-forgotten factory straddling Willow Creek and Sulphur Ridge is exactly where you'd go if you wanted to siphon one and poison the other.

I drop the note. "It's a trap."

"Obviously," Ronan says.

"You don't think she went anyway?"

Ronan snorts. "She absolutely went anyway."

I drag a hand through my hair. "She has no idea what she's walking into."

"She has some idea," Crinkshaw says mildly. "She simply won't let it stop her."

Holly Frost is many things.

Currently, sensible is not one of them.

"Crinkshaw, Wes. Head back to the house. Wake everyone. Make sure they're ready. Full battle gear."

Crinkshaw straightens, all trace of dry commentary gone. "Yes, My Lord."

He moves quickly—actually quickly—which is how I know this is bad.

I turn to Ronan. "You're with me."

His hand settles on the knife at his belt. "Understood."

Outside, the wind hits hard—sleet, woodsmoke, and the sort of cold that suggests something unpleasant is about to happen.

Holly had better be safe.

Not one hair on her head should have been moved out of place. Not one wrinkle should have creased her brow, nor one tremble should have escaped those lips of hers. If any of those things have happened, then Santa is going to regret trying to steal Christmas from her.

She needed me, and I was too busy nursing my own pride to give her what she needed. I should have apologized—properly, plainly—but old habits run deep, and I am not a man accustomed to explaining myself, least of all to mortals.

Holly, unfortunately, has made that position untenable.

I am done pretending otherwise. This morning, I was a brooding, love-sick fool. Now, I am something else entirely. I am a force of nature, the darkness unbound, the patience behind the smile, and the eternal sleep that ushers you somewhere you would very much prefer not to go. If she is hurt, I will ensure they arrive there personally.

I reach for my coat, already moving.

And I am bringing a thermos.

Chapter Nineteen

HOLLY

The old Season's Heart Factory looms ahead, all peeling paint and rusted doors, like the remains of a bad Christmas memory. My breath ghosts in the cold as I stand in the snow, the air biting hard enough to sting—but it's the message pinned to my door that settles deeper, colder still. Behind me, Willow Creek is a smear of warm windows and festive lights; here, the only glow is a failing security bulb that blinks like a nervous star.

I rub my gloved hands together, chasing feeling back into my fingers as I try to piece the note together from memory. The words had been twisted into something that sounded like a carol sung in the wrong key, each line gnawing at me in a way that set my teeth on edge.

I curse under my breath. I left too fast and didn't think to take it with me. Now, the words are slipping away, fragments scattering like shattered glass around me.

Find the place where the tree holds truth and lies,

Wrapped in dusty ribbons, beneath cold, watchful layers.

The rusted handles of the factory doors sag, barely clinging to their broken mounts. I don't see any signs of movement inside, but the shadows play tricks on my eyes, stretching as if something shifts beyond the grime-smeared glass windows. The silence is oppressive, a weight pressing against my chest.

Snow soaks through my jeans as I crouch, studying the building's perimeter. The walls are scuffed and battered, streaks of ice running down the metal like frozen tears. There's a small, shattered window that looks inviting enough to be a terrible idea.

This is probably the moment to tell someone where I am. Marcy, at the very least. But she'd probably tell me to call Nick. And then she'd call him herself. So instead of doing the sensible thing, I edge closer and peer inside.

The flickering overhead lights cast a dim and erratic glow across old conveyor belts and dusty boxes. Nothing seems out of place. Nothing seems wrong. Tension pricks at the back of my neck anyway.

The tree isn't in sight.

My breath fogs up as I creep toward the entrance. The factory doors sit slightly ajar, a thin gap letting out gusts of icy air. It hardly breathes as I slip past and I'm oddly proud of myself for that. Surely my mom never had to deal with quietly sneaking into abandoned Christmas decoration warehouses when planning the Royal Wedding.

Or maybe she did. Royals are weird.

There's a stack of warped crates—maybe that's the 'wood' the riddle meant. I pry one open and find a large stash of eggnog. Potent eggnog, if the alcohol content on the label is accurate. Something skitters between the boxes. Probably rats. Possibly sugar rats—like regular rats, but louder and more unionized.

A tangled mess of red and green wires looping ominously around a corner catches my eye, its glint faint under the overhead lights. Near the wires, a bundle of worn-out elf boots is carelessly tossed aside, their cracked soles pointing like grim sentinels. And a sliver of something shiny reflects the dim light—a crooked, glitter-covered star peeking out like a sinister beacon.

Great.

Just great.

Rogue elves are the last thing I need and, annoyingly, the first thing I should have expected.

A nagging thought creeps in: Nick would've handled this better.

He'd have figured this out faster. Cut through the confusion. Seen the connections I didn't. Trusted his gut while I've been second-guessing everything. He makes a plan, sticks to it, and—annoyingly—it somehow always works.

My skills haven't exactly been stellar over the past few days. Especially for someone whose job is literally organizing events. There hasn't been much of a plan this week, at least not where Nick Draven was concerned. I've been charging in headfirst, powered by adrenaline, stubbornness, and a reckless need to prove I can handle everything on my own.

Usually, I can.

But things would've been a lot smoother if Nick were here.

I hate admitting it, but I've grown used to him being around.

His company.

His ridiculous grin.

His infuriatingly reliable presence.

I didn't listen to him when it mattered. Didn't trust his judgment because I let my pride get in the way. And now I regret every sharp word and every moment I pushed him away. I've been so determined to do things my way that I didn't stop to consider that maybe, just maybe, Mister 'Tall, Dark, and Infuriating' Draven knew something I didn't.

I shake my head and force myself to focus.

Ducking behind one of the old machines, I scurry along the conveyor belt, heading deeper into the factory. Rusted machinery looms. Overturned crates clutter the path. The clink of metal from somewhere ahead stops me in my tracks. There are muffled sounds. Footsteps. Voices. Low muttering. I can't make out the words, but the cadence is unmistakable. People.

Where branches bear secrets and shadows creep

Well, that was accurate.

This is not the type of holiday spirit I signed up for.

I peek around another crate of eggnog and see them. Rogue elves. A small army of them, emerging from the shadows like carolers who swapped sheet music for cudgels. Their ragged little elf hats sit askew, their eyes gleaming with a cold, calculating glint that feels all wrong. They're crouched low, moving with the kind of coordinated menace that speaks of long practice and very bad intentions.

I scan the room again and notice a corkboard pinned on the wall. It's cluttered with hand-drawn maps, notes written in manic handwriting, and photos of suspiciously festive things. Someone's used candy-cane pushpins and awarded gold star stickers. Organized villainy is the worst kind. There are even festive-themed stick-on notes, like someone went to the trouble of ordering stationery for their Christmas heist planning.

The board is boldly titled 'Operation Hollow,' and among the chaos, one drawing catches my attention: a crude sketch of a snow globe with a very wonky, glitter-covered tree inside. The very same snow globe that's been sitting in Nick's living room.

I gasp.

The elves freeze, dozens of tiny heads swiveling towards the noise.

One elf stands tall—as tall as an elf minion can—and his smile is a twisted, sharp thing that chills me more than the freezing air. A laugh cuts through the air—high, delighted, wrong. They form a loose circle, slowly closing in, their eyes locked on me like they've been waiting.

For me.

This was a trap, and like an idiot, I walked right into it.

I'm outnumbered by at least five, maybe six, rogue elves.

My hands clench into fists. I've dealt with obstacles before: spilled eggnog disasters, Christmas-themed escape rooms, and one particularly aggressive nativity play crew. But this is a special brand of holiday peril I'm not ready for.

"Fantastic. I'm the headline act at the Holiday Horror Revue," I mutter.

The rogue elves close the circle around me, and one lunges forward with a grim smile. I lunge back, adrenaline and sheer stubbornness giving me a burst of speed. I manage to shove him off-balance—only for another to grab my arm, his grip like iron.

"Hi," I say, breathless. "I'm Holly. Loving the ambush, very ten out of ten on the menace scale. I'll be sure to leave you a good review. Anyhow...I should probably get going. Kisses to Santa, okay?"

My wit fails to have the desired effect. Which is irritating, because it usually works—and I am at least as funny as Nick, if not funnier.

I wrench my arm free, twisting to break out of the tightening circle. They're playing with me and having a wonderful time doing it. The elves come at me again. I knock a few of them back, but the next hit sends me stumbling across the factory floor until I end up underneath the corkboard.

Close enough to see exactly what's on it.

Strings of red and green thread crisscross the board, connecting photos of the Hollow of Mischief to schematics of the oversized snow globe. Under "Timeline," someone wrote TONIGHT and drew a skull wearing a Santa hat. A larger map of Willow Creek is pinned to the center, and the town square is circled in bold red. Other sketches show the snow globe releasing trails of sparkling magic that spread festive cheer. In the midst of it all is the same unmistakable tree, its lopsided branches glowing faintly like it's alive. Lastly, there's a photo of me labeled 'naughty list, pending review,' and one of Nick with a peppermint 'X' like someone got enthusiastic with craft supplies.

I stare at the notes, then back at the snow globe, and the pieces click together with nauseating simplicity. The ridiculous, tacky Christmas ornament isn't just a gaudy decoration. It's the heart of everything.

"Oh, you've got to be kidding me," I mutter, the confusion evaporating into cold, bitter clarity.

I cannot believe I've—we've—been this stupid.

The realization hits hard. I know exactly why I'm here. This isn't about me. It's about Nick. And the snow globe that's in his house.

"We've had the tree the whole time. Well, Merry *freaking* Christmas."

The rogue elves cackle, a sound that's sharp, grating, and about as festive as nails on a chalkboard. Their eyes glint in the dim light, and the stink of eggnog sweat practically radiates off them. They step closer, forming a tight, glitter-coated circle around me. Vile creatures. I've had enough of them for a lifetime, let alone one holiday.

I glance between the rogue elves and the board, and the scribbled details become clearer with every pass. My brain finally catches up, piecing the rest together faster than it has any right to.

"Great," I huff, a sarcastic grin slipping onto my face. "We've been running around in holiday-themed circles, on a Christmas scavenger hunt designed by the world's worst logistics planner, so you could get into Nick's mansion."

The tallest elf, standing a staggering waist-high level, lifts a tattered clipboard with a checklist that's partially ripped and covered in eggnog stains.

"Gold star for figuring it out," an elf says, voice sweet as spearmint. "We thought the reindeer stampede would lure the vampires out, but they were watching reruns of WKRP in Cincinnati."

"Ronan tells me that Loni Anderson is enchanting," I murmur.

"Anyway," he says, consulting a snowflake pocket watch that pings politely. "We needed something a touch more persuasive. And you walked very neatly into our trap."

"What about—"

"Yup," he continues. "Walked right into it. Like a magpie in the tinsel aisle."

"I got it."

"Like the exceptionally persuadable, seasonally distractible human you are—"

"Got it," I bark. "We can skip the play-by-play. Further description of my role is not required."

He gestures at his clipboard. "There's a whole script here. Itemized. If you don't mind?"

On the one hand, I'm extremely irritated that I'm being dunked on by a group of reject munchkins from the *Wizard of Oz*. On the other, I appreciate the importance of following the to-do list.

"Looks like we've got ourselves a holly-jolly intruder," he sneers, and ticks an item off. "Time to wrap up this little holiday hiccup."

The elves close in, their twisted holiday cheer hardening into something meaner. Like a grandma reaching for the last scone at a buffet. My breath quickens, but I dig my nails into my palms and hold my ground.

I've faced worse.

The Hollow of Mischief. Gingerbread dragons. Reindeer stampedes and candy-cane calamities. Sarcastically hot vampires. This is just another mess to fix. Another holiday crinkle I need to smooth out.

And I am an event *planner*, not an event *ender*.

The rogue elves grab at me. I pivot at the last second, narrowly avoiding one elf's glitter-covered claw as the sound of ragged breaths and creaky boots closes in behind me. Another elf leaps at me, and I drop low, rolling out of the way and scrambling back to my feet. I grab one last look at the map—and then I bolt for the far side of the room.

"Get her!" the tall elf screeches, his voice warping into something carol-adjacent and deeply unpleasant.

"That's exactly what we're trying to do, Greg," another snaps, smacking the first elf on the head.

Greg.

Not Bloodthorn. Not Nightbane. Greg.

I am being hunted through an abandoned Christmas factory by a rogue elf who sounds like he files expense reports.

This is my life now.

I run, dodging rusted machinery and leaping over tangled cords like a deranged caribou on a caffeine rush. The elves' footsteps clatter behind me, their taunts rise into a cacophony of jingling bells and something far less festive.

"Run all you want, sugarplum!" Greg hollers. "We've got the naughty list, and you're at the top! Should've left that Christmas snow globe where you found it."

Right.

Santa didn't want us to take the snow globe.

Maybe he expected us to smash it in the gingerbread house and either ruin Christmas or release all its magic in the Hollow of Mischief. But we didn't. It's still in Nick's house. Which means this isn't over. Not even close.

There's still a way to stop Santa from stealing the festive spirit.

Still a way to save Christmas in Willow Creek.

All I have to do is get past these nasty little rogue elves—who now smell like old gym socks soaked in stale eggnog—and get to Nick. Easier said than done, considering they've managed to corner me in the least jolly corner of this grimy factory.

These elves don't just want to ruin Christmas cheer.

I take a deep breath, preparing to tackle the nightmare before Christmas I've found myself caught in. I should have gotten Nick to help me, but now I'm going to have to do this on my own, and the faint chorus of Christmas music skipping tracks that's started playing in the background isn't improving the mood.

"Where are you trying to run to, sugarplum?" Greg sneers. "We stick around longer than leftover fruitcake. You can't shake us."

I pick up an iron bar and give it a few experimental swings, silently praying that a potent mix of stubbornness, holiday sarcasm, and sheer, reckless optimism will be enough to get me through this twisted rerun of Christmas chaos. So I strike a pose, holding the bar at the ready. If I'm going down, then it's going to be with a fight. I'll never give—

Something slams me in the back of the head, and I collapse to the ground. My cheek hits cold concrete that smells faintly of peppermint and dust. My eyesight dims as I lose consciousness, and the last thing I hear is the footsteps of an elf as it approaches.

"String her up."

Bells jingle somewhere, off-key.

Chapter Twenty

NICK

"Drive faster," I tell Ronan, the first time in close to a century I've uttered those words. Outside, the snow skates sideways, and somewhere a string of Christmas lights blinks SOS in red and green.

Holly isn't picking up her phone.

Another call goes straight to voicemail, and something cold and vicious settles under my ribs.

I no longer care about the holiday, or about the stupid Winter Festival, or even Willow Creek. All of that can hang—and if Santa and his rogue elves have harmed so much as a single hair on her head, I will personally redecorate the North Pole with the fat man's remains.

We fishtail into the factory yard. I'm out before the car fully stops, hitting the ground in a roll and coming up running. Behind me, Ronan's yelling something about slowing down and waiting.

Not a chance.

The trunk slams open and he retrieves that absurd battle axe of his, but I don't look back. My mind tries to supply images of a horror movie I have no interest in seeing, so I override them: Holly bundled in one of Crinkshaw's tartan blankets, cocoa in one hand, with two marshmallows because three is chaos, correcting an elf on the difference between spruce and pine while I stand there and glower.

I hit the factory at speed, fury burning clean and bright through everything else. Charming restraint can go to hell. So can patience. So can anything that isn't getting to her.

The doors don't open so much as fail to remain attached when I kick through them, the impact ripping them from their moorings hard enough to echo.

Inside, the place is dim and dust-choked—and Holly's nowhere to be seen.

But her footprints are.

I'm not sure what she was wearing on her feet, but the mess in the dust tells the story. A larger set, surrounded by a chaotic maelstrom of smaller, elf-sized prints. They surrounded her. Toyed with her. Took her to the back.

She was here.

And now she's not.

I follow.

The shadows shift before I've taken more than a few steps. Dozens of glittering eyes wink into existence, followed by tinkling laughter that scrapes along my nerves. The scent of burnt cinnamon burns my nostrils as rogue elves begin to emerge—from behind crates, beneath broken machinery, and from spaces that should not reasonably contain that many bodies.

They reek of boozy eggnog and pine cleaner—correction: spruce. Even now, accuracy matters.

I crouch, ready for anything. Ronan is still outside. For the moment, it's just me.

One rogue elf steps forward, his sneer stretched too wide, while others fan out across the factory floor. There are at least two dozen. Possibly more. The brave one clasps his hands behind his back. Like he's about to deliver a festive speech.

"Draven," he says. "Finally."

"It's...you," I respond.

"Greg," he corrects, presumably expecting applause. "Your worst nightmare."

I blink.

"I'm sorry, but have we met? I didn't even know any of you had names," I say. "And my worst nightmare involves diving into a swimming pool and emerging in the middle of the ocean. It happened once. Amphitrite was annoyed with me for dating her sister. In fairness, she has fifty. Took me three days to reach shore. This—" I gesture at him, "—is not even in my top ten worst dreams."

"I'm the head elf," he says, puffing up slightly. "Jingle's replacement. You'll be dealing with me now." He flexes what could generously be described as muscles. "Twinkle, twinkle, precious vamp. Do you miss your little tramp?"

"Points for rhyme. Minus points for taste."

"It's time we end this, Draven."

"You've rehearsed that, haven't you?"

I punch Greg, and he bursts apart in a spray of tinsel and bell chimes.

The metallic jangle rings up my arm as if I've struck a particularly festive gong. For a fleeting moment, I find myself wondering whether he was in the middle of "Ding Dong Merrily on High" when he went, which feels like the sort of detail that ought to matter.

The rest hiss and scatter, and I raise a single finger, shushing them all with the authority of a man who has decided he is done with being inconvenienced. They stare back, all glitter and malice, which feels unnecessarily mean-spirited.

"I think we've rather decisively moved past the Marquess-of-Queensberry-but-with-tinsel rules, chaps."

My hands drop to my sides and my fingers clench into fists. Something cold and impatient settles beneath my skin. My knuckles crack, deliberately.

"Let's begin."

I don't wait for agreement.

The first elf goes down under a backhand that sends a shock clean through my shoulder, the second skids across the factory floor with a screech of boots and metal as my kick connects, and a third meets my forehead with a crack that feels deeply satisfying before disappearing into a crate that erupts in a storm of glittering sequins. They scatter everywhere—angels and reindeer and robins flashing in the dim light, sticking to my coat and catching in my hair as I move.

The air fills with it—tinny, sweet, and wrong, all stale eggnog and burnt sugar—and I lean into the fight, faster now, harder, the edges of restraint peeling away with each strike.

They swarm.

One lands on my back, claws dragging hot across my neck. I wrench him off and fling him aside, only for another to latch onto my calf with an enthusiasm I do not appreciate. I kick him loose, but there are too many of them, too many hands and teeth and sharp little laughs, and they pile in with cheerful violence until I'm driven down beneath the weight of them.

I hit the floor hard, and lash out at anything that comes within reach—catching fabric, bone, something that squeaks indignantly—but it's not enough. Their numbers close over me, pressing in, and for a brief, unwelcome moment, I realize I may have made a catastrophic miscalculation.

"BATTLE!!!!!"

The cry reverberates through the hollow factory, and I keep one rogue elf in a headlock and another at arm's length. Yet another elf nibbles on my ankle, and I give him a very firm and deliberate kick in the head.

Ronan stands framed in the doorway, axe slung across his back, his face painted in red Christmas stripes as though he's declared war on the concept of subtlety. Somewhere between the car and here, he has found both time and conviction, and the result is a man who looks like a Viking has been aggressively sponsored by a candy cane.

The elves hesitate, and their twisted holiday glee gutters into something that looks suspiciously like unease. Their eyes dart between each other and Ronan, silently debating who's going to be the sacrificial first strike. The bravest—or most foolish—takes a tentative step forward. Stops. Reconsiders. Then freezes.

"Go ahead," Ronan growls, his voice like gravel and festive violence. "Make my Bloodmas."

The elves exchange another glance.

Ronan grins. "Merry. Freaking. Bloodmas."

He starts throwing knives.

They come from everywhere—jacket, boot, belt, kilt, and at least one location I refuse to think about—each one thwapping through the air with brutal precision. Every throw lands. Every impact bursts into tinsel and bells.

I may have underestimated when I guessed he carried a dozen knives. Now it seems likely he contains a small, well-organized arsenal. I'm briefly concerned about the physics of all of this, and left wondering how he manages to avoid clinking when he walks.

For a man his size, he moves with alarming grace, cutting through the elves in a deadly, spinning rhythm. One of them jerks in my grip as a blade punches clean through its chest and it bursts apart, showering me in glitter. The air fills with it—bright, violent, absurdly festive.

This is less *The Fairytale of New York* and more *Deck the Halls* with casualties.

I take the opening and press the attack, driving into the nearest cluster with renewed enthusiasm. We make a respectable dent, but it doesn't hold. For every elf that bursts, more spill forward to take its place, giggling, slavering, slick with eggnog and bad intent.

I hate elves.

Especially rogue ones.

Ronan's knives finally run dry. He reaches back and hauls the axe free, the blade catching what little light there is as his grin sharpens to match it. The shaft alone is the length of a small argument, and he swings with full commitment.

The axe whistles through the air in a wide, magnificent arc.

Every elf steps neatly aside.

It is, objectively, an excellent swing. Just not especially useful—like a ceremonial parade float with ambitions—and the follow-through takes him off balance, taking him down in a clatter as the axe skids away across the floor.

He looks up at me, sheepish. "I genuinely thought that would work."

The elves surge again, this time with purpose, and the fight turns ugly. Small, sharp wounds accumulate—cuts, slices, the irritating persistence of things that refuse to die properly—and soon my shirt is in tatters. Ronan is faring little better.

We're driven back until we're standing back-to-back, breath coming harder now, weight shared whether we like it or not.

"Is this seriously what kills us?" he asks, incredulous. "Elves? Rogue elves?"

"A soothsayer in the thirteenth century predicted something along these lines. I assumed she was drunk. Or knitting."

We raise our fists as the elves regroup and close in again. We've done damage—considerable, festive damage—but it makes no difference.

There are too many of them.

The circle tightens, and I brace for the next rush, already calculating how long we can hold before something important starts detaching.

Holly should not be part of that calculation.

I was meant to keep her out of this. Keep her somewhere sensible, preferably far away from weaponized sparkles and homicidal holiday décor—and instead I've managed to lose her in the middle of it while I get myself thoroughly, and somewhat humiliatingly, overrun.

Ronan and I share a look as the next wave gathers itself. We're both breathing hard, clothes in ribbons, bleeding from what feels like a thousand paper-cut assassins.

"I always hoped I'd go out in a blaze of glory," Ronan says. "Slightly more tinsel than anticipated, but I'll take it—"

The front wall of the factory explodes.

What was once a structural wall is abruptly replaced by a truck, a great deal of noise, and the sort of impact that removes one's feet without consultation. Ronan and I hit the floor in tandem as elves scatter in all directions, the air filling with dust, splinters, and the consequences of poor planning.

I push myself up through the debris, coughing, waving a hand through the haze. "I would like," I say, to no one in particular, "one problem at a time."

The dust settles enough for me to make out what is coming.

The coven.

The truck idles where the wall used to be, and Crinkshaw steps down from the driver's seat wearing an expression so profoundly unimpressed it may, in fact, be celebration. Behind him, the rest of my brethren pour through the gap like a particularly well-dressed disaster.

Wes first, baseball bat over his shoulder and grinning like this is exactly the sort of evening he'd hoped for.

Damian, one of the first to join us, wields a mace laden with spikes.

Ranu, a dark-haired former priestess, moves beside him, her staff angles just so, the blade at its end already promising unpleasant outcomes.

And more behind them—my coven, my thoroughly unreasonable, deeply competent coven—fanning out across the factory floor with the sort of calm that suggests this is not their first festive ambush.

Something in my chest loosens. Just a fraction.

Even Crinkshaw joins the line, straightening his cuffs as if preparing for a particularly aggressive dinner engagement.

They advance as one.

Armed.

Decided.

The rogue elves groan, which I take to be a positive development.

"I don't have a clever line," Crinkshaw says, surveying the scene with mild distaste. "Ghouls do not, as a rule, do quips. However," he adds, adjusting his sleeves, "I am prepared to make an exception."

He cracks his knuckles.

"I guess you must have...a crink in your neck."

A rogue elf coughs into the silence.

The fight resumes.

The coven fans out and tears through the first row of elves, and in seconds the factory turns into a blizzard of glitter, streamers, and chiming bells thick enough to choke on.

With renewed force, Ronan and I battle to the back. Toward Holly. It's slow going, and if we were mortals, we'd already be dead. Still, we make the door.

"Go," he gasps, punctuating it with savage chops that send an elf spinning. "I'll hold them back."

"The coven..." An elf's fist connects mid-sentence.

"I'll keep them safe, Sire." He catches my forearm and hauls me in, grip iron tight. "Save her."

I clap his shoulder once.

"I want it noted," he adds, voice hoarse, "that I kicked an elf fourteen feet."

A laugh tears out of me. "You win, friend."

Then I'm through the door.

The corridor beyond is dim and close, all steam and dripping pipes, and the noise of battle falls away as I push forward. A thin strip of light outlines a doorway in front of me, and I race toward it.

A steel door waits at the end. Locked.

I hit it once. Twice.

The hinges scream on the third strike. On the fourth, the entire thing gives way and goes flying through the air.

I step through—and stop.

Holly is suspended from the ceiling, bound to a chair that swings over a vat of bubbling, brown liquid. Below her, elves caper and skitter in looping circles, their celebration turning the scene into something grotesque. The place stinks of burnt sugar.

"Is that caramel?"

God help me. It *is* caramel.

They are going to turn her into a Christmas candy apple.

"NICK! WATCH OUT!"

I don't look to see why. I move.

A blade carves through the space I just vacated, close enough that air rushes past me as I hit the ground and roll.

When I come up, a giant, grinning snowman is beaming at me.

Not the friendly, lopsided kind—this snowman looks like he has strong opinions about upper body training. He smirks at me, red hat tipped at a menacing rather than cheerful angle, and there's a red and green sash tied at his waist like he's about to host something both Christmassy and violent.

I stare at it for a beat.

"Is that...*an aggressively competitive snowman*? You're joking."

Holly screams as the snowman charges, hauling a grotesquely oversized claymore that gleams in the low light. I throw myself sideways just in time as the blade slams into the concrete where I stood with a crack that sends shards skittering across the floor.

"Why does he have a six-pack?" I demand, scrambling up. "What's next? The Yule Goat with a machete? Snowarzenegger?"

The snowman declines to engage in dialogue. Apparently, he's not big on conversation, nor does he embody the gentle, polite charm one might expect from a monster made of marshmallow.

Pity.

He's also the only thing between me and Holly.

The claymore comes again. I duck inside the swing this time, close enough to feel the rush of it over my shoulder and drive my fist into his ribs. Then I hit it harder again.

It's like punching a cathedral.

Absolutely not.

The marshmallow monster will not win.

I am a Lord of Darkness, and I have a reputation to uphold.

Holly is watching.

That matters. Perhaps exactly as much as I'd like.

I break away, landing lightly and glancing over my shoulder. The elves have formed a loose ring, perfectly content to spectate. One of them has found popcorn. He's eating it with enthusiasm.

"Holly," I call, circling outside the range of the claymore. "Are you all right?"

"What do you think?" she shouts back. "They're going to candy-apple me!"

"Don't worry. I'll be there in a minute."

The snowman presses forward, relentless, the claymore carving wide, brutal arcs through the air. I duck, pivot, slip inside his reach when I can, striking where I find openings—but it makes no difference.

Every hit lands like I'm arguing with stone.

And stone, as it turns out, is not easily persuaded.

Holly screams as the elves lower her closer to the boiling vat of caramel, and that—more than anything—focuses my mind. The caramel's at a proper rolling boil. Ideal for confectionery. Less so for the woman I'm profoundly attached to.

The claymore whistles past my shoulder close enough to take a suggestion of skin with it, and I pivot away, angling toward the vat. The elves scatter readily, unwilling to interfere with whatever this has become. Sensible of them.

I run up the metal stairs, two at a time. The platform rattles underfoot. Behind me, the snowman follows, his sword still carving great, lethal arcs through the air.

Just a few more steps.

A few more seconds and this giant marshmallow puff will be where I need him to be.

He raises the sword with both hands, committing to the strike.

"Alright, Snowzilla," I say, buying half a heartbeat and coming up empty on anything wittier. "Time for you to be tragically *hurt*."

I'm a blur of motion—past him, behind him—and then both my feet drive hard into his back.

For a second, nothing happens.

Then he pitches forward, straight into the vat.

Caramel erupts around him, bubbling furiously as it swallows him whole. There's no sound worth noting. Just a brief, undignified struggle before the sugar does what sugar does best and takes him apart, marshmallow first, like a snowball melting in a hot chocolate.

"Couldn't handle the heat," I say, deciding some things deserve to be said.

A small scream cuts the moment short.

"Holly—"

"Get me down!" she yells.

She kicks her legs, sending the chair swinging hard enough that it twists to face me. For a second she's all motion—rope creaking, breath catching—and then she stills, eyes locking onto mine.

Relief hits first. It breaks across her face so fast it almost looks like laughter.

Then it fractures.

Her hands are bound, her shoulders straining against the ropes, and her breath comes too shallow. There's fear there—real, immediate, and not going anywhere—but it's tangled up with something fierce and almost disbelieving, like she wasn't entirely certain I would come and is now forced to revise her opinion on the spot.

It is, I realize bewilderingly, a devastating combination.

And entirely my undoing.

The woman dangling over a vat of molten sugar looks at me like I might actually pull this off, and that—more than anything—is a responsibility I am suddenly, acutely aware I cannot afford to fail.

Behind me, the elves break. Their confidence presumably evaporates as they scatter in all directions. Garlands drop in their wake—

spruce, not pine, accuracy persists even in retreat—and the rest of my coven pours into the room, efficient and decisive.

It doesn't take long.

It never does, when they're like this.

It's over. We won.

I bend slightly at the waist, more from the sudden drop in momentum than anything resembling exhaustion, while someone—Ronan, I think—takes charge of the ropes and starts lowering Holly down. What remains of my shirt is hanging on by optimism alone, so I finish the job and discard it. Tinsel clings everywhere. Shallow cuts mark the rest, already closing, already fading.

A quick glance confirms everyone's accounted for. Glitter drifts lazily through the air like slow snow, and somewhere a bell jingles itself out of tune.

Holly hits the ground, and Ronan makes short work of the ropes. She doesn't hesitate—racing until she's in front of me. Close enough that I can see the flush still high in her cheeks. Close enough to catch the way her gaze flicks—briefly, and not entirely unintentionally—over the state of me.

I don't lean in.

I want to. God, I want to.

But I have no idea if I'm allowed.

"Are you okay?" I ask, because it seems like the safest possible ground.

She nods, once. Her eyes are still wide, still bright, still carrying too much of everything at once.

Holly opens her mouth—whatever she's about say, no longer matters.

She's here. Alive, breathing, and standing in front of me. For now, that's enough to make my doubts feel distant. Somewhere nearby, a carol stumbles through a verse and finds the chorus. With her, I do too.

Chapter Twenty-One

HOLLY

I open my mouth to say something—anything—but the words catch in my throat. There's too much to say and no time to say it. Apologies, anger, and relief churn inside me, tangled and chaotic. Unhelpfully, he is very shirtless, and tinsel confetti dusts his shoulders like glitter someone forgot to sweep. He looks unfairly good for a man who just survived chaos.

None of it matters right now.

All I want is to feel Nick, solid and real, and remind myself that we both made it through this in one piece. Before I can talk myself out of it, I throw my arms around him, burying my face against his chest. His skin is warm, and the smell of wood smoke and something distinctly Nick settles the panic thrumming in my chest. He stiffens for a fraction of a second, then his arms close around me, strong and sure.

"You're okay," he murmurs, his voice rough, like he's convincing himself as much as me.

I nod against him, my throat too tight to speak. I don't care if he's shirtless, battered, and probably freezing. I don't care if I'm still mad at him, or at least I *was*. Annoyance can wait until later, preferably when he is wearing a sweater.

We stand like that for a moment, the chaos of the factory fading into the background. The muffled sound of Ronan's grumbling and Crinkshaw's bony footsteps feels miles away. The vat of caramel bubbles happily, and I try not to picture that snowman mascot melting into it in some horrifyingly sticky cautionary tale. I've acquired a new seasonal slogan: *avoid a rolling boil—buy local, ethically stirred candy canes.*

Finally, I pull back just enough to look up at him.

"We need to go," I say softly, my voice steadier than I expect. "The snow globe—it's the actual festival tree. The real one."

His brows knit together, confusion flashing across his face. "The tacky bauble in my living room?"

"This whole thing was a diversion. Santa didn't expect us to take it from the Hollow of Mischief. He needed you and the coven distracted so he could break in and steal it back. Once he has it, he can continue siphoning its built-up gloom and piping it straight into Sulphur Ridge."

Nick's arms tighten around me. He exhales sharply. "A small army of rogue elves powered by enough negative energy to start a war and turn his Crapmas idea into a reality."

My stomach twists. "Tell me your house is protected?"

"From thieves and routine burglary? Sure. From an immortal wind sprite with a grudge? Probably not. He'll have gone down the chimney already," he says, his tone bitter. "That's what he does, right? He plays by his own rules. Who needs locks or alarms when you've got the ultimate Santa trick. I bet he's ruined my carpets with his sooty footprints too."

Ronan roars something unintelligible, slinging his oversized axe across his back like it's a bag of holiday shopping. Crinkshaw picks his way through the remnants of rogue elf weaponry and melted candy canes with an efficiency that's both horrifying and impressive. The rest of Nick's coven trails behind, looking various degrees of unimpressed with the entire situation, as though battling rogue elves was a mild inconvenience compared to running out of mulled wine at the Winter Ball.

Nick turns to Ronan, his voice sharp. "Get the car. Now."

Ronan stomps toward the exit with heavy, deliberate steps. "Why is it always me? I yearn for glory. Crave blood spilling forth in rivers of my own creation. What I get is being the vampire who drives a reasonably priced car. It does zero to sixty in eventually."

Crinkshaw follows, muttering about the structural integrity of chimneys and how Santa's methods lack elegance and leave a mess to clear up. And all the while, Nick refuses to let go of my hand as we head to the door.

I yank out my phone and fire a message to the Willow Creek Volunteers group chat: 'Emergency meet at the square—thermoses, salt, spare lights, first-aid, and the choir. Dress warm.'

Three dots appear at once. *On my way*, from Marcy. *Salt-spreading truck warming up*, from Mr. Patel. *Carolers assembling*, from Meribel, who adds six bell emojis and a triangle. What does a triangle emoji even mean?

"This isn't over," Nick says quietly.

"Not even close," I reply, my steps quickening to match his.

As we step out into the cold night air, the weight of what's ahead hangs over me. Santa has the snow globe, and if we don't stop him, Christmas in Willow Creek, and probably everywhere, will be lost.

I should never have come here alone.

Now it might be too late to fix this, even with Nick's help.

Santa might be about to ruin Christmas and turn it into Crapmas—and it's all because of me.

"This isn't your fault," Nick says, almost like he can read my thoughts. "I should have dealt with Santa the last time we had a run-in. I didn't, and he's had centuries to plan his revenge. Bet he's been waiting for the opportunity."

"But I made it easy for him," I mumble.

"No," he replies. "We wouldn't be here without you. You're

determined to save Christmas for Willow Creek. We'd have solved this already if I hadn't been so arrogant."

The icy night air bites at my cheeks as we walk through the parking lot, where Ronan stands, axe in hand. He glares at the stack of crates sitting next to the old present-wrapping factory. The boozy eggnog sits in crates with labels promising guaranteed holiday cheer, and Ronan eyes them as if they're technically legal but morally indefensible.

"Ronan," Nick warns, his tone laced with exasperation.

"We don't have time for this," I add.

"Oh, we have time." Ronan hefts the axe with a flourish, his grin a terrifying mix of glee and menace. "This stuff isn't innocent holiday cheer. It's how Santa controls the rogue elves."

Nick and I exchange glances. "And?"

"And...I figured it out."

Ronan beams like he's discovered plutonium, and it's sweet, even if the reveal—boozy eggnog—has been on our radar for days. Thankfully, Nick steps in.

"That you did. What would we do without Ronan?"

He claps him on the shoulder, and Ronan practically glows. There's no tease in Nick's voice, none of the sly edge I've come to expect—just warmth. He's giving Ronan the win because Ronan wants the win. He cares for his coven in a way that's plain and protective, and yet again, I find myself reevaluating my opinion of the deeply complicated vampire who is Nick Draven. And to my surprise, a small, prickly pang of jealousy blooms. I want to feel that.

Nick points at the crates. "You'd better destroy them, old friend. Then we'll go."

"With pleasure."

Ronan swings the axe down with the force of a holiday berserker, splintering the first crate into a rain of wood shards and sloshing eggnog. The sickly-sweet smell of alcohol fills the air, so potent it makes my eyes water.

"Say goodbye to Santa's secret sauce!" he bellows, decimating the stack of crates. Eggnog spills across the icy pavement in a sticky, boozy flood.

Crinkshaw steps back with a grimace, his skeletal frame leaning away from the mess. "Well, that's going to freeze solid. Congratulations, you've made the parking lot undrivable."

"And uninhabitable," I mutter, wrinkling my nose.

Ronan pauses, surveying the carnage. "There. Problem solved. Now they're just regular rogue elves, not liquored-up, supercharged rogue elves."

Nick surveys the wreckage. "Well done. And now it's time to get going."

Nick's coven begins filing into the truck. The vampires, each looking various degrees of irritated, jostle for space among the scattered crates and some broken Christmas decorations. A few of them exchange muttered complaints about the sticky smell clinging to the air from Ronan's blitz on the rogue elves' supply.

Crinkshaw bustles up to Nick, carrying what looks like a perfectly pressed shirt that is, somehow, untouched by the chaos of the night.

"Sire," he says with an air of theatrical disapproval, "if you're going to confront a rogue Santa Claus, might I suggest you do so with a modicum of dignity?"

Nick raises an eyebrow as the zombie hands him the shirt. "You think Santa cares about my wardrobe?"

"Perhaps not. I, however, do. Deeply." Crinkshaw gestures to the rapidly healing cuts on Nick's still naked chest. "You look like you've been mauled by a reindeer. I have standards to uphold."

Nick snorts but shrugs into the shirt, buttoning it efficiently. "Happy now?"

"Delighted," Crinkshaw sighs. I'm unsure he's aware he's the definition of deadpan. "Sire is now suitably dressed to save Christmas."

With everyone loaded up, the convoy rumbles onto the snow-covered road. Up front, Ronan is already muttering about babysitting immortals and dealing with eggnog-related disasters.

"I am not trained for this," he snaps at no one in particular. "There are no manuals. There should be manuals."

"You'd ignore them," I say automatically.

"I would improve them," he shoots back.

Nick doesn't join in. He's got his phone pressed to his ear, voice low, trying to get a read on what's happening at the mansion. I watch his expression instead—jaw tight, shoulders locked, the kind of stillness that means whatever he's hearing isn't good.

The call ends.

"Well?" I ask.

"Not good," he says, which is not helpful and also exactly what I expected.

The car settles into a tense quiet, broken only by the hum of the engine and the steady sweep of the wipers. My hands knot together in my lap before I force them still.

"The snow globe," I say, aware I can't not say it. "He's got the tree."

Nick glances at me.

"The glitter, the star, the whole...aggressively terrible aesthetic," I go on. "It's all in there. Mímir told us—just...badly."

Nick exhales through his nose. "He does enjoy a riddle."

"'Where glitter gathers, snow flurries,'" I mutter. "Which apparently translates to 'it's in the snow globe, you absolute idiots.' I swear, if this whole god thing falls through, he could have a thriving career writing flat-pack furniture instructions."

Ronan snorts from the front. "That explains a great many things."

The lights of Willow Creek begin to bleed into view—soft, familiar, stubbornly cheerful. Porch lights blink along Maple and Third. Mr. Patel's truck idles at the curb, salt spreader already whining to life. Outside the library, carolers huddle under an awning, voices carrying faintly through the glass. The chocolatier's window fogs like a kettle while fairy lights blink Morse code along Main Street.

For a moment, it almost feels normal.

Then the red light hits.

It pulses out from the direction of the square, slow and wrong, washing over the town in a crimson glow that drains the warmth from everything it touches. The lights don't look festive anymore. They look...consumed.

Nick leans forward. "Faster."

"Did you just say—"

"FASTER."

"I am already driving on ice," Ronan says. "We will arrive in one piece or several festive ones."

My chest tightens.

"We're not too late," I say, mostly to convince myself.

No one answers.

"Santa's already here," Ronan says, breaking the silence before it can settle.

"Yes," Nick says, his voice edged with something akin to violence. "I've confirmed it. He had the snow globe before we even left the factory. The mansion's already been hit."

The thought makes my stomach churn.

The snow globe—the tree, the heart of our gala, the thing holding Willow Creek together—is already in his hands.

Great.

No pressure.

"How are we going to do this?" Ronan asks.

"We're Willow Creek," I say, almost like I'm trying to convince myself, "and Willow Creek doesn't fold. I've seen that much. Whether we're recovering from a disastrous Halloween with an authentic haunted house, or that time an errant fog machine disrupted weather patterns on the entire eastern seaboard, magic destruction is as common here as chocolate cake experiments. We show up. Put our boots on, roll up our sleeves, and get our opinions ready. We fix things. Loudly if necessary."

I finish my quite fantastic speech by holding up my finger.

"And we're not done yet."

Nick's silver eyes hold me. "You never give up, do you?"

"Nope."

The town sharpens through the snowfall as we approach, lights blinking stubbornly against the dark—but the red glow underneath it all is wrong. It pulses, slow and heavy, stretching shadows too far across the streets.

By the time we reach the square, the air itself feels off.

Ronan brakes. Hard.

We pile out.

Santa stands at the center, the snow globe raised beside him on a platform. Inside, the glitter churns violently, the crooked tree glowing like it's under strain. Around him, rogue elves scramble, stringing lights that pulse instead of shine, their glow casting everything in something that isn't festive anymore.

My stomach turns.

And the crowd—

They stand in a loose ring, swaying gently, eyes unfocused, like they're nutcrackers that have been set down and forgotten. Not cheering. Not singing.

Just...waiting.

"Oh no," I breathe. "Why do they look like carolers who've forgotten the words and are hoping someone else remembers the next verse?"

Nick leans forward, gazed fixed. "He's twisted it. The tree isn't skimming off the gloom anymore—it's taking everything. The good, the bad...even the bit that knows the difference between spruce and pine. He's hollowing them out."

"Why do this?" I ask. "Why go through all of this?"

"It's obvious," Crinkshaw says. "The elves got a bit too fired up on boozy eggnog. After they stole the tree, Santa took it to the

Hollow of Mischief until he could figure out a way to get at the magic. Frank must have placed some wards on it and the transition would have altered the tree, reducing it to a snow globe. It's Elementary Metaphysics, not Eldritch Geography."

I join the others in staring at Crinkshaw, mouth open.

"We stole it before he could change it back," he continues, "and now that he's got it, he's using the town's energy to give him enough power to alter it. Simple, really."

"That's obvious to you?" Nick asks.

"That's more complicated than calculus," Ronan says.

A pang of guilt hits me. Hard.

"This is my fault. If I'd realized sooner—"

"No," Nick cuts in, sharply. "Santa's had this in motion for a long time. We've been at it for—what—twenty minutes? And we've done it with a group chat, two thermoses, and Ronan's flair for dramatics."

From behind, Ronan yells, "It is not flair. It is commitment."

"How do we stop him?" I ask.

Nick doesn't hesitate. "We take back the tree. Then we make sure he never tries this again. Are you ready, Frost?"

I meet his gaze.

The doubt is still there, loud and persistent.

But so is everything else.

"Born ready, Draven," I say. "Let's go ruin Santa's Christmas uncheer."

Chapter Twenty-Two

NICK

We step away from the cars, ready for anything.

Santa doesn't notice us.

The air shifts—not dramatically. Nothing so considerate. Just wrong enough that the back of my neck prickles. The red glow deepens, the light flickers, and something in the center of the square…unravels.

His veneer has gone. No more jolly, cherubic man in the red suit, but him as he really is. A wind sprite. He isn't even solid.

He's there, but not quite present. A smear across the air, like a painting rubbed while the paint was still wet. His face pushes through the middle of it, wrong and shifting, familiar only in the way a nightmare sometimes borrows a face you recognize. The beard remains, but it's no longer hair—it fractures into crystals of frost that catch the light and splinter it. The red suit clings to the shape of him in pieces, darker now, like the color's gone off.

He looks like a snowflake that's turned on you. Not the charming kind you embroider on a tea towel. The other sort.

"Oh," I say, because that's apparently all I've got. "That's… different."

The townsfolk sway in loose, vacant unison around him, eyes glassy, expressions smoothed down to nothing. Whatever's coming off him—whatever he's pulling through that grotesque snow globe at the center—isn't harmless. The air is thick with it, a cloudy, creeping miasma that curls through the square and sinks into everything it touches.

I've dealt with terrible things.

A basilisk in Bruges who knitted.

This is worse.

A low hum vibrates from the snow globe, a sound that pulses through the air and settles in your chest. It's pulling in all the energy, the corrupted glow deepening with every second.

Vampires don't really need sleep—not properly—but something in me is dragging anyway. Not physical. Not quite. Just the slow, grinding exhaustion of someone who's been at this too long and would like five uninterrupted minutes of peace.

I suspect this is what it's like to be a woman with an opinion on the internet.

I shove the thought aside before it can become a personality.

We're far enough away that he still hasn't noticed us, the corrupted snow globe holding his full attention. The red glow pulses, thick and insistent, while rogue elves scurry at his command, and the hum of dark magic rises steadily beneath it all. The air tastes like frost and old pennies; the spruce garlands hang limp under the red throb of the globe.

Before I can say anything, Holly produces a clipboard like a magician pulling a rabbit from a hat and brandishes it with alarming authority.

I have no idea where she got it.

At this point, I'm forced to assume she simply generates them as needed.

She squares her shoulders and takes command of the night—brisk, bright, entirely unflappable—the sort of person who can turn chaos into a checklist and make you grateful for the opportunity to comply. The clipboard even catches the light as she gestures with it, like a general who prefers stationery to swords.

Even now, Holly Frost is completely in her element.

And I—

No.

We'll come back to that.

"Ronan," she says, "take half the coven and circle round behind Santa. Quietly. No yelling about battle or glory. Tiptoe. Can you do that?"

"Aye!" Ronan roars.

Holly smacks him on the arm.

The warrior who has inspired poetry about violence looks faintly chastened.

"Quiet," she says.

"Aye," Ronan whispers, then leans in with great solemnity. "It will be my honor to show these elves that Ronan doesn't just fight. He creates legends. Blood, tinsel, and sheer unhinged grit will etch our tale into the annals of battle, and they shall sing our names—"

Holly ticks a box on her checklist labeled 'Ronan: pointlessly dramatic monologue' and moves on.

"Wes, take the rest. Shadow us. Peel two off to the choir—get them humming something steady, just not "Carol of the Bells," we don't need panic. Keep some vampires by the bakery: cocoa, blankets, first-aid, spare mittens. Nick and I go first and figure out how to wake the townspeople. If it goes wrong, plan B is loud carols and louder thermoses."

"You okay with this, boss?" Wes arches an eyebrow at me, lounging against the car like we're about to run errands and not confront a deranged Santa with apocalyptic tendencies.

Holly flushes. It suits her.

"Oh my god. Nick. I'm sorry. I didn't mean to—"

"All good," I say. "Do what she says, Wes. She's the event planner."

Wes flicks me a salute. "Aye, boss." Then to Holly, with sudden gravity, "Ma'am."

Holly flashes me a tight grin, and it's like the sun breaking over a gray morning. Bright, quick, gone again before I can decide what to do with it.

I should have kissed her in the factory.

It occurs to me now, with the clarity of someone who has made an excellent decision approximately ten minutes too late, that there was a moment—right there, between the homicidal elves and the questionable caramel—when it might have worked.

Now we're here, and she's looking at me like that—like I'm worth trusting—and I have absolutely no idea if I've earned it or how quickly I might lose it again.

Inconveniently, I would like very much not to.

She turns away before I can do anything foolish. Or more foolish.

"Damian—take a small strike team, thin the elves on the flanks. Ranu—set up recovery: Nanaimo bars, cocoa, seats by the diner heaters. Borrow extension cords if you have to. Three on the roofs—there, there, and there—if it jingles and isn't festive, sing out."

And there it is again. That stubborn miracle of Willow Creek. A town that brings casseroles and extension cords when the world misbehaves. A place full of stubborn, ordinary people who keep showing up, again and again, and who somehow expect that to be enough.

Absurdly, it usually is.

The coven moves. No hesitation. No debate.

Just...movement.

I watch her for a second, the way she stands there with that clipboard like it's a weapon of mass organization, turning chaos into something almost reasonable.

She is, infuriatingly, very good at this.

And I—equally infuriatingly—am a little in awe of her.

I give the barest nod as the others pass, which is all the permission they need. We're doing this her way.

Assuming we survive, I suspect they'll be doing it her way rather often.

"Our priority is waking up the townsfolk," Holly says, already moving onto the next crisis. "We can't do anything while Santa's got them magically captured. We use carols, cocoa, and contact. Warm hands, warm voices, familiar faces. We start bringing them back and get them to help us rouse the others."

My brethren spread out, serious in their tasks. In short order, we're divided and slipping through the streets toward the town center.

On impulse, I take Holly's hand.

Her fingers are cold from the night, faintly dusted with sugar and glitter—evidence of her recent proximity to festive sabotage—and they fit into mine with a kind of alarming precision.

She startles, glancing at me, and for a moment I think I've overstepped.

Then she doesn't let go.

That steadies me more than it has any right to.

When I moved the coven to Willow Creek, it was meant to be another distraction. Something to occupy immortals who've already fought most of their wars—including the one that got us banned from Christmas in the first place.

In hindsight, defeating Santa and expecting him to take it well was optimistic.

Now there's a town being slowly hollowed out by a corrupted ornament, a centuries-old grudge unfolding in real time, and a woman beside me who has decided—clipboard in hand—that this is a logistical issue we can solve if everyone would just cooperate.

Against all available evidence, I find that reassuring.

It has been a very long time since I've had a reason to involve myself in anything quite this enthusiastically. Longer still since I cared whether I got it right. But I'm walking next to the woman who is Holly Frost, marching toward a supernatural disaster like it's a poorly managed gala with inadequate staffing and a theme that's gotten out of hand.

I tighten my grip on her hand, a fraction.

We creep forward until we reach the first line of townsfolk. I lean in, close enough that her ridiculous blood-orange-and-cinnamon scent threatens to derail my concentration entirely.

"The last time I fought Santa, it was just the two of us," I murmur. "He didn't have this kind of reach. He's drawing on the globe—look. You can see the pull. We'll need to be careful. He's not just a man in a suit. He's an elemental, and he's very good at holding a grudge."

"How did you beat him last time?"

"I tricked him." I shrug. "It was close, though. He had me beat, but elementals are notoriously fickle and rely on others for their power. If we make him sip from a source that isn't fuel—something thin, dissonant, disruptive—it'll gum the works. Elementals are fickle engines. Foul their intake, and you stall their storm."

"Who's got the energetic profile of cold porridge?" she asks. "A person so hollow and emotionless that there would be nothing to drink. Utterly unsurprising. Passion-free. Bureaucratic, ideally. We'd need someone completely devoid of passion or life. Someone who flattens the energy of a room simply by existing. Who'd even come close?"

There's a brief, terrible pause while the answer assembles itself.

Holly inhales.

I wince.

"Crinkshaw," we say together.

The zombie is the definition of functional despair. Every bony, shuffling step suggests he's already filled out the paperwork for the worst possible outcome and filed it somewhere inconvenient. His suit predates at least three of my coven members, and the pockets contain string, receipts, and exactly one boiled sweet of uncertain vintage. He never smiles, never hurries, and approaches catastrophe like a forms-in-triplicate problem.

If apathy ever required a patron saint, it would nominate Crinkshaw.

Holly grins and nods, and I smile back. Ten out of ten from each of us. My knees tremble.

"I think this will work," I say. "If we can get him close enough, Santa will absorb his energy. It will be like pouring concrete down a water slide. The entire thing rests on Crinkshaw."

"I think I'm going to throw up."

"It's...not ideal," I agree. "But if anyone can save Christmas, it's Crinkshaw, the depressed ghoul."

"You do hear yourself, right?"

"I'm trying not to."

I squint across the square, the cold needling my eyes, and pick out Ronan and his team taking position. Subtle as ever, Ronan moves like a raccoon approaching a dumpster—committed, enthusiastic, and not especially concerned with stealth—while the others fan out behind him, weapons ready. On the other side, Wes slips into place. His jaw sets as his eyes scan the area with practiced focus.

Past him, more headlights blink as if they're waiting for our signal. Scouts hold salt and shovels. Mrs. Lee steadies a rolling urn of cocoa like it's a sacred object. Meribel's carolers stand poised to shake out harmonies like blankets.

For now, they're still. Held under Santa's control.

But Willow Creek has a way of starting itself. A familiar name called across the square. A cookie pressed into a mitten. The choir catching the next verse.

That's all it will take to shake it free.

And when that happens, Santa is going to learn that you can't out-magic a town with grit, glitter, and a group chat.

We crouch behind snowbanks and improvised cover—Crinkshaw tucked in behind us like a disapproving coat rack—outside Santa's line of sight. His focus is locked on the tree, the thing pulsing and twisting at the center of the square, and for once, his obsession is working in our favor.

This is the moment.

The hinge.

If it swings our way, we get Christmas back.

If it doesn't, we get...January.

"Okay," I murmur, giving Holly's hand a brief and very deliberate squeeze. "Let's go get Christmas back."

Chapter Twenty-Three

HOLLY

My grip tightens on the edge of the abandoned market stall until the wood creaks in protest.

After everything we've been through, Santa has the sheer nerve to stroll into Willow Creek and try to take it over.

The square is a mess of pulsing red light and churned snow, and there he is in the middle of it. A very not-jolly fat man with his hands up like he is conducting a carol no one agreed to sing.

"Nick," I whisper. "What's he doing?"

"I think he's trying to transform the tree back," Nick says, his mouth set in a straight line. "Maybe he can't get at the energy while it's in that form. I'm not well-versed in the intricacies of tree-based magic batteries."

Despite everything, a smirk tugs at my mouth.

The tacky snow globe is holding its ground. It splutters and hisses like a kettle refusing to boil for someone it dislikes, giving off a stubborn, sulky swirl of glitter instead of doing what it's told.

Honestly, I feel the same.

Around him, the townsfolk stand frozen, eyes glassy, under the grip of Santa's enchantment. They sway slightly, like something's pulled the strings too tight and forgotten how to let go. It should terrify me.

It does.

Just...later.

We've made it close enough that we're within twenty feet of Santa, huddled behind a flipped-over market stall that smells faintly of cinnamon sticks and overambitious fudge samples. From here, we can see everything. We're close enough to act.

Close enough to get caught.

Which would be a problem.

It also means Nick and I are pressed in beside each other, and the awareness of him—warm, solid, entirely too distracting—is doing its level best to derail my focus.

Now is not the time.

"We need to stop him," I say, fists clenching. "We can't let this happen to Willow Creek. This is not part of my festive party plan."

Nick nods, his gaze unwavering. "We stick to the plan. Wake the townsfolk up, and then we deal with Santa."

The streets are littered with snowmen that have been trampled into mush, candy canes snapped in half, and Christmas lights dangling like broken spiderwebs. The air smells like burnt cocoa and reindeer sweat—an oddly fitting metaphor for the holiday disaster we've gotten ourselves into.

The vampires slip along the periphery, somehow escaping notice. I consult with my clipboard and tick off the last few items, trying to ignore the way my pulse is climbing.

Everything's in place. Or close enough that it's going to have to be.

Which means all we have left is the part where we actually do it.

The plan that relies, somewhat alarmingly, on Crinkshaw saving the day.

"Hey." Nick's breath brushes my ear and his expression catches me off guard when I turn. The silver in his eyes looks dimmer than usual, like the shine's been dulled at the edges. I don't like it. Not one bit.

"You be careful, okay?"

"Promise." I draw an X over my heart, aiming for light, but he doesn't quite buy it.

That's new.

Nick is usually the one who moves first and figures it out later, all sharp instincts and impossible luck, the kind of man who lands on his feet even when there isn't anywhere obvious to land. Seeing even the hint of hesitation in him—just a flicker—is enough to make something twist low in my chest, something I'd very much prefer to ignore.

So I do.

Or at least, I try to.

The square is a mess of shadows and broken light, and Santa's magic is pressing down over Willow Creek like a storm that doesn't intend to pass, and whatever this is between us, it's going to have to wait its turn.

"Time to get to work, Draven," I say, flashing him a grin that feels steadier than I do. "You ready?"

"Ready, Frost."

The look he gives me lands somewhere behind my ribs and lingers there, long enough to make breathing feel like a conscious decision instead of an automatic one.

I manage it anyway.

Barely.

I sprint toward the townsfolk, snow crunching beneath my boots, adrenaline kicking my pulse into something unhelpful. The plan—such as it is—is distraction. Noise. Enough chaos to give everyone else a fighting chance.

I wave my clipboard over my head like it's a weapon of last resort and start shouting.

"Hey! Hey, listen to me! This isn't over! We don't let Santa take Christmas. Not here. Not ever!"

A few heads twitch. Eyes flicker.

It's not much, but it's something.

Mrs. Christie, who runs the bakery on Main Street, stands near the front. Her bakery apron is dusted white and her expression is flattened into something distant. I push closer, like I can force my way through whatever's wrapped around her.

"Mrs. Christie!" I call. "Remember the bake-off? You beat three mayors and a sous-chef with that gingerbread cathedral. Flour, icing, glory. That was you. You don't lose to anyone!"

Her gaze shifts. A fraction.

But it's there.

Behind me, something changes.

I feel it before I see it—the pressure, the attention snapping into place.

Santa turns.

His face twists, all the jolly scraped off it. "You think you can stop me? With snowballs and holiday spirit?" His voice drips with contempt as it cuts through the square. "I'll show you what real power looks like. *I'm* the one making the party rules now."

"Great," I fire back, breathless, "then you won't mind if we bring our own playlist."

He lifts a hand.

The magic hits like a rolling wall, sweeping through the square and sending people staggering. It catches me full-on, knocks my feet out from under me, and I hit the ground hard—but momentum is a beautiful thing. I roll, shove myself back up, lungs burning, vision sparking at the edges.

Still here.

Still standing.

Nick doesn't bother with subtlety.

He roars—louder than Ronan—and charges, his immaculate shirt finally losing its composure along with the rest of him. A discarded candy cane snaps in his hand, and suddenly it's not festive anymore—it's a staff.

Crinkshaw plods behind him like he's preparing to be a backup dancer in "Thriller." I can make out his faint muttering about wardrobe standards and battlefield etiquette. He stops in front of an elf reeking of boozy eggnog and fixes it with a look of such profound disappointment it almost feels educational.

"It pains me to say it—one might even call it a shot to the heart—but you give elves a bad name."

Trust Crinkshaw to butcher a perfectly good lyric.

Ronan's attempt at subtle reconnaissance concludes exactly as expected, and he emerges from the other side of the square with a look of joy spreading across his face, axe already raised. His eyes gleam with chaotic delight, a warrior's joy filtered through something distinctly seasonal.

"Time to get festive!" he bellows.

Several dozen elven heads snap toward him.

I glance down at my clipboard, where I have underlined *quiet* several times.

There is patience, and then there is Ronan.

"Attack them, my elves!" Santa yells. "Keep them away from the globe."

Chaos answers.

Boozy rogue elves scatter into the crowd like cats dropped onto a hot griddle, all claws and noise and terrible decision making. It's madness. One launches itself at me, but it never gets close—Nick knocks it clean out of the air with his cane in a move that is, regrettably, extremely impressive.

I feel a brief and deeply inconvenient flicker of swoon.

"Keep waking up the town," he calls, "I'll handle these pests."

I nod and pivot, scanning the square until I spot a young man caught in the spell, his expression stuck somewhere between confusion and mild regret.

Casey, I think.

Mostly, I remember his unfortunate relationship with Sarah

Waterson. His Christmas karaoke and how his attempts to win her over have spectacularly failed to work out.

I push through the crowd and grab his hand.

"Hey!" I shout. "Christmas karaoke—last year! You sang 'Jingle Bell Rock' like it was legally binding. You got half the town dancing. You wore those awful elf ears and said they were lucky!"

For a moment, a flicker of recognition crosses his face too. His eyes sharpen, his posture straightening as the fog of Santa's magic is lifting ever so slightly.

"Let's show Santa that the heart of Christmas isn't something he can steal," I say, pressing on before the moment slips away. "It's in us—right here, right now!"

For good measure, I dump a handful of cold snow down his back.

He yelps, jerking upright, and whatever hold Santa had on him snaps clean through. He blinks at me, dazed.

"Miss Frost?"

"Welcome back." I squeeze his shoulder. "Now go help your neighbors."

He nods—still shaky, but there—and turns to the nearest cluster of people.

"Come on!" he shouts, his voice gathering strength. "We don't let anyone mess with Christmas in Willow Creek!"

The ripple starts small, then builds.

At the edges, my musical swat team gets to work. Meribel lifts a hand, and the choir finds a note. *Silent Night*, soft as breath at first. The sound threads through the square, and the fog on people's faces loosens like old tape being peeled back. Carolers shake out their scarves and step forward. The Scouts form two neat snowball lines without being told. Mr. Patel's gritter noses up to the curb like a faithful old reindeer, engine rumbling in support.

All around us, people blink and stir, waking like they've been pulled from a restless sleep. They look dazed, faintly irritated—the particular expression of someone who has been woken far too early on Christmas morning and intends to complain about it later.

But they're waking.

That's what matters.

Song, touch, noise—whatever it takes—the spell is cracking, and Willow Creek is coming back to itself one stubborn, slightly grumpy resident at a time.

And now it's about to show him what happens when you mess with it.

Mrs. Christie has shaken off the last of the daze and produces a rolling pin from her apron pocket with terrifying efficiency. Apparently, she's been armed this entire time. I make a mental note to never annoy her. She taps it against her palm twice and strides into the fray with the calm of a head baker calling order, directing teenagers to form a cookie-sheet shield wall, assigning cocoa-mug artillery to the choir, and claiming the front line for herself.

"No one steals Christmas from Willow Creek!" she roars. "Holly throws this party, thank you very much."

I appreciate the sentiment. The phrasing needs some work.

I sprint back toward the center of the square, shouting over the chaos. "Grab whatever you can! Snowballs, candy canes—anything festive. If it can be thrown, it's a weapon. Come on! It's time to fight!"

The townsfolk surge into motion, confusion hardening into something determined and only slightly unhinged. Someone starts frisbeeing shortbread at the rogue elves. The elves screech and hiccup nutmeg. Another group overturns the cocoa cart and hands out mugs as shields. Strictly lukewarm, because safety comes first. A gaggle of teenagers packs slush into weaponized snowballs, stacking ammunition like they've been training for this their entire lives. The Scouts call out ranges like artillery officers and start a tidy stack of ammunition beside the bandstand.

Someone claps me on the back as they charge past, swinging a garland like an axe pole.

I turn, catching sight of Nick and the vampires already deep in the fray, cutting through rogue elves with a blend of strategy and sheer, chaotic force. Ronan's axe flashes as it sends a cluster of elves scattering like festive bowling pins. Crinkshaw moves through the chaos with quiet inevitability, flicking candy canes with unnerving precision. Mr. Patel salts a clear path across the square. Mrs. Lee stations her cocoa urn on the church steps like a field command post.

The choir shifts into "Joy to the World," and the notes ring like little hammers.

And then there's Nick, right in the center of it all, his shirt slightly askew, his movements fluid and deliberate and full of controlled violence. He cuts through the chaos like he belongs there—but it's the moment his eyes find mine that knocks the breath out of me.

For a moment, the madness fades.

He holds my gaze, and there's something in it—warm, unmistakably proud—that lands harder than it should, like he can see exactly what I'm trying to hold together here and trusts me to do it.

"Enough!"

Santa's voice cracks across the square before I can move, magic flaring in a surge of cold red light that rolls outward and sends people staggering.

But Willow Creek doesn't fold.

"Snowball fight!" someone yells, and it's like a switch flips.

The square erupts.

Snowballs fly in every direction. Rogue elves scatter, shrieking as they're pelted from all sides. The brass band lurches into "Good King Wenceslas" like it's a war march. Teenagers run supply lines from the gazebo. Someone's dad is attempting a fairy-light lasso with alarming confidence. The reindeer sweep the flank, bells jangling like cavalry.

Mrs. Christie plants herself beside me, still tapping her rolling pin against her palm like a threat with excellent follow-through, and fixes me with a look that brooks absolutely no nonsense.

"Holly, this is your moment," she says, her voice firm. "We're behind you. Every single one of us. Just say the word."

The words hit hard—harder than they should—and for a second, everything tightens in my chest.

Not fear.

Something bigger.

It's not just her. It's all of them. The town, the vampires, the chaos and the carols and the absolute madness of it all—and somehow, impossibly, they're looking at me.

Waiting.

I draw in a breath and stare at the snowball melting in my palm—and decide that I am absolutely not letting a wind sprite masquerading as a very unjolly fat man take my Christmas from me.

"LET'S SHOW SANTA WHAT WE'RE MADE OF! CHARGE!!!!!"

Mrs. Christie doesn't wait for a second invitation. She barrels forward, rolling pin raised, letting out a scream that is both impressive and deeply concerning from someone her age. Eighty-something or not, she moves like a woman with purpose and excellent upper-body strength.

Behind her, the square detonates into holiday chaos. Snowballs, candy canes, and the occasional pie fly through the air with surprising accuracy. A rogue elf lunges at me, shrieking something unhelpful, but I duck, snatch up a fallen snow shovel from the ground, and swing.

It connects.

The elf bursts into a spray of tinsel, its shriek dissolving into a warped fragment of "Jingle Bells" that echoes across the square.

More elves go down in glittering explosions, confetti spiraling through the air in festive shapes that would be charming under literally any other circumstances. Carols clash with questionable Christmas hits, and the whole thing teeters on the edge of beautiful and completely unhinged.

I'm trying not to think about the clean-up.

"Keep going!" I shout, dodging another rogue elf that leaps from behind a collapsed popcorn garland. "We've got this!"

Nick is deep in the fray, moving with sharp, ruthless precision. The candy cane staff in his hands looks less decorative and more like it was forged for exactly this purpose, and he wields it accordingly, sending elves bursting into festive debris without breaking stride.

I scoop up another snowball as I move, hurling it straight into an oncoming elf. It hits square in the chest and detonates into streamers, the creature releasing a cheerful line of "Ding Dong! Merrily on High" as it vanishes.

I still cannot get over how weird that is.

They seem to be getting the message, keeping their distance for the moment, and I take a second to catch my breath and get my bearings.

Then Santa roars again.

His magic surges again, and the red glow from the corrupted tree flares brighter as a shockwave tears through the square and forces everyone back. The rogue elves regroup instantly, snarling, and the townsfolk falter.

Inside the dome, the glitter whips into a tight, violent cyclone. The crooked star trembles like it's trying to shake itself free, and the tree strains against the glass, its light flickering in jagged pulses as though it's feeding on the fear and chaos around us.

Nick glances at me.

Just for a second.

And in that second, there's nothing but certainty in his eyes—the infuriating belief that we can win this. It steadies me, even as the corrupted tree pulses brighter and the globe itself starts to glow like a warning beacon.

My stomach drops.

Whatever Santa's doing, it's working—and we're running out of time.

I grab another snowball, my fingers numb now, shaking with cold and adrenaline.

"Don't stop now!" I shout, forcing my voice to carry as people stumble back. "We've got him on the ropes. Keep fighting!"

The words feel thinner than I'd like.

Santa throws back his head and laughs, the sound booming across the square. "You think you can stop me with snowballs and tinsel? You can't steal my holiday. Christmas belongs to me!"

Nick charges.

The candy cane gleams in the crimson light as he closes the distance, and behind us the choir holds the note, the Scouts reload, and Mrs. Christie keeps time with her rolling pin like this is a very aggressive baking schedule.

Willow Creek is awake now.

All of it.

And my heart is in my throat as I watch him go, because whatever happens next is going to come down to this—to him, to me, and to whatever magic we have left to find.

Chapter Twenty-Four

NICK

The battle unfolds around me as I carve my way through rogue elves, trying to get closer to Santa. The town square has become a demented holiday diorama—townspeople fighting elves, elves fighting vampires, and, at the center of it all, a deranged wind sprite cackling as he tries to siphon magic from a snow globe.

It is, without question, the fourth strangest Christmas I've ever attended.

Wes is holding his own beside the young server from the diner, both of them moving with surprising coordination. Across the square, Marcy and Ronan have somehow formed an alliance and are laying waste to anything pointy-eared and festive.

Notably, no one is teaming up with Crinkshaw.

Holly swings her snow shovel into the side of a rogue elf's head with admirable commitment. The impact knocks her slightly off balance, but she recovers quickly and, catching me watching, flashes a lopsided thumbs-up.

It's adorable.

The tide is turning in our favor, but a pulsing barrier of magic still surrounds Santa, keeping everyone just far enough back. We need to break through it—get close enough to stop whatever he's doing with that cursed globe.

Around us, Willow Creek has escalated this into a full seasonal production. Someone has set up speakers and a DJ table, blasting aggressively remixed Christmas music. Others fall back to the Nanaimo-and-cocoa station my vampires have established, regrouping before diving back in.

Despite the circumstances, people appear to be enjoying themselves.

I spot an opening and make for Holly, dodging a stray elf and a poorly aimed snowball as I go. She sees me coming and grins.

"Holly—" I start.

She shushes me.

"No time, Draven," she says. "We've got the rogue elves on the run. It's time for us to stop Santa."

"Have you seen Crinkshaw?"

"Right here, Sire."

The zombie materializes at my shoulder, and I react with all the dignity of a startled cat flung into a bath.

"Gah! Don't do that. Where did you come from?"

"I've been standing beside you the entire time," he says.

"I didn't notice you."

"That was what they carved on my tombstone."

I stare at him for a beat, deeply unconvinced by both the statement and the universe that allowed it, but his timing is inconveniently perfect. He's exactly where I need him to be. All we have to do now is feed his existential disappointment to Santa.

Right then.

"Time to end this," I say.

Holly gives me a single nod. Crinkshaw shrugs, which for him counts as enthusiasm. We press forward into the maelstrom.

Willow Creek rises to meet us—shoulder-checking the elves, battling back the gale with snowballs, cookie sheets, garland lariats, and candy-cane staves—holding a narrow, glittering lane open straight to Santa. Holly and I push through it, winds tearing at us hard enough to sting, forcing us to shield our eyes as wrapping paper, splintered candy cane, and tinsel whip past in a festive attempt on our lives.

Santa stands with his hands raised, dragging what power he can from the snow globe. He still can't force it back into the tree—thank every minor miracle available—and that failure is the only reason we're still in this fight.

We press on, shoulder to shoulder. Crinkshaw follows with the air of someone attending a particularly inconvenient meeting.

Then, with one final surge, we break through the wind and step into the eye of it all.

Santa's eyes burn with manic delight, his form flickering at the edges like he can't quite hold himself together. He shifts from foot to foot, jittering with stolen power, frost-crystal beard rattling softly as red and green energy spits and snaps from his fingers.

He notices us instantly.

"Holly Frost!" he says, voice threading through the wind like it's being dragged across broken glass. "And Niklaus Draven. Of course. You always did have a talent for arriving just in time to fail." The air tightens around him. "You won't stop me now. Not with this much power. Not when I'm this close."

"Holly—" I begin.

She's already stepped forward.

"You're done, Santa," she says, in a way that feels almost offensive in this storm. "Your elves are losing. The town's awake. You're not taking Christmas away from people who actually like it."

His grin widens—too wide, stretching oddly through the blur of him.

"Oh, really? Think you're going to win now you've brought the vampires into this?" he asks, delighted. "How wonderfully ironic. Shall we let the wolves guard the pantry as well? I do admire a bold strategic error."

"Enough." I step in front of Holly before he can build

momentum again. "It's over. Walk away from Willow Creek and don't come back."

"Eat Christmas, Draven."

The magic hits before the words finish landing.

A blast of red and green energy tears toward us, sharp and violent, the air screaming as it goes. Instinct takes over—I shove Holly aside, hard enough that she stumbles clear, and twist away as the strike scorches past me. Heat and frost rake across my skin in the same breath.

It slams into the snowbank behind us, detonating in a spray of hissing steam and charred ice.

Santa laughs.

The sound is wrong—like sleigh bells dragged over broken teeth. The wind coils tighter around him as he lifts his hands again, power gathering fast, unstable, eager.

I roll to my feet and sprint back toward Crinkshaw and Holly. He's still standing like a man waiting for a delayed train and expecting worse news. She's already pushing herself up, her green eyes bright and blazing with determination, and the sight of her cuts through the noise in my head.

"Nick, he's insanely powerful," she says.

"I know."

"We've got to get some Crinkshaw in him."

"Please don't ever use that combination of words again."

Her gaze sharpens. "How though?"

"Follow my lead."

Without waiting, I grab a bewildered Crinkshaw and manhandle him a few steps closer to the malevolent wind sprite, who's still cackling like a mall Santa three eggnogs past good judgment.

"Holly!" I bellow, pitching my voice toward full theatrical catastrophe. "We can still win this with him," I jab a finger at Crinkshaw, "as long as Santa doesn't get to the magic Christmas goblin!"

"I'm a what now?" Crinkshaw asks, deeply unimpressed.

Holly doesn't miss a beat. Her face shifts instantly—alarm,

horror, urgency—all dialed up to a level that suggests she's missed her true calling on the stage.

"Oh no!" she gasps, clutching her chest. "None of this matters—the tree, the town, not even one strand of its tinsel—if we don't keep the grotesque Christmas goblin away from Santa. Please," she adds, with an escalating desperation that would make a seasoned actor blush, "anything but that. He's horrible."

"I am standing right here," Crinkshaw says.

Santa stills.

His head tilts, the wind around him stuttering as suspicion gives way to curiosity.

"...I beg your pardon?"

"Oh no," I say, committing fully now, dragging a hand down my face. "We're too late."

And then I shove Crinkshaw forward.

He stumbles straight into the pull of Santa's magic, coat flapping as his expression settles into a kind of resigned offense.

"I feel I should object to this," he begins.

Santa's attention locks.

The pull sharpens.

"Oho," Santa murmurs, delighted. "And what, exactly, do we have here?"

His hands curl like claws as he reaches out, seizing Crinkshaw by the head with a grip that seems more ceremonial than required. The air thickens, dark magic coiling as Santa pulls deep, inhaling Crinkshaw's energy like a vampire at an all-you-can-drink buffet.

I don't actually need to breathe, but I hold my breath anyway.

Holly's fingers tighten around mine.

For a moment, there's nothing.

Then Santa drops him.

He hits his knees with a strangled groan, and the storm dies instantly. The wind vanishes. The pressure lifts. Even the fighting falters, as if the entire square has collectively decided to pause and see how this goes.

Crinkshaw, for his part, straightens his coat.

Completely unaffected.

Holly and I tense.

Willow Creek freezes mid-throw—snowballs suspended, cocoa halfway raised—as the town leans in.

Santa sways.

His face tightens in confusion.

Then—horror.

Pure, unadulterated horror.

"What...what *is* this?" he gasps, clutching at his chest like something inside him has gone profoundly wrong.

I offer him a smile. "You've been Crinkshawed."

A strange, rattling groan escapes him. Not pain, exactly. This is far worse. Meaninglessness. Weariness. The slow creeping certainty that everything is an administrative burden with no clear resolution.

"It's awful," Santa wails. "What agony, this life? Are we little more than cosmic motes? What's the point? What is any of this for?"

Santa's manic grin twists, falters, and finally collapses under the full weight of Crinkshaw's Crinkshawness. It's not just the emptiness, or even the apathy—it's the bone-deep weariness of existence without punctuation, the dull ache of eternity stretching on with nothing particularly worth hurrying for. His face contorts like he's bitten into a fruitcake laced with despair, and for a moment, it's clear even he can't stomach the crushing weight of Crinkshaw's ennui.

A third wave hits.

Santa's expression slackens, horror giving way to a void of enthusiasm that only Crinkshaw's existential dread could create.

For a brief, glorious moment, Crinkshaw's entire outlook makes perfect, terrible sense. He carries an eternity of dread around with him like it's a light inconvenience, and now Santa is drowning in it.

Crinkshaw watches him with mild interest, as though this is a perfectly reasonable reaction to being himself.

"Now!" I shout.

While Santa wrestles with the full emotional burden of

Crinkshaw, Willow Creek closes ranks around him. Ronan digs in and sweeps a cluster of elves aside like he's clearing snow off a stubborn driveway. The teenagers loose a marshmallow volley. Mr. Patel nudges the gritter enough to blunt a slicing gust. Mrs. Lee sends a plume of peppermint steam straight into the chaos.

For a handful of seconds, the town holds.

That's all we get.

I move.

Without hesitation or flourish—just forward. Throwing fists, shoulders, whatever lands with everything I have. Every strike is driven by the increasingly personal desire to end this ridiculous wind sprite and his festive-themed holiday tantrum.

Holly is right beside me, wielding her snow shovel like a seasoned warrior with a legendary blade. She swings it like she's been waiting her entire life for this exact moment.

Santa buckles.

The manic energy drains out him, replaced by something smaller. More frantic. He tries to rally, to gather himself, but Crinkshaw's influence clings like damp wool.

"Wait," he grunts, holding up a hand. "Wait—"

"You're finished," Holly snaps, stepping in before he can find a second wind. She plants her shovel like a line in the snow. "Your elves are done. The town's back. The tree's ours. Whatever this is—it's over. Leave Willow Creek and don't come back."

"EVER!" Mrs. Christie yells from somewhere behind us.

Santa scrubs at his eyes with a shaking hand, then looks up, his face twisting into a snarl of pure hate.

"This isn't over." He spits. "I won't forget this, Frost. When I come back, your little town—your precious tree, everything you've built here—I'll grind it down to slush."

"Get out of here, Santa," Marcy shouts, appearing at Ronan's side before she launches miniature mince pies with a surprisingly accurate aim. "Hit the road, you hoary old sprite."

"Away, vile demon of questionable origin," Ronan adds, hurling an ornament that cracks squarely against Santa's forehead.

That seems to open the floodgates.

The entire town joins in—snowballs, candy canes, ornaments, and one deeply suspicious fruitcake all arc through the air like festive missiles. Laughter and shouting collide with half-sung carols as the square descends into coordinated nonsense.

The bakers escalate to flour bombs, which burst in soft white clouds and turn Santa's beard into a damp, collapsing meringue. Meribel rings a handbell in time while the choir leans into a refrain that makes his magic wobble like a loose bauble. Mrs. Dapplewhite, guardian of the town archives, produces a roll of red ticket tape and efficiently trusses two elves, reciting infractions as she works: disorderly jingling, unlicensed wreathing, glitter spill, late fees already accruing.

The last of Santa's storm gutters and fails, magic flickering out in uneven bursts like a dying string of bargain-bin lights: one bulb pops, then another, then the whole strand goes out. He staggers, hat slipping, bravado leaking out of him like air from a punctured balloon, while Willow Creek closes in and keeps him there.

"We can make a deal, Draven," he snarls.

I let one eyebrow arch.

The barrage falters, if only out of curiosity.

"You may have knocked me down," he says, voice tight, "but I still hold Christmas. The spirit, the current, the whole infernal system. And I will keep it from your kind—unless you hand over the tree."

A murmur runs through the crowd—uncertain at first, then hardening from uncertainty to resolve.

I hesitate.

The coven has been shut out of Christmas for so long. Longer than most of them can even remember properly. I see it in Ronan's face, in Wes, in Ranu—the brief flicker of want they'd never admit to out loud.

And I nearly—

"No deal, Santa."

Mr. Patel steps forward, jaw set like he's about to argue over parking permits and win.

Mrs. Lee joins him without hesitation. "These are our vampires."

Marcy elbows her way to the front. "Leave, and take your Crapmas with you."

A hand lands on my shoulder.

Mrs. Christie.

Her rolling pin trembles—not with fear, but with the kind of fury usually reserved for overworked dough and underbaked opinions.

"You've got it wrong," she tells Santa. "They're already part of this town. We don't need your permission, and we certainly don't need your magic." She glances up at me, and the look she gives is warm, certain, entirely unshakeable. "They've got us."

We came to Willow Creek after I'd run out of better ideas. Another town, another stretch of time to fill—something to keep the coven from turning in on itself.

It was never meant to be permanent.

Not the eternal kind of permanent.

Now, people are standing between us and the thing coming for us. Not because they owe us something. Not because we asked. Just because we're theirs now—and they've decided that means something.

I don't know what to do with that.

I don't think I've ever had to.

"Keep your Christmas, Santa," I say lightly, flicking a glance at Holly before looking back at Santa. "It sounds absolutely exhausting."

Holly threads her fingers through mine.

"We've got something better," she says. "People who show up. People who stay. People who bring spare mittens, and too many cookies, and refuse to leave when things get strange." She glances at the crowd, then back at Santa. "You can't bottle that. And you don't get to take it."

Santa's expression curdles, the air around him cools as what little magic he has left twitches in response.

"You haven't seen the last of me," he snarls. "I'll ruin it. Maybe not today. Maybe not tomorrow. But I will."

"Not here," I say.

"NOT IN WILLOW CREEK!" the town roars—bells ringing, cocoa sloshing, and snowballs cocked back with deeply personal intent.

With a sharp, sucking gasp, Santa folds inward like a blizzard pulled down a drain. The air ripples, shimmering as he shrinks into a tight whirl of red and green. One last pulse snaps—glitter and soot skitter across the square—and he's gone. What lingers is a single, off-key jingle, a bell note that wobbles, fades, and leaves a hush like fresh-fallen snow.

The square holds still for a beat, as if expecting him to snap back into existence out of sheer spite.

He doesn't.

The cheer hits all at once—loud, messy, immediate. People laugh, grab each other, talk over one another as if the volume will convince the night to stay won. Someone starts singing half a carol and forgets the words halfway through. It doesn't seem to matter. Somewhere in the square, a kettle clicks to warm, and for the first time all night, the lights blink in time.

I glance at Holly.

Her grin is as bright as the tree lights we've fought so hard to save, and something settles in my chest.

I could have taken the deal.

I didn't.

The coven is still behind me. The town is still standing. No one's been traded away for a cleaner ending—and that is the right kind of win. The kind you plan for, fight for, and refuse to let anyone take from you.

Chapter Twenty-Five

HOLLY

Relief floods through me in a hot, overwhelming wave. For a single, glorious moment, everything feels possible. The townsfolk's cheers echo through the square, a triumphant noise that mingles with the lingering hiss of Santa's vanishing magic. The remaining rogue elves stumble over each other in their rush to retreat.

Around the square, Willow Creek exhales as one. The Scouts stack sleds into impromptu benches. Mr. Patel pivots his gritter so the hazard lights throw a warm amber blink across the snow, and Mrs. Lee wheels her rolling urn forward and starts pouring cocoa with vigor.

Mrs. Christie wipes glitter off her cheek with the brisk efficiency of someone who has seen twelve bake-offs and a blizzard.

"You did it, Holly. You and Nick." She takes in the scene. "Christmas belongs to us now. Let's make sure we keep it that way."

Ronan laughs, and the loud, boisterous sound bubbles up through the chaos. He lifts his massive axe in mock toast. Wes, bruised but standing tall, gives me a nod of solidarity. Even Crinkshaw, with his perpetually gloomy expression, manages a small, reluctant smile—and I immediately wish he hadn't. Behind him, vampires and neighbors trade nods that look suspiciously like ease; someone hands Wes a cookie, someone else takes a selfie with Ronan's axe. No one—not one single soul—approaches, or even looks at, Crinkshaw.

I drop my shoulder and exhale for a single beat.

The collective spirit of the town and the vampires feels like a real, tangible force now, a bond that glitters brighter than any holiday decoration.

Nick steps towards me, his head dipping before that wide, confident grin that warms my chest. I crane my neck, half-wondering, half-hoping he'll wrap his arms around me—but he shoves his hands in his pockets instead.

I glance around, and amid the celebration, a nagging thought creeps in. The snow globe. Santa might be gone, but that glittering monstrosity still sits in the middle of the square, the tree inside twisted and glowing with that unsettling, corrupted light.

It's not right.

And it still needs fixing.

It's perched ominously on the raised platform where Santa had stood, the distorted tree flickering despite my very best event planner glare. Its crooked star teeters, a perfect little symbol of everything we've fought through.

"Good work, all of you. But we're not quite done yet."

Frank's gravelly voice cuts through the noise just as Meribel taps her triangle and the square hushes like a curtain falling. I turn to see the town mayor trudging over, his glasses sliding down his nose, a smudge of soot on his knitted Christmas sweater. His eyes—sharp even behind the weariness—scan the square before settling on me.

Authority settles with him. The square quiets.

He strides over, brushing soot from his sleeve as he stops in front of me.

"Holly, that snow globe needs changing back. I didn't hire you as my event planner for nothing."

I blink and the celebratory haze slips away. "I don't think I know how, Frank."

He rests a hand briefly on my shoulder. "You do. You've been doing it all night. We don't force it—we turn it. All that fear, all that pressure...we let the town carry it together. That's what fixes things here."

I nod, and something behind my sternum sharpens through the exhaustion. I glance at Nick, who's still standing nearby, his face illuminated by the glow of holiday lights. We've fought together, bickered together—and now, we have to finish this together.

Our eyes meet, and there it is: trust.

Not borrowed, not bargained. Earned.

Nick coughs, clearly forced.

"Before we begin, Frank," he says, grinding his heel into the churned snow, "where, exactly, have you been? We could have used you when we were dealing with a particularly violent wind sprite who was distributing anything but cheer in a frankly hostile manner."

Frank gives a lopsided, unapologetic shrug. "Here. Just...not in the way you wanted. You know the rules. Power answers power. If I'd stepped in directly, we wouldn't be having this conversation—we'd be filing reports about the crater."

He brushes his hands together, as if that settles matters.

"So I kept it small. Strengthened the ward lines. Ringing the volunteer phone with directions. Boosting the choir's morale using mince pies. That sort of thing." His gaze flicks between us. "And I may have...adjusted a few schedules and made sure a certain vampire and event planner were assigned the same tasks."

I drop my hands to my hips.

"I wasn't forcing anything," he adds quickly. "Just making sure the right people kept ending up in the same place. When you two work together, the town steadies. I didn't know Santa would go this far—but I knew Willow Creek would answer better if you were working together."

"Wait." I hold up my hand as the realization lands on me like

Christmas morning. "Are you saying that you did all of this just to bring us together?"

Frank shakes his head with a low, knowing chuckle. "No. That's not how this works. I had no idea Santa was going to steal the tree, or half of the rest of it. But I saw what happened when you two work together. It brought out the best in everyone, so I simply stayed out of the way. Ninety percent of being a good cupid is knowing when not to interfere. And look, here we are. The rogue elves are gone. Santa's gone. The snow globe's back. Not bad for a reluctant partnership."

Nick raises an eyebrow, clearly skeptical, but lets it pass.

"You were both...persistently difficult," Frank adds, dryly. "I nearly stepped in more than once. Santa had more bite than expected, and I've got a town to keep in one piece—not to mention a reputation to maintain."

"Well," Nick says, with a faint sigh, his gaze flicking to mine, "glad we could be of service."

I'm not entirely sure how I imagined teaming up with Nick would end, but now we have and I don't want it to be over. He gives a half-smile, like he's read my thoughts, and his usual confidence settles back into place.

"Looks like stubbornness actually got us somewhere after all," he says.

"What about the tree, though?" My nerves catch up with me and my voice tightens. "How do we restore it? It's the centerpiece of the entire festival. And—" I check my watch and groan. "We've got until tomorrow. Look at this place. It's a disaster."

Frank laughs, the sound warm and unexpected enough to cut through my panic. His eyes twinkle as some of the weariness fades from his face, a surprising lightness settling in his gaze.

"Well, Holly, we've already established that Christmas can survive broken eggnog, rogue elves, and a frankly irresponsible amount of glitter. Restoring a snow globe is practically administrative."

He gestures toward the platform.

"The tree can be fixed. All it needs is people who care for each other. I wonder if we have anyone—"

"Oh!" Casey barrels forward, practically vibrating with enthusiasm. "Is it me and Sarah Waterson? We've got really strong feelings. She gave me a candy cane once. That was a real moment."

Frank closes his eyes and pinches the bridge of his nose. Somewhere behind him, Sarah Waterson goes crimson and disappears into her friend's shoulder.

"For the love of tinsel," Frank murmurs. "No, Casey. Not every candy cane is a lifelong commitment."

He exhales, then fixes him with a look.

"We need the sort of love that survives washing up and weather. Something quieter. Less...sugar-fueled. More enduring."

I take a shaky breath, and the uncertainty in my chest eases. I glance back at Nick. The skepticism is gone, replaced by something solid that's been built, piece by piece, whether either of us meant it to or not.

"We can do this together," Nick says, his voice low and sure. "Let's fix that tree. Let's remind Santa what real Christmas magic looks like."

"Together," I say, meeting his gaze.

Nick nods, his cocky smile fading into something more sincere. "Always together, Frost."

My heart promptly forgets how to heart, which is going to become a problem if it has an arrhythmia every time Nick looks at me.

We set the globe back on the plinth and rest our palms on the glass. Around us, the town draws in—vampires on one side, neighbors on the other—closing the circle with cold hands, wool gloves, and the occasional sniff. Meribel lifts her arms and the choir hums the first safe notes everyone knows.

Inside the globe, the light brightens—then falters, as if it's waiting.

I glance at Nick. He's still looking at me like that.

It's nicer than nice.

Like a chair that never wobbles.

We step forward, the snow globe sitting menacingly on the raised platform, its crooked star glinting with unsettling brilliance. The glow inside flickers, throwing warped reflections across our faces. My unreliable heart kicks up again, and this time it's not fear doing it.

Around us, Willow Creek closes ranks like a quilt being pulled up to the chin—people and vampires shoulder to shoulder, mittens brushing leather gloves, a handbell chiming the town into a shared purpose. There's no speech, no fuss. Just everyone doing their bit and holding their place.

I reach out, and with a nod from Nick, we lift the globe together. It's heavier than it looks, dense with too much magic. Cold bleeds through my gloves, sharp enough to bite, but I don't let go.

The square settles into a hush. Bruised, exhausted, still here.

Nick glances at me, his expression steady.

"This is the part where we don't mess it up," he says quietly.

I huff a breath that might be a laugh. "Define 'mess it up.'"

"Best case? Nothing happens and we stand here holding a cursed ornament while everyone politely pretends this was a good idea."

"Mm."

"Worst case?" He tilts his head toward the globe. "It explodes, the tree stays corrupted, and Santa comes back brandishing a naughty list with two names on it."

"Festive."

"Extremely."

I shift my grip, feeling all of it—the everything—pressing in. The town. The night. The ridiculous, stubborn fact that everyone's still here.

"And just to check," I say, tightening my grip, "are we working with a method here, or are we leaning heavily on vibes?"

"Strong, decisive vibes," Nick says.

"Excellent. Love that for us."

Nick glances at me, then out at the square.

"Ready, Frost?"

"Always, Draven."

Together, we close our eyes. For a heartbeat, everything else drops away.

I reach for something solid. Something Willow Creek. Marcy, cheeks smeared with chocolate after a long day in her shop, handing me a coffee. Ronan, destroying doors with an enthusiasm that makes general contractors salivate. Wes mixing a cocktail, stylish and smoldering, still standing where he said he would.

The town—messy, loud, impossible—showing up anyway. Karaoke in pajamas. Snowstorms and shared shovels. People who argue about fairy lights and still turn up with ladders.

I hold onto that. Tight.

The globe answers.

Light bleeds out from beneath our hands—thin at first, uncertain. The tree inside twitches, its crooked branches dragging themselves toward something straighter, like it's remembering how. The star flickers, slips—then catches.

"More voices," Frank calls.

The square obliges.

Mrs. Lee flips the urn lid so peppermint steam billows like incense. The Scouts snap lanterns alight in a rough circle. Mr. Patel swings the gritter's lights toward us like we're on stage whether we like it or not. The choir finds a note and holds it, and even the vampires join in, adding a harmony that hums through bone.

The light swells. Warmer now. Stronger.

The tree pulls straighter—almost there—

—and then it stutters.

The glow falters, flickering at the edges like it might gutter out entirely. The warmth thins. The star wobbles, wrong again.

A ripple of unease moves through the square.

It's not enough.

Not yet.

I tighten my grip on the glass, cold biting deeper now, like the thing is pushing back.

Come on.

"It's not working," I say, the words slipping out before I can stop them.

"It is," Nick says quietly.

I shake my head. "No, it's...look at it. It's falling apart again."

"Frost."

His thumb brushes against my hand. Deliberately. Steadily. There's no magic. Just him.

"Don't look at the tree," he says. "Look at me."

Everything else drops away—the noise, the light, the pressure of a hundred people holding their breath—until doubt slips in right behind it.

I only got this job because my mom made a call. Celeste Frost wouldn't be standing here second-guessing herself with a cursed snow globe in her hands and half a town watching. She'd already have a plan, a backup plan, and a clipboard color-coded for festive emergencies.

And me?

I'm standing in the middle of the town square, holding a cursed snow globe that might decide the fate of Christmas, making it up as I go.

Brilliant.

"You're thinking too hard," he says.

"I'm trying not to ruin Christmas."

"You won't."

He doesn't budge. That's the thing I keep coming back to. When everything else tilts, Nick doesn't. He just...holds.

And I relax.

The glass doesn't so much shatter as sigh. It softens into light, lifts like a glittering snowfall, and drifts through our hair and coats without a single cut. When it clears, the globe is gone—and in its place stands a real tree, full and green, spruce and not pine, hung with warm white stars. The crooked topper turns, thinks better of it, and sets itself straight.

The wrongness is gone.

Warmth rolls through the square—not so much the air, but the people in it.

The cheer rises, but it doesn't scatter. It settles. Arms link, lights are straightened, cups passed hand to hand. A note lifts, holds. For a moment, the whole town seems to realize what it's done—together—and the glow belongs to them as much as the tree.

I glance at Nick.

He's smiling, really smiling, and when he looks at me, it feels like I've finally stopped bracing for the next thing to go wrong.

We did it.

When I look around, reality refuses to be ignored.

The square is littered with broken crates, smashed Christmas decorations, and snowbanks turned into slushy obstacles. Snowballs lie abandoned, candy canes are shattered, and the inflatable snowman is as deflated as he was when the rogue elves stole the tree.

Right.

Time to get to work.

"Okay, everyone," I say, clapping once like a headmistress you do not cross. "Teams of ten. Lights, litter, ladders. Cocoa breaks on the half hour. Choir, sing something brisk, nothing by Bach."

A cheer goes up. Brooms appear from nowhere. Someone already has a spreadsheet. Willow Creek has pivoted from battle to tidy-up without even pausing for breath.

"And after that?" someone calls. "We've still got a square to rebuild and three miles of tinsel in knots."

"Then we follow Holly's list," Marcy calls back. "She points, we sparkle."

I scan the square, already slotting pieces into place—what goes where, what can be salvaged, what needs replacing. Candy canes lie in pieces. Tinsel is tied in knots. It's a mess, but it's a fixable mess.

"You still want to put the gala on tomorrow, don't you?" Nick sighs, lacing his fingers through mine. "You're not letting this go, are you, Frost?"

"I'm not giving up on Christmas," I reply, shaking my head.

Nick squeezes my hand. "Good. If anyone can pull this off, it's you."

I look out over the square—my town, our town—already moving, already rebuilding.

Hope feels less like a wish and much more like a plan.

It's time to get to work.

Chapter Twenty-Six

NICK

I'm wearing overalls.

Faded blue, baggy in the wrong places, and almost certainly purchased by Crinkshaw sometime near the end of the last war, when ration books were essential and sophistication was not. They do not so much fit my frame as drape upon it like a tarp over a sculpture that used to have dignity.

I've been relegated to rebuilding the carolers' stage with Wes, who is conspicuously not wearing overalls. That feels deliberate. Possibly strategic. Certainly noted. And while I am working, Wes is engaging in an ongoing social event with an endless rotating cast of twentysomething females who just happened to be in the area and who appear to be composed primarily of perfume and giggles.

I knew I'd pay for telling Holly I was good at everything. As it happens, I do know how to build a stage—and, annoyingly, I'm quite good at carpentry. That said, this feels beneath my ancient mystique, which is not the same thing as being beneath me, and therefore technically acceptable.

I hammer in another crossbeam.

I've barely seen Holly since yesterday. She's turned Willow Creek into a cheerful machine. Choir scales drift from the bandstand, a clipboard command center has sprung up beside a nest of extension reels, and there's an assembly line where cocoa, biscuits, and encouragement are dispensed. In that order. Every ladder has three extra hands already assigned to steady it.

It's...effective.

And it's hard not to notice the tree, either. Restored. Blazing at the center of the town square. Holly's pulled all of Willow Creek into orbit and set it spinning in the right direction, and the Winter Wonderland Festival is going to happen.

Everyone has a job, and I mean everyone. She's even made Frank string popcorn.

She's a wonder.

With some irritation, I keep building, because whatever my ego says about mystique, I am not the man who lets Holly down. I set the cleat, fix the batten, admire a frankly excellent stage, and attempt to share my brilliance with Wes, who is busy conducting a field study on blushing.

Miffed, I hop down and look for my next task.

It's remarkable, watching the town come together. I've noticed over the centuries that there are weeks that last entire years, and there are years that happen in a week. This feels like the latter. Everyone's smiling and engaged. The coven looks more alive than I've seen them in a very long time.

It feels like home.

That's...wonderful.

Holly has threaded herself through my days in a way I did not see coming. Detached cynicism used to be a cloak, and now it is a napkin. She's reminded me that enduring the years isn't the same thing as experiencing them.

I have feelings again. The inconvenient real kind.

And, against all expectations, I find them rather splendid.

God help me, I wrote a line of poetry last night. It didn't scan, but the sentiment was devastating.

As I admire my handiwork, Marcy and Ronan approach, each

armed with a clipboard, and I find myself smiling at how thoroughly Holly has taken over my coven. I don't mind. Not even slightly.

I've also noticed Ronan seems to be finding reasons to be in Marcy's company.

Interesting.

"More chores, Nick," Ronan says by way of greeting. "That lass of yours has an endless list. She'll keep you busy for an eternity."

I do hope so.

"What's on your list?" I ask, keen to steer the conversation away from anything that might lead to further revelations about my feelings for Holly.

"You don't seem very full of Christmas spirit," Marcy teases. "I'd have thought you'd have been delighted you defeated Santa, and instead you're sulking."

"I'm the lord vampire of an entire coven. My name is used to terrify children in some parts of the world. I once dined with—"

"Eleanor of Aquitaine." Marcy cuts in, rolling her eyes in an extraordinarily clichéd move. "We've all heard it. Was that your only dinner, or do you pace them out over the centuries?"

"Excuse me for not including Johan de Witt."

"Who?"

"My point exactly."

"Mm." She taps her clipboard. "Anyway, I'm in charge."

"Of course you are."

She bounces on her heels, aiming for innocent and landing somewhere near smug. It's alarming how much authority a clipboard confers. Her satisfaction shouldn't be this effective on me, not when I am a Lord of the Night, and yet here I am, waiting on instructions like a well-behaved menace.

"Holly had to run home to change. Someone spilled cold cocoa all over her," Marcy adds. "Wes, Ronan, and I can cover you for a while. And if not—" she gestures to the square "—the rest of Willow Creek's got this."

Ronan nods, entirely too quickly.

Interesting again.

Let's hope this doesn't develop into something where his actions could be misconstrued. Such as following her home late at night. Or offering any other man who comes too close an eager, friendly, tavern-bouncer smile that's wrapped in cashmere.

I hand him my hammer. "Try not to build a catapult."

"No promises."

I take one last look at the square. Someone's testing the fairy lights; a hundred bulbs blink in hopeful sequence, like the town itself giving me a nudge.

Right.

I turn and head out at speed, chasing after the woman I've somehow failed to see for several hours—a frankly unacceptable state of affairs.

Two weeks ago, we could barely stand each other.

Now...

Well.

Let's not examine that too closely. I'm in a hurry.

Her house is a vampire's sprint from the square. Warm light leaks from the window, spilling gold across the snow. Fairy lights blink with the stubborn rhythm of a heart that refuses to quit, and the wreath smells pleasantly of spruce—which is not pine, and everyone should really know the difference by now.

Last time I was here, we argued.

I'd prefer not to repeat the experience.

I stop at the foot of the steps.

Through the centuries, I've managed my life with reasonable competence. This—standing on a doorstep, unsure what to say—feels disproportionately difficult. There's no strategy for it. No elegant solution. Just the uncomfortable truth that I was an idiot, and she has every right to shut the door in my face.

I don't knock. Not immediately, because once I do, this becomes real.

And I would quite like not to ruin it.

...again.

I exhale, take the steps two at a time, and knock before I can reconsider. The sound lands too loud in the quiet.

The door opens, and there she is.

Holly Frost.

She's wearing a soft sweater that clings to her shoulders in a way I am absolutely not equipped to deal with, her hair loose and curling around her face like it's made a series of excellent decisions without consulting me. Glitter sticks to her skin. The faintest flush of pink brightens her cheeks.

She looks like she lost a fight with a festive beverage and won anyway.

Her green eyes widen when she sees me, and for a second, I forget how words are meant to function.

She's covered in cocoa.

She's never looked better.

"Nick?" she asks, cautious but curious.

"I'm sorry," I blurt, immediately, like a man with no sense of pacing or dignity. "I'm sorry for being an idiot. For breaking your trust. For making you think—" I stop, drag a hand through my hair, and try again. "For making you think I'd ever hurt you. Or this town. I was trying to help, and I made a mess."

She just looks at me.

Which, historically speaking, is worse than yelling. People who yell tend to declare terms. This is...silence. Open-ended. Dangerous.

"I mean it," I add, committed to digging myself into a deeper hole. "All of it. I'll fix it. However you want. I don't—" I huff out a breath. "I don't care how long it takes."

A beat.

Still nothing.

Right. Excellent. I've faced down warlords with clearer feedback.

I step closer. Retreating now would be cowardly and I've already committed to a course of action that can only be described as *emotionally reckless*.

"Holly," I say, quieter now. "I've done a lot of existing. I'm very good at it. Centuries of practice. Empires rise, empires fall, one acquires a decent coat and a tolerance for disappointment." I shake my head slightly. "But you—"

Her expression shifts. A sliver.

"You make it feel like that's not enough," I finish.

The words settle between us.

"I don't want to just pass time anymore. I've done that. Very successfully. Centuries of it. You learn how to let years slide past without catching on anything. It's a skill," I say, deploying far more honesty than I intended. "I want...this. You. The ridiculous town. The chaos. The cocoa incidents. All of it."

I let out a breath that feels like it's older than I am.

"I've watched cities burn and be rebuilt badly. I've seen men swear eternal devotion and forget it by spring. I've had entire decades I can't distinguish from one another except by the cut of the coat—and it all blurs, eventually. But you don't."

Her gaze doesn't move.

"I'm not good at this," I admit. "Which is not unfortunate, as I'm good at almost everything else. This, however, appears to have no interest in being managed, categorized, or sensibly ignored. And it refuses to behave like anything I understand."

That earns the smallest flicker in her eyes.

Encouraging.

"I choose you," I say, more steady now. "Not as a grand declaration. I've seen those. They tend to end in wars or despots." A small pause. "I choose you because you don't blur. I don't want anyone else."

Another beat.

"If you'll have me."

She takes a shaky breath, her eyes glistening unnervingly.

"Nick," she whispers, her voice barely audible. "You're the most infuriating, ridiculous, impossible man I've ever met."

I brace, because that feels like the beginning of a very thorough rejection.

"And I like you for it," she finishes, like she's decided it mid-sentence.

That...was not the direction I prepared for.

"You do?"

Admittedly, it's not my strongest line, but it's the one that makes it out.

She huffs out a small laugh, stepping closer, closing the distance like it's the most obvious thing in the world.

"Yes, I do. You're a menace, you barrel into everything, and you say things like 'I've watched cities burn' in the middle of a conversation like that's normal."

I open my mouth to defend myself.

She doesn't let me.

"But you showed up," she says, softer now. "You stayed. You fought for this town—even when it would've been easier not to."

I close my mouth.

"And you don't get to decide for me what I can handle," she adds, a little spark breaking through. "If you spiral off into something dramatic and ill-advised, I'll be right there to drag you back out of it."

Now does not seem like the time to argue the technicalities of my so-called spiraling.

She steps in fully now, close enough that the cold doesn't matter.

"And yes," she adds, a touch lighter, "you are absolutely an idiot."

Another step closer.

"But you're *my* idiot," she says despite the tremor in her breath. "Not because you're perfect—clearly—but because you try. And you keep choosing us, even when you think you shouldn't."

"You do?" I ask, aware this is apparently the best I can manage.

She laughs softly, brushing at her cheek. "I do."

I blink. Then again, just to be certain this isn't some elaborate hallucination brought on by festive trauma.

"Would you say that again?"

Her smile deepens, a little steadier now.

"I choose you, Nick Draven," she says. "Even though you drive me completely insane." She lifts a hand when I start to grin. "I was scared, okay? Of letting someone in. Of how fast this was happening. I should've listened. I should've let you explain."

Her fingers tighten in her sleeve.

"That part's on me."

I shake my head. "Holly—"

"No," she says, softer but certain. "Let me finish."

I do. Immediately.

"Because the truth is..." She exhales, then meets my gaze properly. "You make me feel safe. And that's terrifying. But it's also—" she huffs a small, disbelieving laugh "—really, really good."

That lands somewhere critical. Possibly fatal.

I'm not sure I'm ever going to recover from this moment.

From this woman.

Not that I have any particular desire to.

"You mean it?"

She nods, a soft smile breaking over her face. "I think I realized it somewhere between being captured by rogue elves and being suspended over a vat of boiling caramel."

"A classic progression," I say. "Kidnapping. Peril. Emotional clarity."

"Standard," she agrees.

Something in me settles in a way that is both unfamiliar and dangerously permanent. I didn't know it was possible to feel this... much and still remain upright. But here I am. Defying the laws of metaphysics.

"I want to kiss you," I say, certain subtlety has clearly abandoned me for the evening. "More than anything. But not here. Not while

I'm dressed like a cautionary tale." I gesture at my attire. "You deserve better than slush, glitter, and overalls that have seen at least one war."

Holly blinks—then, thankfully, laughs. The sound fixes several structural issues I hadn't realized I had.

"It has nothing to do with the cocoa," I add, quieter now, my voice catching slightly as I lean in. "You look—" I stop, recalibrate. "You look like yourself. Which is, unfortunately for me, devastating."

That earns me another laugh, softer this time.

"When I kiss you," I say, brushing a stray curl back from her face, "it's going to be deliberate. Possibly intoxicating. Definitely memorable." I pause. "I'd prefer not to have it upstaged by festive debris."

I pull her into my arms before I can overthink it, holding her close. Holly fits there easily, like this was always the plan and no one thought to inform me. She exhales against me, something in her finally unwinding, and I rest my chin lightly against her hair.

I close my eyes and, for once, don't think about leaving. I think about staying. Through the clean-up. Through the next disaster. Through whatever comes after that.

"You're an idiot," she murmurs, her voice warm against my chest.

"I've built a reputation," I say.

She pulls back just enough to look up at me, her eyes holding mine, not letting me look away.

"I really do like you like this," she says. "All of it. The chaos, the terrible decisions, the dramatic speeches you pretend you didn't rehearse."

I open my mouth to object to that last point.

She stops me.

"And you," she adds, "are coming with me to the Willow Creek Winter Wonderland tonight."

I blink. "Isn't that now?"

"It starts in an hour."

I glance down at the overalls, then back at her, weighing the situation with all the seriousness it deserves. There are, as far as I can tell, no viable alternatives that don't involve leaving her. For now.

"...I'll need to change," I say.

"Oh, I recall your very specific conditions. Vividly. Which is why you should probably run. Fifteen minutes."

"Cruel."

"Efficient."

Her fingers lace with mine as if this is simply the next logical step, and I realize, not for the first time, that I have been comprehensively outmaneuvered by an event planner. And at this point, the only sensible course of action is to stop arguing and go where she leads.

Chapter Twenty-Seven

HOLLY

The aftermath of battling an evil Santa should probably leave me ready to crawl into bed and hibernate until New Year's Eve, but instead, I'm standing in front of my closet, trying to decide if the sequined dress is too much. My hair is a mess. My arms ache from hurling snowballs. I'm fairly certain there's still rogue elf glitter embedded somewhere in my scalp, plotting a long-term residency.

But none of that matters right now.

Tonight is the Christmas gala, and after everything this town has been through, it's going to be perfect.

Or at least aggressively competent with moments of sparkle.

I yank the sequined dress off the hanger and hold it up to the mirror.

"Too much?" I ask no one in particular, tilting my head.

It would be helpful if Marcy were here. She'd have an opinion. Several, probably. All laminated.

The sequins glare back like they're trying to flag down passing reindeer. I'm not dressing for aerial navigation.

Back on the hanger it goes.

I reach for something more practical. A cozy patterned sweater with just the right amount of sparkle—the kind that says *I can run a gala and a snow-shovel brigade*—paired with thick black leggings and my favorite knee-high boots. Functional. Festive. Unlikely to cause any more incidents.

I'm halfway through pulling my hair into a loose braid, still brushing rogue elf glitter off my arms, when there's a knock.

My heart stutters and I somehow make it to the front of the house. I take a breath and open the door.

And—

Right.

That's unfair.

He's standing there in dark jeans that fit like they were tailored by someone with a vendetta against breathable fabrics, a black coat that manages to be both elegant and dangerous, and a gray scarf looped loosely enough to suggest this was accidental and not, in fact, extremely deliberate. His hair is slightly wind-tossed, his silver eyes catching the porch light—

—and apparently I've forgotten how to form sentences.

In his hands, he's holding a bouquet of holly and roses, the red blooms bright enough to look almost theatrical against the snow.

"For you," he says, softer than I've ever heard him.

I blink, caught off guard. "Holly and roses? That's aggressively on-brand botanical punning, Draven."

His smile widens. "Perk of dating someone several centuries old. Our commitment to wordplay is absolute."

I take the bouquet, my fingers brushing his, and the contact sends a warm jolt through me. "Thanks," I say, failing to be casual by a noticeable margin. "They're beautiful."

"You're beautiful," he murmurs—and then, as if realizing he's said that out loud, he clears his throat and offers me his arm like some kind of dangerously well-dressed holiday problem. "Shall we?"

I hesitate for half a second, caught between swooning and pointing out how absurd this all is. But the way he's looking at me—

like I'm not just part of the evening but the reason for it—makes the decision for me.

"Let's," I say, slipping my arm through his.

The cold bites at my cheeks as we step out into the night, but with Nick beside me, it barely registers. The air carries a mix of cocoa, woodsmoke, and whatever questionable decision someone's made with peppermint schnapps, and somewhere a voice calls for more string lights like it's a matter of national security. Ahead, the glow of the town square spills into the street like a promise that's already been kept.

Windows shine up and down the street; silhouettes move behind glass, adjusting lanterns and straightening wreaths. A hand-painted sign in candy-cane script offers directions: Cocoa right, Choir left, and perhaps a bit optimistically, General Merriment lies ahead.

The town isn't just decorated. It's decided.

"Are you ready for this?" Nick asks, his tone light on the surface, but not quite casual underneath.

"I have no choice," I reply, smiling. "The gala's happening, chaos or not. Willow Creek deserves it."

Nick stops mid-step, drawing me to a halt. His hand settles at the small of my back as he turns me toward him, his eyes glittering like frost-kissed silver under the streetlights.

"I wasn't talking about the gala," he says softly, his voice threaded with something protective and also teasing. "I meant you. Everyone's going to be looking at you tonight. And for the record, I don't think I'm going to be particularly gracious about it."

"Gracious about what?"

"Watching them admire you," he says. "Because they will. Extensively. And I'll be standing there, centuries old, allegedly composed, trying not to develop a reputation for glaring at humans."

My breath catches before I can stop it.

"Do you know how insufferable you are?" I manage, though it comes out far softer than I intended.

Nick's mouth curves. "Deeply. It's one of my more consistent traits."

His fingers brush mine before he offers his arm again, like this is all perfectly normal and not doing alarming things to my internal organs.

"Come along, Frost," he adds lightly. "Let's go see your kingdom."

Despite myself, I grin and slip my arm through his.

"Careful," I say. "I run a tight ship."

"I've noticed. I'm both impressed and mildly afraid."

We make our way toward the square, and the closer we get, the more the light builds. Warm. Layered. Undisputedly festive.

And then we step into it.

The transformation takes my breath away.

Where there was chaos, there's now structure. Where there was wreckage, there's now intention. Strings of lights crisscross overhead, steady and bright, casting everything in gold instead of glare. The tree stands at the center—tall, whole, unapologetically itself—its ornaments catching the light without that wrong, corrupted flicker.

People move through the space with purpose now instead of panic—adjusting, laughing, calling to each other across the square like this was always the plan.

It's not perfect.

It's better than that.

It's ours.

Christmas in Willow Creek has become a strange and entirely successful blend of traditional holiday cheer and vampiric charm. The twinkling lights glitter like stars, but there's a faint red hue to them. Garlands loop between posts—some of them threaded with garlic bulbs in what feels like a pointed compromise. The baubles gleam, and tucked among the snowmen and angels are bats in tiny Santa hats and small, tasteful coffins filled with chocolate.

Even the icicles have been...adjusted. Their tips are dipped in red, as though they've taken up a dramatic new hobby.

The square isn't perfect: a few broken decorations have been nudged into corners with optimistic intent, and someone has absolutely repurposed a candy cane fence into a barrier that now poses a mild legal liability.

But it's alive.

It feels like Christmas. Not pristine—just perfectly *Willow Creek*, which is better.

Nick glances at me, his expression soft. "It's amazing, Holly."

"It's not bad," I say, aiming for modesty, but ending up in the vicinity of proud.

At the edge of the square, Ronan is laughing loudly as he demonstrates his axe skills by splitting chunks of firewood for an already aggressive bonfire.

"For roasting chestnuts!" he bellows, demonstrating how little he appreciates the size of a chestnut.

Nearby, Wes is attempting to string lights around a precarious stack of crates that have somehow become a cocoa station. His progress is being actively managed by Marcy, who is standing on one and issuing instructions with the authority of someone who has appointed herself Queen of Christmas Decorations and intends to keep her title.

"Higher, Wes! It needs to look like the North Pole threw up on it!" she demands, pointing dramatically at an empty spot.

I giggle, and my eyes find Crinkshaw, who, bless his eternally gloomy soul, is stationed at a table laden with baked goods. His skeletal hands move deftly as he arranges trays of gingerbread zombies that are less cheerful holiday treats and more terrifyingly detailed nightmare snacks. Each one is somehow desiccated yet fresh, with green icing which I assume is meant to represent ghoul blood.

He remains utterly unchanged by his interaction with Santa, as if he truly is a renewable resource of despair.

As we pass, he inclines his head. "I've been up all night. This batch was supposed to scream when you bite them. They've settled on a disappointed wheeze."

Nick pauses. "Of course they have."

I pick one up, eyeing it cautiously. "That's...is that worse?"

"It lacks conviction," Crinkshaw says.

Nick gestures to the tray. "Have you considered giving them tiny existential crises instead?"

"They already have those, Sire," Crinkshaw says. "It's the after-taste that's wrong."

I snort, quickly setting the gingerbread zombie down.

"Impressive work," Nick adds, gently. "Truly festive."

Crinkshaw sighs, the sound of centuries of disappointment distilled into one breath. "I aim to unsettle."

We move on before I'm tempted to test the wheeze.

The square hums around us—people milling, laughing, voices overlapping in that easy way that means no one's bracing for disaster anymore. Vampires and townsfolk mingle with surprising ease, dark mugs in hand, the whole thing a little chaotic, a little uneven, and entirely ours.

We make our way toward the towering tree, and I can't help but stop. The ornaments catch the light just right, scattering a kaleido-scope of color across the square, and the once-crooked star now glows warmly—a beacon of what we've overcome.

Nick glances at me, his silver eyes soft. "You did this, Holly."

I shake my head. "*We* did this."

I glance up at the star crowning the tree, its light steady now. There's no flicker. No strain. No sense that it might all decide to turn on us at any moment. It feels like nothing is waiting to go wrong.

Which, frankly, is suspicious.

But also...nice.

Around us, the square hums on. Without caution. People are enjoying the evening. They're unworried. Laughing too loudly, arguing about marshmallow versus hot chocolate ratios, and building a snowman that has, through some combination of enthu-siasm and questionable judgment, acquired fangs, a cape, and a level of personal dignity that is not, in any meaningful sense, earned.

"Do you think this would have happened if the Christmas tree hadn't been stolen?" I ask.

Nick considers the square, the lights, the entirely unnecessary number of snow-based initiatives currently underway.

"No," he says. "I think you'd have had a perfectly respectable evening. Minimal peril. Modest decorations. More caramel and less property damage."

I nod. "We were so close to that."

"A near miss," he agrees. "Shame about the rogue elves. And the reindeer stampede. And the wind sprite attempting to redecorate the town on a conceptual level."

"It wouldn't have been the same. And yet," I say, glancing around.

Nick follows my gaze again.

At the cocoa station, Mrs. Christie hands a mug to one of the vampires with the air of a woman who has decided this is fine and will remain fine if everyone behaves. He accepts it like it might bite him back.

"It's all just...working," I say.

Nick hums softly. "It is."

Which, after everything, feels faintly improbable and earned.

I watch as Ronan claps one of the older vampires on the shoulder with enough enthusiasm to knock him half a pace sideways, then proceeds to explain firewood like it's a subject no reasonable person could be expected to understand unaided.

"They're not even standing out anymore," I add.

"No," Nick says, a quiet note of something easing in his voice. "They're not."

I look back at the square—the noise, the lights, the fact that no one's waiting for it to go wrong.

Willow Creek doesn't do seamless.

But it does, eventually, decide who belongs.

Nearby, a group of teenagers launches into an impromptu snowball fight, their aim questionable but their enthusiasm impeccable.

Marcy has somehow established a competitive snowman-building league, complete with judging criteria that appear to reward poor decision-making and structural instability. Carrot noses are aggressively overused. Sunglasses have been introduced. No one is asking why.

Further along, someone has organized a snowshoe relay that seems to consist primarily of falling over with commitment and being applauded for it. No one wins. Everyone insists they did.

"So," Nick says, glancing at me, "what do you want to do now?"

"Aside from lying down for a week and pretending none of this happened?" I say.

"A tempting plan. Deeply unrealistic."

"I could supervise from a horizontal position."

"I'd support that," he says, his eyes glinting. "Heroically."

As if summoned by the word *heroically*, a booming voice cuts through the square.

"Holly! Nick! Mistletoe—two paces left of the lamppost!"

I close my eyes briefly. Of course.

Frank emerges at the edge of the square, glasses halfway down his nose, sweater collecting soot like it's a hobby. He points—firmly, theatrically—at a sprig of mistletoe hanging from a slightly crooked lamppost.

"By order of the mayor," the voice continues, "and seasonal bylaw twelve-b: unattended sprigs must be immediately attended. Shoo!"

"We could ignore him," I whisper.

"We could," Nick agrees, already steering me in that exact direction.

"That is not ignoring him."

"It's ignoring him in spirit."

The crowd notices.

"Oh, here we go," someone calls.

"About time," Marcy adds, appearing from nowhere and absolutely not helping.

"Ten gold bullion says he trips," Ronan offers, entirely uninvited.

"No one uses bullion anymore," Wes says.

"More fool them," Ronan replies.

"Focus," I hiss, but I'm already smiling.

Nick leans closer as we reach the lamppost. "Willow Creek is very invested in this."

"The town's had a long week."

"They've decided this is the payoff."

We stop beneath the mistletoe—slightly lopsided, mildly questionable, and now the most important botanical object in Willow Creek.

Nick turns to face me, and just like that, the noise dims. Not gone, just...respectfully distant.

"This feels appropriate," he says, quieter now.

I tilt my head. "Why's that?"

"Because after everything we've been through," he says, "I think we've earned a moment that isn't trying to kill us." He brushes a loose strand from my face. "Ambitious, I know."

"Wildly optimistic."

"But worth attempting."

His hand finds mine, and whatever's been skittering around under my ribs all night finally decides to behave.

"I think we should," I say.

"Good," he murmurs. "The mayor is watching, and I'd hate to be fined."

I laugh, and it breaks whatever last bit of nerves I had left.

And then he leans in.

The kiss is slow. Soft. Not sweeping. Just right. Warm, inevitable, and a little bit amazed at itself, like it can't quite believe it made it through rogue elves, weaponized confectionery, and a frankly unreasonable amount of emotional growth.

I lean in, and he pulls me closer. For a moment, the rest of the world obligingly minds its own business. Somewhere, a cork pops like a starting pistol, someone immediately cheers too early, and Mrs. Dapplewhite shouts "Not yet!" with the authority of a woman who has waited her entire life for timing to matter.

When the kiss deepens, it's not about proving anything. It's just...staying. Choosing it. Choosing him.

Choosing us.

There's a cheer when we finally pull apart—inescapable, enthusiastic, slightly off-beat—but it lands somewhere far away, like background music to a very specific victory.

"Merry Christmas, Frost," he says.

"Merry Christmas, Draven."

The square surges back into motion around us—music, voices, someone starting a dance that no one has agreed on but everyone is joining anyway. The triangle, having found its purpose, *tings* like a star. Lights blink, mugs reappear, and the whole place hums like it's remembered what it was for.

But right now, it's still just us.

No speeches. No saving anything.

Just...this.

We did more than survive the week. We didn't just patch things back together and call it festive. We made something out of it—messy, stubborn, held together with effort and choice and the occasional questionable decision.

Which, as it turns out, is exactly how Willow Creek likes things.

Not flawless. Not polished. Not the kind of Winter Wonderland my mom would design, where every ribbon matches and every act unfurls on cue.

This one runs on last-minute decisions and borrowed ladders and a general agreement to sort it out as we go. Structurally questionable in places, but emotionally sound.

And it works.

I glance at Nick, still smiling, still here, and feel it settle properly this time—

Not a miracle.

A choice.

One we'll keep making.

"Ours," I say, half to him, half to the night.

"Dangerous word," he replies lightly.

"An accurate one."

I smile.

"Also," I add, "I'm fairly certain someone's left a thermos on the sleigh."

He follows my gaze. Nods.

"Then, clearly," he says, offering me his arm again, "this evening continues to improve."

Chapter Twenty-Eight

NICK

January has draped itself over Willow Creek like a knitted blanket that smells faintly of frankincense, smoke, and road salt—comforting, provided you don't ask too many questions. The lights on the square are still up after Holly decreed they can stay until the last thermos of cocoa is empty and the final casserole dish is returned to its rightful, faintly passive-aggressive owner.

Which means February. Possibly March.

The town has agreed, without discussion, that this is now a tradition.

My coven is content too.

Ronan runs wood to anyone who so much as thinks about being cold. He calls it the 'War on Chill.' He has a roster and has begun referring to himself as a one-man logistics division. Ranu has taken over Tuesday Story Hour at the library and reads ancient epics to children who don't blink at the word sacrifice and clap enthusiastically for dragons, which bodes...interestingly. Wes has discovered the intoxicating combination of fairy lights and a staple gun and is daydreaming about expanding Hemoglow. Even Crinkshaw—who would deny enjoyment under oath—consults for one of the beignet bakeries twice a week and has developed a gingerbread recipe that does not bake so much as judge. It scowls when you open the oven. Customers find this reassuring.

As for me, I am wearing an Aran sweater.

It isn't black.

Midnight blue, which Holly insists counts as growth. It is warm, indecently soft, and cable-knit within an inch of its life. She gave it to me as a belated Christmas present, handed over with a look that said she would keep handing me colors until one of us broke. I didn't argue. I put it on and discovered a new and terrible weakness: I like the shade. I refuse to tell my coven. They will orchestrate matching knits, and I will retreat to a pressing appointment with meaning.

"You're staring at it again," Holly says from the sofa.

"I'm assessing it."

"You're petting your own sleeve."

"It's a tactile assessment."

She snorts without looking up from her phone. "You love that sweater."

"I tolerate it with distinction."

"That's not a phrase."

"It is now."

She twists a strand of hair around her finger.

"You've worn it two days in a row," she adds.

"That was strategic."

"For what?"

"I wanted the town to adjust gradually."

She lowers her phone, looks at me over the top of it. "Nick. They know you fought a gingerbread dragon."

"Which behaved with considerably more dignity than the things Crinkshaw baked."

Her mouth twitches. "The wheezing ones?"

"I will not be judged by confectionery. Not now. Not ever. Not even during the Grand Sugar Covenant of 1672."

"It's insane that you have an opinion on that."

"I've been alive a very long time," I say.

I move the mug within reach and place a kiss on the crown of her head because I can. She shifts under the blanket, glancing toward the window as if she can still see the square from here.

"I'm sure this Christmas will become a cautionary tale in your ever-expanding collection of arcane historical references no one understands."

"Just look at it," I say, glancing toward the window. "The town is intact, no one has been permanently caramelized, and Willow Creek appears to have become famous for its cocoa. By most metrics, the Winter Wonderland was a success."

"High bar," she says, but there's pride in it. "We pulled it off."

"We did."

It settles between us, that fact—no fanfare, just there, like it's decided to stay.

A light flickers outside, followed by the distant sound of a man discovering that electricity is not, in fact, optional.

Tonight there is frost on the windows and stew on the stove. Holly has curled up on one of my sofas in socks with little trees on them. I cannot tell if they are spruce or pine, which feels like a test I am failing on principle. She is reading messages on her phone and humming the way she does when a problem is a puzzle instead of a headache. Every now and then, she looks at me, finds me looking, and does that scrunch with her nose that would, in an earlier time, have ended empires.

I make a show of reorganizing my bookshelves, but I am really just orbiting. Medieval Botany does not belong beside Eldritch Geography, but I leave it there anyway, distracted by the way her braid has come loose and the small tilt of her mouth when someone sends a photo of Meribel leading a surprise singalong in the grocer's frozen aisle.

I have seen stranger things.

This may be my favorite.

"You're staring," she says without looking up.

"Only with both eyes," I say.

She smiles into her phone. "Flatterer."

"The stew will be done in five minutes, the way you like it. With reckless amounts of thyme."

"Is this domestic bliss?" she asks, still smiling. "Or your latest campaign to distract me from the fact you rearranged the mugs by height again instead of category?"

"Both can be true."

Her laugh runs across the room like a string of lights finding the outlet. She tucks her feet under her and glances past me toward the mantle. On it sits the most contentious compromise of the season: a miniature snow globe we never speak about. It is non magical. Not too tacky. Progress.

I wander back to the kitchen and stir the stew because it is satisfying to do so. At least eighty percent of the therapeutic value of stew comes from the stirring. In the distance, a pair of teenagers slides across the ice while pretending they are not holding hands. They are failing admirably.

There is a feeling in Willow Creek that I have not tasted in a very long time.

The taste of after.

Not aftermath, which is its officious cousin—the one that arrives with recriminations and the unavoidable sum of what's happened and what went wrong. No. After. The better relation. The one where you remember how to sit.

Holly appears beside me with the stealth of a cat and the temperature of a furnace. She steals my spoon, tastes the stew, considers it with alarming seriousness, and drops in three more grains of salt with the gravitas of a microsurgeon.

"Perfect," she says.

"You are the only human I know who salts by millimeters."

"Salt is an art form. Besides, you like it when I meddle."

I do. It is not a secret.

We migrate to the small table by the window because that is

where Holly likes to eat, and I have learned that preferences, once established, are to be treated as law. She tucks one leg under herself, steals my glass of Cabernet Sauvignon, and takes a sip without asking.

She nudges my foot under the table. Keeps it there.

I blow on a bite of stew. "Ronan complimented Marcy's confectionery skills today."

Holly pauses mid-chew. "I'm sorry—he what?"

"The way she beats eggs," I say. "Apparently, it's impressive. Figures that Ronan would be impressed by what is, essentially, a culinary assault."

She lowers her spoon slowly. "That's either courtship or a hostile takeover."

"I am monitoring the situation," I assure her. "There may need to be guidelines."

"For chocolate or axes?"

"Both."

She laughs and reaches across to pinch a piece of bread off my plate like it has always belonged to her.

We circle like that for a while—small things, local things, things that would once have struck me as dangerously unimportant. The stew disappears. Her knee stays pressed to mine as our legs have their own gravity.

When we're done, I collect the plates out of habit.

"Don't you dare vanish into vampire efficiency," she says, pointing her spoon at me like a warning.

"I am incapable of doing anything inefficiently."

"You're humming."

I pause. "I am not—"

"You are," she says, delighted. "Keep it. It's festive."

This is how I find myself at the sink, washing dishes at a pace that would embarrass my ancestors, while she dries them with exaggerated care and commentary.

"This one survived the Great Cocoa Spill," she says, holding up a mug.

"A veteran," I agree.

"Bit chipped."

She passes it back. Our fingers brush. Neither of us makes a point of it.

"Nick," she says, and it lands in me the way it did the first time she said my name without flinching.

"Yes."

She looks at me like she's already decided something and is just waiting for the rest of the world to catch up. Her hand comes to rest on my chest, catching slightly on the cable knit, and I still without meaning to.

I had intended to wait. There was, at one point, a structure to this. Timing. Atmosphere. Possibly a line that did not involve accidental rhyming.

She ruins all of that by being here, and it is perfect.

"I love you," she says.

It happens in a kitchen that smells of thyme with a hint of overconfidence. The tap drips once. The stew cools. The books on the shelf lean into one another like they've agreed not to fall tonight.

And still—

Everything shifts.

"Oh," I say, as several centuries of language fail me entirely.

Her mouth twitches. "That's all I get?"

"No," I say, quickly. This is not a moment one fumbles without consequence, and I will not be a man who fumbles anything, especially not anything that involves Holly Frost. "No, you get considerably more. I'm simply reorganizing my entire internal landscape."

She blows out a laugh, but her hand stays where it is.

"I was going to do this properly," I admit. "There was a plan. It involved patience, and dignity, and possibly a poem that would not have survived scrutiny."

"You wrote a poem?"

"One line," I say. "It was...ambitious."

She smiles, and that is the end of any remaining strategy.

"I love you," I say.

I take her face in my hands—not because I practiced it, but because it feels like the correct thing to do when presented with something I intend to keep.

"I love you when you're certain," I add, "and when you're not. When you're organizing a town like a military campaign, and when you're stealing my spoon and calling it instinct. I love you in the middle of chaos and at the end of it, and—" I glance around the kitchen, at the quiet, the ordinary miracle of it— "I love you here as well."

Her eyes shine, and then—predictably, sensibly—she stops me talking.

The kiss is not the kind that announces itself. It's not trying to prove anything. It's familiar already, like it's been waiting for us to stop pretending we didn't know how this would end.

She presses herself against me. I follow, because I am not an idiot. Not about this.

Her hands slide up into my sweater, and I feel her relax—properly relax—under my hands like this is not a risk anymore, only a decision.

That does something far more dangerous than any declaration.

When we part, she doesn't go far. Neither do I. Neither do her hands. This appears to be a part of our new arrangement.

"Good," she says.

I nod. "Good."

We return to the kitchen in theory. In practice, we orbit it. Plates are washed, eventually. A glass is dried twice. She confiscates the towel on the grounds that I am leaving philosophical streaks.

"You're smudging," she informs me.

"I am contemplating," I correct.

"You're contemplating in circles."

"Then we should take a stroll through town," I say. "We can test whether my newfound emotional competence survives the weather."

We walk through town, and habit pulls us back to where we first came together. The tree's still there—mended and luminous—hung with ornaments that are better for having been broken. People wave as we pass. Some say thank you as if we did more than arrive with unfortunate timing and a tolerance for chaos. Others press confectionery into our hands and refuse to negotiate, which is how I come to be carrying a paper bag of lemon squares like a man with purpose.

The lanterns take us past the shops and down toward Sunmirage Lake. In June it will pretend to be a beach and throw a party for the solstice, but now it's frozen into a broad sheet of pale glass. Someone has set up two nets, and a game of hockey has broken out. Others skate in lazy circles alongside children who dart between their legs playing tag.

"Home," Holly says.

"Yes," I reply.

She loops her arm through mine, and we stand like that until the cold insists on being noticed. Then we turn back, following our own footprints.

I had thought I understood power. I did not. It does not conquer. It does not announce itself. It looks, it turns out, like being handed another chair and trusted to place it well. Or a midnight-blue sweater I was not meant to like. Or a town that keeps choosing itself. And exactly like the woman who reaches for my hand without looking, because she already knows I am there.

We reach her porch. She turns to me, cheeks flushed from the cold, eyes bright with something that has nothing to do with winter.

"Stay," she says.

Simple. Open.

An invitation I have wanted since she marched into my life with a clipboard and a frown and a heart that could move an army.

She laughs as she welcomes me in, at whatever expression I'm making as she pulls me along by the front of my sweater.

The radiator ticks. The house smells of cloves. Outside, Willow Creek settles into its winter breathing. Tomorrow will bring lists and errands and an argument with the council about whether bats should wear reflective vests.

But tonight—

Tonight, there is her.

A sofa meant for cocoa and conspiracies.

And a love that surprised a very old vampire by being louder than the dark.

For the first time in a very long time, Christmas is a season and not a sentence.

I am home. And I am staying.

Thank you for reading! Did you enjoy? Please add your review because nothing helps an author more and encourages readers to take a chance on a book than a review.

And don't miss more in the *Hexes and Holidays* series with book two, BLOOD AND BEACHES, coming soon!

Until then read CJ Holmes' fantasy novel, LABYRINTHINE. Turn the page for a sneak peek!

Also be sure to sign up for the City Owl Press newsletter to receive notice of all book releases!

Sneak Peek of Labyrinthine

BY CJ HOLMES

Starsfall was once sacred. Then, the gods abandoned it, and us, to the mercy of a man who had none.

My father.

The priests say it was necessary. That the gods were merciful. Clever. Brilliant. That they saved Starsfall and Larkshind from the curse of magic and stopped the war that had turned into a feast of fire and flesh. From the blight that made our rivers run red with the blood of youth and choked our skies with smoke from the pyres that never stopped burning.

But it's what men don't say that tells the real story.

They don't speak of the way silence settled like ash after the gods turned away, or how my father stepped into that silence. How he shaped himself into the image of a savior, but there were always fractures in the mask—hairline cracks where his cruelty leaked through.

They don't say that binding the magic in Starsfall smothered the kingdom's heartbeat, or that even the gods could not unmake it. For even they don't hold that power. So the priests don't tell tales of sorcery that is more than mere destruction. More than spells and storms and fire. That is power born from pain, woven into the land and its blood.

They say the binding was a sacrifice.

But it wasn't made by them.

It was mine.

Made without my consent, breathed into me the moment I was born—for when the gods bound Starsfall's magic, they bound me with it. Because the curse they feared wasn't the land's fury or a king's wrath. It was his daughter's.

What lives in me is old and patient. Made of darkness and death. Power that remembers. Magic that seethes and rebels and waits. That doesn't forget the sound of screaming. That seeks the light—that hunts for it through the small hours of the night—to destroy it.

They say the gods locked Starsfall's magic away in a contest whose rules are written in blood. That the Reaping is the cost of peace. A sacred rite. The priests whisper that the gods found a way to contain two monsters who might ruin the world. My father, with his craving for power and his eternal quest for more. His child, with her magic that could destroy all the gods had created. But what they really did was put a blade in my father's hand and called it mercy.

Each year, ten men from Larksbind enter the Reaping. Ten lives offered like prayer, like tribute. They hope to win my hand in battle, and with it, the magic bound inside my blood. If I marry a man from Larksbind, the power returns to them. Peace, they say. Balance. But if a man from Starsfall wins my heart and earns redemption through love, our kingdom's magic stays with us.

And that makes my father hungry. A man who would bleed the world dry to have magic on his side.

The gods must have thought a balance had been found. That mortals would rise to meet the trials of combat or the heart. That someone would survive long enough to reach me, and that mortals would, somehow, learn compassion through suffering. Perhaps they even thought that my father's hunger would burn itself out.

But he is not the kind of man who fades with time. He is the kind that rots deeper.

Over the years, he's made certain no suitor survives the Reaping and none comes close to claiming me.

He's twisted the trials until they're nothing but slaughter. Changed the rules, the terrain, the odds. Turned them into a show of blood and fear. The people cheer. The priests bless the carnage. No one remembers it was meant to be anything else.

And each year, the outcome is the same.

I remain unmarried.

Unclaimed.

And with every failed Reaping, my father comes closer to claiming what should never be his.

Because long ago, he made another bargain. One hidden in the fine print of gods and law, a deal no one speaks of.

If no man reaches me before my twenty-fifth name day, the magic bound in the Reaping reverts to him. Not to the kingdom. Not to the land. Not to me.

Him.

So he waits. And bleeds them all dry.

Until only I remain. A crown with no court. A throne with no allies. A girl with no choices left but one.

Or so they say.

Don't stop now. Keep reading with your copy of LABYRINTHINE

And sign up for CJ Holmes' newsletter and Michael Ashwood's newsletter to get all the news, giveaways, excerpts, and more!

Don't miss the book two of the *Hexes and Holidays* series with BLOOD AND BEACHES coming soon!

Until then, read the fantasy novel, LABYRINTHINE, by CJ Holmes, available now.

Every generation, the gods take their due. This time, they might take her.

Princess Azhara was born cursed. Marked by ancient magic. Promised to an unholy bargain sealed in blood. When the Reaping begins, suitors will descend into the labyrinth beneath the palace—each one fighting to win her hand or die trying.

She's never had a choice. Not in the Reaping. Not in her future. Not even in the power buried beneath her skin.

Until now.

The golden prince arrives with charm too slick to trust and eyes that gleam with secrets. Her quiet guardian—once her only constant—has begun to keep dangerous truths from her. And as the labyrinth trials unfold, Azhara realizes the maze isn't her only trap.

It's the men.

One lies. One loves. One kills. And she's not sure which is which.

As suitors fall and secrets surface, Azhara must choose what's worth saving—her kingdom, her heart, or herself.

Labyrinthine is a seductive, myth-woven romantasy of deadly trials, cursed bloodlines, and a love born in shadows.

Please sign up for the City Owl Press newsletter for chances to win special subscriber-only contests and giveaways as well as receiving information on upcoming releases and special excerpts.

All reviews are **welcome** and **appreciated**. Please consider leaving one on your favorite social media and book buying sites.

Escape Your World. Get Lost in Ours! City Owl Press at www.cityowlpress.com.

Acknowledgments

Books are never written alone, and co-written books perhaps least of all.

First, our enormous thanks to the team at City Owl Press for helping bring *Blood and Bells* into the world. To Tee, our editor, for her insight, patience, and care; to Tina, for believing in the book; to Yelena, for helping guide it through the many stages between manuscript and finished novel; and to everyone else at COP who worked behind the scenes on edits, production, design, marketing, and all the thousand invisible things that make a book possible—thank you.

We also owe a great deal to the writers whose stories taught us that fantasy can be strange, warm, absurd, moving, and very, very funny. Terry Pratchett and Douglas Adams showed generations of readers and writers that comedy and imagination need never come at the expense of heart. Their influence can be felt throughout the genre, and certainly in the kind of book we wanted this to be. We are also grateful to the many fantasy, romance, and comic-fantasy authors whose work made us fall in love with magical worlds, impossible creatures, small communities, and characters who find one another in the middle of chaos.

From CJ

To my husband, my children, and my family: thank you for living alongside the deadlines, the edits, the strange questions, and the periods in which I was physically present but mentally somewhere in

Willow Creek. Your love, patience, and support mean more than I can say.

To Karina, my wonderful PA, thank you for keeping so many plates spinning, often before I have even noticed one is wobbling. To Mandie and Courtney, thank you for all the admin, organisation, encouragement, and calm competence that allow me to keep writing when the practical side of publishing threatens to swallow the day.

And to the Shadow Court: thank you for every post, recommendation, message, review, graphic, cheer, and act of bookish enthusiasm. Having a street team so generous with its time and excitement is something I never take for granted. You make every release feel less like sending a book out alone and more like opening the doors to a very enthusiastic, occasionally chaotic court.

From Michael

To my wife, my son, and my family: thanks for putting up with me through the hours of Dev Calls with CJ, the endless bizarre questions (how much memory do you think a severed head would reasonably take? What is the ratio of prophecy to memory theft? Three point five to one?), and for listening to me go on about Willow Creek. You're the reason I'm here.

To Kristin, my PA: thank you for helping me to get up and running and your support in rebranding, which, as it happens, is quite a bit of work.

Finally, thank you to every reader who chose to spend Christmas in Willow Creek with a stressed event planner, a sarcastic vampire, several badly behaved supernatural creatures, and a town determined to celebrate whether the universe cooperated or not.

We hope this book made you laugh, gave you a little escape, and reminded you that sometimes the best things happen after the plan has gone completely wrong.

Love,

Mike and CJ

About the Author

MICHAEL ASHWOOD writes stories that sit at the crossroads of cozy fantasy, modern fairytale, and weird fiction, blending inventive worldbuilding with a dry, slightly sideways sense of humour and a quiet belief that gentleness can change the world. He lives outside of Toronto with too many notebooks, not enough shelf space, and a running list of ideas that are all, deeply, deeply funny to him. When he isn't writing, Michael can usually be found doing Canadian things—apologizing, remarking on the weather, that sort of thing.

www.michaelashwood.com

instagram.com/michaelashwoodauthor

About the Author

CJ HOLMES lives in England, where it's cold and damp, and it's always raining—which provides her with enough time to write stories about magic, fantasy and romance. She'd like to escape to somewhere warm but that might mean that she spends too much time sunbathing and not enough time writing books.

She lives in a quaint English cottage that would have one of those idyllic gardens if her fingers weren't the opposite of green. Fortunately, her husband doesn't seem to mind that almost everything she tries to grow dies instead. She enjoys drinking wine and gin, which conveniently coincides with her love of reading and writing.

cjholmeswriting.com

instagram.com/cjholmes_writing
facebook.com/cjholmeswriting
tiktok.com/@cjholmes_writing

About the Publisher

City Owl Press is a cutting edge indie publishing company, bringing the world of romance and speculative fiction to discerning readers.

Escape Your World. Get Lost in Ours!

www.cityowlpress.com

facebook.com/CityOwlPress
x.com/cityowlpress
instagram.com/cityowlbooks
pinterest.com/cityowlpress
tiktok.com/@cityowlpress

www.ingramcontent.com/pod-product-compliance
Lightning Source LLC
Chambersburg PA
CBHW061737140826
49883CB00030B/333
* 9 7 8 1 6 4 8 9 8 6 0 3 1 *